Your Neighbour's Wife

TONY PARSONS

C

CENTURY

1 3 5 7 9 10 8 6 4 2

Century
20 Vauxhall Bridge Road
London SW1V 2SA

Century is part of the Penguin Random House group of companies
whose addresses can be found at global.penguinrandomhouse.com.

First published by Century in 2021

www.penguin.co.uk

A CIP catalogue record for this book is available from the British Library.

ISBN 9781529124736 (hardback)
ISBN 9781529124743 (trade paperback)

Typeset in 14/17.75 pts Fournier MT
by Integra Software Services Pvt. Ltd, Pondicherry

Printed and bound in Great Britain by Clays Ltd, Elcograf S.p.A.

The authorised representative in the EEA is Penguin Random House Ireland,
Morrison Chambers, 32 Nassau Street, Dublin D02 YH68.

Penguin Random House is committed to a sustainable future for
our business, our readers and our planet. This book is made from
Forest Stewardship Council® certified paper.

Your Neighbour's Wife

Also by Tony Parsons

The Murder Bag
The Slaughter Man
The Hanging Club
Die Last
Girl on Fire

Digital Shorts
Dead Time
Fresh Blood
Tell Him He's Dead

For Jonny Geller and Selina Walker,
who helped me tell the story

SHOPPING FOR PAIN

They call it shopping for pain.

My husband leaves the room with our son in his arms and I snatch up the phone that he has left on the coffee table and I start scrolling through all the secret corners of his life.

His text messages. His WhatsApp. His email. I quickly ransack them all. The possibility of pain – real life-wrecking, heartbreaking, how-could-you, tears-of-rage pain – is everywhere. There are so many places now for him to leave the evidence of betrayal. Or the thought of betrayal. Or the flirtatious foreplay of betrayal. Or the sordid sweet nothings of real betrayal. All the damning, undeniable proof of his secret life.

Soft voices crackle on the child monitor. Christian, my husband, is reading Marlon, our five-year-old, his bedtime story.

'Buck was neither house-dog nor kennel-dog,' *he reads.* 'The whole realm was his …'

The Call of the Wild, *I think. Our son loves that book. But a five-year-old is far too young for Jack London. I should go in there right now and tell Christian to read something more age-appropriate. Five years old is the time for* The Tiger Who Came to Tea *and not* The Call of the *bloody* Wild.

But I don't. Instead I carry on scrolling through Christian's phone.

The ball of my right thumb moves faster but it's thin pickings in the pain market today. Christian's old texts scream with innocence. The only unread WhatsApp message is a reminder to bring the car into the garage for a service. His inbox contains a dozen unread emails but they are all junk from mailing lists.

Christian gave up work to look after Marlon – although perhaps it would be more accurate to say that work gave up on Christian – and his phone is not stuffed with the urgent pleas for attention that constantly fill my desktop. But then I have the inbox that never sleeps, the inbox of someone with a growing business to run. Christian is spared all of that.

On the child monitor I hear his calm baritone. 'He plunged into the swimming tank or went hunting with the Judge's sons. He escorted Mollie and Alice, the Judge's daughters, on long twilight or early morning rambles. On wintry nights he lay at the Judge's feet before the roaring library fire.'

I shake my head. I mean, I love that book, too. But not now. Not at five. *And yet I can't help hoping that Christian plans to read Marlon the whole chapter. Because his phone just beeped importantly.*

A new message!

But it is only his friend – our friend, Spike – confirming tomorrow's appointment at the gym.

And then I remember Instagram. My husband bloody loves Instagram.

And as I am scrolling through Instagram I feel the first sharp stab of guilt. Because, you see, unlike some people I could mention, my husband's life is good.

Christian's timeline abounds with all of his favourite things – physical fitness and electric guitars and images of amusing animals being unselfconsciously adorable. This is what my husband has lurking in the secret corners of his phone.

A skateboarding French Bulldog. And vintage Fender Telecasters. His personal posts are full of family, full of us. Christian, Marlon and me and not forgetting Buddy, our yellow Lab. I am shopping for pain but the shelves, I see now, are all empty. Christian's phone comes with a delete button, of course. Any keeper of secrets with any kind of experience knows that you do not leave anything on your phone that you would not want written in letters of fire.

And you can always have a second, secret phone.

That's what I did.

But in my heart, I know that my husband has not been compulsively pressing his delete button or conducting his extracurricular activities on a second phone. Because some people have nothing to hide.

Some people are simply – that word again, because there is no other word – good.

Look how casually Christian leaves his phone lying around for his wife to secretly plunder. In my experience, the truly innocent, the good souls with nothing to hide, are never suspicious because they live with the delusion that the rest of the world is as honourable as them. It is only the guilty who are tormented by suspicion. It is only the guilty who ever go shopping for pain.

I hear Marlon yawn and stretch and protest that – honestly, Daddy – he is not even remotely sleepy. And then much scuffling as the dozing dog is lifted from the bed.

'Just rest your eyes,' Christian says, his smile in his voice.

In our family we are always telling each other to, 'Just rest your eyes.' Just resting your eyes means there is no pressure to sleep. And without the pressure to sleep, you inevitably sleep. It works for us.

I hear Christian kiss Marlon on the top of his blond mop and I take one last look at our happy faces on his phone, his loving witness of us.

This is his world, I think, a sob of real grief buried deep in my heart.

Me and Marlon and Buddy. This is Christian's life.

Which makes him sound much duller than he is.

Christian may be a stay-at-home-dad but he is still a major dude. He is tall, lean, muscular, a natural athlete who hones his genetic blessings in the gym three times a week under the watchful eye of friend Spike. In those long hours when I am slumped in my office chair, over-caffeined and carbed-out and work-stressed, Christian is clocking up the high-intensity cardio.

Women look at him. I've seen them. Not staring so much as taking a second glance. Or a first look that lasts a moment too long. In the street, in a restaurant, at the school gates (those mums really should know better). He wears glasses – big black-rimmed things, more Buddy Holly than John Lennon – but that just seems to add to his allure, and they look at him as if he is Clark Kent, undoing the top button of his shirt.

And he doesn't even notice.

But this is really the true measure of how good he is – when he comes back into the living room holding the Puffin Classics edition of The Call of the Wild, *Buddy the yellow Lab padding behind him, Christian sees that I am holding his phone.*

And he doesn't flinch.

How many men can you say that about? How many women?

Christian is still smiling as he puts The Call of the Wild *on the coffee table.*

I gently place his phone on top of the book and then I go to him and find his mouth with my mouth. He laughs when I squeeze him tight. He hugs me back, and I melt into him, enjoying the sweet warmth and hard bulk of him, as familiar to me as what I see in the mirror every morning.

'Love you,' I whisper.

'Love you too,' he returns.

We do not say it all the time but God knows I need to say it tonight. I feel what is between us and it is the bond that only comes with time. You can't get it in a bar. You can't get it in a club. You will not – trust me on this one, for I am a bit of an expert – find it swiping through the gallery of a dating app.

Having a child together. Having a dog together. Sleeping side by side for hundreds – thousands by now – of nights. Watching your parents grow older. Watching them getting ready to die. Knowing another human being in a way that only all those shared experiences, big and small, can bring.

I embrace him too hard. I kiss the side of his face, his end-of-the-day stubble sandpaper rough against my lips. I knock his big Buddy Holly glasses slightly skew-whiff.

'Tara,' he chides, laughing, straightening his specs. 'It's not even Saturday night!'

It's not you, I think, suddenly on the edge of weepy exhaustion.

It's me.

His smile fades when he sees my eyes shining with tears.

And I decide that it's time.

I must tell him tonight. I must tell him now.

Frankly, I have no choice. He is about to discover that everything he thinks he knows about our life together is wrong.

His phone begins to ring.

'Don't answer it,' I tell him.

He holds me at arm's length.

'Tara?'

His phone stops ringing.

'What? Tell me? Come on, I want to know.'

I look at his face and I take a breath.

Then I hear the sirens and I feel my husband pulling away from me, and there is a look on his gorgeous face that breaks my heart, because it shows that he really does not understand what I have brought to our little family's door, and into our home, and into our good life.

The blue lights of the police cars fill the room.

And I know that they have come for me.

WANTING

10 Days Ago

1

CHRISTIAN

'Fancy a bottle of Prosecco?' Tara said, smiling.

All married couples speak their own language and, in our home, this translated as – *you up for a date night, big boy?*

In the morning Tara was going away for three nights. One night in the air, two nights at a conference in Japan. We were not a family that was often apart and so the moment definitely demanded Prosecco.

'I'll chill two glasses in the freezer,' I said.

Which translated as – *A date night? You bet, beautiful.*

Our home buzzed with excitement. An adventure was about to begin and Tara's suitcase was packed but still open, a copy of *The Rough Guide to Tokyo* sitting on top of her clothes, as she stood in front of the full-length mirror in our bedroom, sheaths of scrawled notes in her hand, trying out her speech.

Marlon, our five-year-old boy, was in his pyjamas and up way past his bedtime, teaching the dog new tricks. Sort of.

'Roll over,' Marlon commanded, holding up a treat.

Buddy bobbed his head, grinning hopefully, that knowing Labrador grin, and slowly eased himself down onto his side.

'*Good* boy,' Marlon said, scratching Buddy behind the ears and slipping him the hard-earned treat. Our son lifted his face to us. 'You have to watch, both of you.'

Buddy got up carefully.

'We're watching,' Tara said.

'Play dead,' Marlon said, and Buddy gamely eased down onto his side again, keeping his head raised and his shining eyes on the treat.

'I'm calling Simon Cowell about you two,' Tara said, miming the telephone with her hand. 'Hello, Mr Cowell? Simon?'

Marlon was wide-eyed at the game. 'What does Simon say?'

Tara listened. 'Wait a minute.' She covered the mouthpiece of her invisible phone. 'Simon says – I don't like it ... I *love* it!'

Then she stared at herself in the mirror, biting her lower lip.

I went to her and slipped my arm around her waist.

She shook her head and scrunched up her mouth. The notes for her speech hung by her side. Sometimes married couples don't even need their secret language. 'They'll love you,' I said. 'They'll go crazy for you. Don't worry.'

Tara looked doubtful.

'You made such a great speech at our wedding,' I reminded her.

'To a bunch of drunks who all quite like us. They don't count. And I *cried*.'

'Only a bit.'

'Mama?'

'Yes, angel?'

'What does Simon say now?'

'Simon says – it's bedtime, kiddo!'

Marlon scowled darkly. At five, he wanted any game he loved to go on and on and on, preferably forever.

Tara placed her fingertip on the dimple on his right cheek.

'I'm going to kiss you right there,' she said.

A reluctant smile. He was such a sweet, gentle boy. He shyly placed a fingertip on his mum's undimpled face.

'And I'm going to kiss you right there.'

I took *The Rough Guide to Tokyo* from Tara's suitcase and sat down on the bed. There was a young white-faced woman in a kimono on the cover. I turned the pages, and Tokyo looked like a city that had absolutely nothing to do with today. It looked like a place that lived in the future and the past all at once.

'There's a bar in Tokyo that only plays Led Zeppelin on vinyl,' I read. 'And only serves red wine. And only one kind of pasta.'

'I'm not going to have any time for bars.'

'Shake, Buddy,' Marlon said. 'Shake hands, boy.'

The dog grinned at him.

Marlon grabbed his front right paw and shook it.

'That dog still needs his evening toilet break,' Tara told me. 'And you, young man, need to brush your teeth and head for bed.'

So I walked Buddy around the block, our quiet corner of Camden Town already turned in for the night, Buddy patiently checking the lampposts and the recycling bins and the bushes for the stories that lived in the splashes of a hundred dogs, a thousand dogs, for all dogs live in a world of scent.

Buddy finally did his business and I lavished praise on his handsome yellow head as I crouched with a poo bag. When we got home I set him free and collected the chilled glasses from the freezer and the Prosecco from the fridge.

Marlon had hung a new artwork on the fridge door. *My Family*, it was called. He had left his stick people phase behind him, like Picasso moving on from cubism, and the limbs of his figures were far rounder now, their lines softer, as if the subjects were made out of cartoon sausages. A woman – her hair an explosion of yellow scribble – holding a black briefcase was being waved off by a man in thick black glasses and a child with a dog at his feet. Who could that be? The tall go-getting, world-conquering mummy and the myopic brown-haired (OK, mousey) stay-at-home daddy holding the hand of a little boy with a dog glued to his side, the kid's mop of blond hair exactly the same shade of melted butter as his knockout mother's crowning glory.

That's us. That's our family.

I smiled at the drawing and then carried the bottle and the glasses to the bedroom.

Tara was sitting up in bed in her T-shirt and pants, Marlon sleeping soundly by her side. She grinned ruefully.

Sometimes a bottle of Prosecco doesn't mean a date night. Sometimes it is only a bottle of Prosecco.

'When I get back?' she said, sighing. 'I really don't want to go.'

'It's Japan. It's Tokyo. You've never been. It will be great.'

'But this bloody speech . . .'

'They're going to love you,' I promised again, opening the bottle. 'Who could ever do anything but love you?'

We had a glass and we kissed and then I turned off the light.

Tara was soon sleeping – she was a great sleeper – but I lay awake, listening to the cars that drive too fast down our street, and smelling our son sleeping between us, that special Marlon scent of paint and dog and toothpaste and books.

I must have slept because the first light of a spring morning was seeping into the bedroom when Buddy jumped up on the end of the bed and settled, keeping very still, hoping nobody would notice him.

Tara turned to face me across our sleeping son.

She touched my face.

I held her hand and kissed her fingertips.

'What will you boys do without me?' she said, her voice husky with sleep.

I will miss you, she meant.

'We're going to be teaching the dog tricks at midnight,' I said.

I will miss you too.

And then she turned her face from mine, and for reasons I could not explain, I found myself on the edge of tears.

2

TARA

They are all sleeping when I slip from the bed and quickly shower, dress and put on my face.

I take one last look at them from the bedroom door – Christian contentedly snoring on his back, Marlon somehow on top of the duvet with Buddy curled up between his feet – and, resisting the urge for final kisses all round, I quietly make my way downstairs to the hallway where my suitcase is waiting and, I can see through the old-fashioned frosted-glass of our front door, my car to the airport is idling on the street.

But then I linger, breathing in my home, listening to the sounds it makes without us, feeling my love for it, prolonging the actual moment of leaving, feeling sad to leave my boys but – there's no denying – also a mounting excitement. Our elderly, endlessly difficult boiler sounds like it is playing up again and its arthritic moans and choking gurgles echo mournfully through our house, a cavernous Victorian terrace that we converted from multiple dinky flats to family home with the considerable help of my father, who does that sort of stuff for a living.

I listen to the song of the wonky boiler as I stare up at the framed blown-up magazine cover that has pride of place in our hallway. Every home has these little grace notes that proclaim – *among all this brick, stone and slate, once occupied by generations now long dead, this is who* we *are, and this is what makes* our *family and* our *house so special.* This framed poster is definitely one of those grace notes because that's me on the cover, wearing a black dress from Stella McCartney that is slightly too short and an amused smirk that makes me look slightly too pleased with myself.

At the urging of the photographer, I have all my weight on my front foot and my other leg casually cocked, like the head girl after hockey practice, and my arms folded across my chest. I am biting my lower lip as I grin. My hair took two hours for the stylist to get it that fashionably unkempt. The headline is 'Your Next Date?' and the piece inside was about dating apps, which is what *I* do for a living. The article covered five fledgling dating apps, but I had the cover all to myself. I look like a little minx. And I love that picture because it makes me look far more successful and beautiful and confident than I ever feel in normal life. That's why – no matter how scared and sad it makes you feel – it is always good to be the one who goes. Because we all become someone else when we are unanchored by home, don't we?

Christian is probably going to need an emergency plumber over the next few days but I will be gone, worrying about other things, no doubt, like looking a stuttering fool whose speech sucks in front of a conference hall full of clever strangers.

I pick up my suitcase and step out to the street and Phil, my regular driver, eases his considerable bulk out from behind the wheel to rush to help me. And it begins almost immediately, this transformation that takes place when we are unmoored from all that we love.

I feel it in the back of the car, watching the first planes of the day coming in for landing at the airport, these thin slivers of molten silver that look as if they are moving in slow motion, and I feel it after I have said goodbye to Phil and I am pottering about in the shops after security, buying all this stuff that I am fully aware I don't need, treating myself to a triple espresso and a newly released paperback and some Clarins duty-free double serum.

By the time I am at 35,000 feet stretched out in my flatbed seat at the important business executive end of the cabin, an early morning glass of champagne wickedly cold in my hand, fussed over and pampered and euphoric to be above the clouds, the transformation is complete. I feel free, free at last, thank God almighty, I am free at last. More champagne? Oh, go on then.

But here's the thing that I never really understand.

This person that you become when you are far away from heart and home – that independent, exciting and excited person, unencumbered by the mundane, knocking back the guilt-free fizz first thing in the morning, flying across the planet towards Tokyo. Is that just a role that you are playing? Are you on a minibreak from yourself?

Or have you become the person that you were meant to be all along?

I did not want to make a speech. The prospect terrified me.

The jet lag from the twelve-hour flight from London to Tokyo was kicking in as I found an aisle seat in the conference hall. I felt disconnected and scared, the notes that I had worked on after one glass of Australian Shiraz too many on the flight suddenly unfit for purpose – my insights banal, the statistics dull, my spiel nowhere near good enough to impress all these start-up-building, high achievers gathered here today from every corner of the planet. I could feel it in my tired, slightly hungover bones. This would not go well.

The conference hall itself was massive, the space far bigger than I was expecting and half the speeches were not even in English. Delegates bleary from their own long-haul flights bolted early morning coffee and fiddled with flimsy black plastic headphones that provided simultaneous translation in the language of your choice.

Up on stage an image of my face appeared on the screen behind the moderator. As she began a brief introduction to my company, I stared beyond the huge tinted windows of the hall where Tokyo was luminous with the pink cherry blossoms of spring. I could just go now, I thought. Just ... go. But as I seriously contemplated running away, I heard my father's voice.

'*You bought the ticket, Tara!*' my dad would have told me.

He had been telling me exactly the same thing all my life. Thought you were a big girl who could ride her bike without stabilisers? Well, you bought the ticket! Thought you could get away with drinking vodka shots with your mates without getting sick? You bought the ticket! Whenever I took an uncertain step, from my early childhood memory to my wild teenage years to starting up my own company, my dad would be there to remind me – not unkindly – that what went wrong was usually nobody's fault but mine.

You bought the ticket, Tara! Meaning – *your choice, your consequences.*

I had not literally bought the ticket to come here, of course. My travel expenses – a non-flexible business class return on British Airways, two nights in a junior suite at the Park Hyatt Tokyo – had been paid for by the conference, which was bringing together a few hundred scrappy young female entrepreneurs who had built their businesses up from nothing. Women like me. I could have found a hundred ways to get out of coming. But flattered by the invitation – despite that magazine cover, my firm was only a three-desk operation jammed into a small office at the end of a mews – and excited to see Tokyo for the first time, I said – *count me in*. I bought the ticket, didn't I?

'*So please welcome ...*'

Then I felt the light touch of a hand on my arm. The man in the next seat. Unlike most of the people in the hall, he was wearing a suit and tie. And he was older than most of us, though not yet old.

His eyes were friendly but he did not smile. He was dead serious. He leaned forward, his words meant just for me.

'Be sincere, be brief and be seated,' he told me.

I stared at him.

On stage, my name was being announced to a smattering of half-hearted, never-even-heard-of-her applause in the hall. A tough crowd. But I was staring at the man in the suit and tie. He had craggy good looks, like middle period Harrison Ford. *Witness* and *The Mosquito Coast*, around there. An attractive grown-up with a few miles on the clock. There was a big expensive watch on his wrist, some sort of Rolex, as showy as a dowager's bracelet.

'What?' I said.

'Be sincere, be brief and be seated,' he repeated. 'Remember those three things and you'll be fine. I promise you.' He lightly squeezed my arm. 'Go now, Tara.'

I stared at him for a moment longer and then I nodded.

I left my inadequate notes on my seat and I went up on stage and I took a breath and I told them how it all started with my best friend – Ginger.

Ginger was – and Ginger still is! – this beautiful, smart Aussie girl who moved to London from Sydney and who could not get a date. Imagine God's second attempt at Elle Macpherson, I told them. That's Ginger. The audience smiled at that. They were waking up.

Ginger had surfed all her life, I said, staying with Ginger, being sincere. She had played beach volleyball on Bondi until the day she got on that Qantas flight to London ten years ago. This incredible young woman who would hang out with me and my boyfriend Christian – who eventually became my husband – because there was no man in her life.

Ladies and, er, ladies – it was *insane*. It was *nuts*. And it was just plain *wrong*.

And I was personally going to do something about it. So I started my company because my lonely, lovely friend Ginger deserved to meet a good man.

I rattled off some statistics, the stuff I knew by heart that I had in my abandoned notes. Our digital traffic. The latest figures for our subscribers. Our reviews and ratings on Trustpilot. But really the speech was all about Ginger. That is how I came to start my company Angel Eyes. An online introduction agency. A dating app. Because of Ginger.

Court someone worth catching was our slogan.

I could see smiles in the audience, even from people wearing their little plastic headsets, the delegates getting my story in a second language. The speech worked, even in translation, because I spoke from the heart.

And because I followed the man's advice.

I had been sincere, I had been brief and now I was going to get the hell off this stage while I was ahead and be seated as soon as I had spoken to the scrum of media waiting stage left. That was the way the moderator was steering me after I wound it up.

But I glanced back to see the man in the suit and tie on his feet, grinning and clapping, leading my standing ovation.

As if he was proud of me.

I slept until the maid arrived to turn down the bed in the early evening. Outside it was already dark and the piercing red emergency lights on top of all the tall buildings lit up the Tokyo night. Those red lights were everywhere, making the sky a constellation of man-made stars, a Milky Way in scarlet.

I phoned home. 'They bloody loved me!'

Christian laughed with triumph. 'I *knew* they would bloody love you! You should have more faith in yourself, Tara. I *told* you they would love you.'

It was true – he had kept telling me they would love me. Before I left home, when I was fretful and sleepless at the prospect of public speaking, Christian had predicted that they would love me at the conference. But I knew I would never have nailed it – and they certainly would not have loved me – without the advice of the man in the next seat. But I didn't mention the advice, or my neighbour in the next seat, and I was happy for Christian to feel that he had been proved right.

'How's Tokyo?'

I looked out of the window at the city fifty floors below. This high up, Tokyo seemed infinite but totally empty of all human life. It felt like a long way from home.

'It's great, but I wish you and Marlon were here.'

There was some child-and-dog disruption at the other end of the line.

'Marlon? Buddy doesn't *want* you to kiss him, OK? Marlon? Not on the mouth. That's – no, you listen to me – that's how humans express affection, not dogs.'

Our son. Our dog. A debate about one of them kissing the other.

'I'll let you go,' I said.

'Never let me go.'

'Hah! Love you.'

'Love you too! And well done, Tara. I'm so proud of you. See you in a couple of days. Enjoy Tokyo. You've earned it.'

I let my husband, my son and our dog carry on with their day on the other side of the world and I stared out the window at the winking red skyline of the Tokyo night.

Eight hours ahead of home, the day was winding down out here.

And suddenly I was nowhere near sleepy.

3

TARA

He was sitting alone at the bar on the fifty-second floor, a different kind of attractive from my husband. I could tell that women had told him he was good looking all of his life, and he had believed them. I walked over to where he was sitting.

'Hey, thanks for the public speaking tip,' I said.

He shook his head and smiled. Good teeth on a man pushing forty, just a shade too white.

'I wish I could claim credit for the advice,' he said. 'They're the words of Sir John Mills.'

'Sir John Mills?'

'Won the Best Supporting Actor Oscar for *Ryan's Daughter*? No? Before your time. But it's brilliant, isn't it? *Be sincere, be brief and be seated*. When the nerves are kicking in, and a room full of faces are staring up at me waiting for me to say something interesting or enlightening or entertaining, I remind myself of those lines.'

I couldn't imagine him being nervous before making a speech.

'James Caine,' he said, holding out his hand. 'And I already know your name.'

I shook his hand, slid onto the seat next to him and ordered a draught Kirin. He was drinking some kind of complicated cocktail with fruit in it.

'And did it work?' he said.

'I never had a standing ovation before,' I said. 'So I guess it must have worked.'

'I meant your friend – Ginger. Did your business do the trick for her? Did you manage to find her someone?'

The *someone* was well judged. He didn't say *true love*. He didn't say *a man*. He didn't try to make light of it or to dismiss her loneliness – and Ginger was very lonely when she first came to London, she was lonely for years – as somehow trivial. I liked that a lot.

'Ginger found someone,' I said. 'She's married now. To Spike.'

'Spike?'

'Not his real name. At least I don't think it's his real name. But – ironically enough – it had nothing to do with me. He was another Aussie in London and they met in the gym. The old-school way.'

'But your company took off,' he said, raising his cocktail glass in salute.

I smiled. It was easy to be modest about my business success.

'Tinder are not losing any sleep about us just yet. But there are a lot of wonderful women out there on their own, men too. It's five years now and we have been turning a small profit for three and a bit. I didn't think we would last so long.'

'What's your secret?'

'A good idea with low overheads. If you keep the costs down, all you need is a web designer, someone to answer the phones and your good idea. And we're hard on catfishing.'

'Catfishing?'

'Catfishing is the plague of all online dating. People pretending to be something they're not. You know – the fifty-year-old man pretending to be twenty-five. The man with a wife and ten kids pretending to be young, free and single. The men who take off their wedding rings on a date. And women catfish too, though nowhere near as much as the men. We're one of the few dating apps that gets clients to upload a passport or a driving licence. You need photo ID to join a library, so why shouldn't you need it to join a dating agency?'

'But how does that stop people pretending they still look like their fifteen-year-old profile pictures? Or Brad Pitt? And how does it stop them fibbing about their marital status?'

I didn't like the *fibbing*. It's horrible to pretend you are free when you are not. It's rotten to trick someone into liking you.

'It doesn't,' I said. 'It can't. But it encourages honesty. At least, I hope it does.'

'You're very idealistic.'

I shrugged. My Kirin arrived. I took that first glorious sip.

'At Angel Eyes we never pretend there's some magic formula to meeting someone,' I said. 'And we never promise happy endings, because everybody has to work out their happy ending for themselves. But we're sincere, and we're well run, and we can put our subscribers in touch with some like-minded body and soul who lives within a comfortable drive or commute. Then it's all up to them. And there's no stigma to online dating any more.'

James Caine leaned back on his bar stool.

'So you had a good idea at the right time. Social lives revolving more around phones and the Internet and less around someone you meet in a bar or at the office. And you have a great slogan – *Catch someone worth courting.*'

I smiled. 'Close. It's actually *Court someone worth catching*. The other way round.'

'Ah. Sorry.'

I took another sip of my beer. 'We thought about doing it that way round but *Court someone worth catching* seemed playfully romantic while *Catch someone worth courting* sounds a bit too much like a stalker. We're not here to help you *catch* someone. We're here to help you *court* someone.' We had both turned our bodies half-sideways to talk and I saw that our knees were almost touching. 'And what do you do?'

'I'm not an entrepreneur like you and most of the people at this conference. I'm just a suit. I work for an investment bank and I'm here to look for interesting start-ups, small businesses that have the potential to become big ones.'

He took out his wallet and gave me a business card. James Caine of Samarkand Wealth Management. Address at a top floor in one of the new glass towers next to London Bridge.

'When you finally decide to sell your company, someone like me will come through the door to do the admin,' he said.

I laughed. 'I'm never going to sell my business.'

'But if you *did* – if one day you went public, if you sold a percentage of your company in the form of shares to be traded in the Stock Exchange – then someone like me would turn up to arrange the IPO.' He hesitated. 'The Initial Public Offering.'

I picked up my beer. 'Yeah, I know what IPO stands for.'

'Of course you do. Sorry, sorry. It's my jet lag. And how's yours?'

'The jet lag's been bad. You don't have any tips for that, do you?'

If James Caine tells me something about jet lag, I thought, then I know it will be good advice.

'The best cure for jet lag is sunshine,' he said with supreme authority. 'Melatonin is the hormone that controls wakefulness in the body and sunshine is nature's melatonin. Try to get out of your hotel room early tomorrow morning and put your body clock on the local time. How long are you in Japan?'

'Just for the conference. I'm going home the day after tomorrow.'

'That's not long enough to get over jet lag. It takes a day for every hour's time difference. Can't you stay longer?'

It sounded too much like an invitation. I shook my head.

'Got to go home to my son, my business and my dog.'

'Shame you can't see more of Tokyo. Or Kyoto. Or Mount Fuji. Or the Nagano mountains. The real Japan.'

'My husband told me about a bar that only plays one kind of music, and only has one kind of drink and only serves one kind of food. As much as any temple or mountain, that mad bar sounds like the real Japan to me.'

He nodded. 'When the Japanese love something, they *really* love it,' he said. 'I mean, they're *crazy* about it, they're *obsessed*. I admire that.' He indicated my empty glass. 'Another?'

But one was enough. I wanted to look for that bar. I signalled for the bill.

'I'll remember your speech,' he said. 'I go to a lot of these things and I see a lot of people who have started very successful companies. But I never heard a speech as good as your one.' He raised his glass. 'Honestly,' he said.

'All thanks to you.'

'No, all thanks to Sir John Mills.'

'Well, then God bless Sir John.'

The bill arrived. Predictably he tried to pick up the tab but I would not let him.

I definitely owed him and Sir John Mills a round.

And I could buy my own drinks.

The bar I sought was a pink glow at the end of a dark side street in deepest Shibuya. Inside, there were maybe a dozen seats, half of them occupied, a mixture of sleek Japanese couples and well-heeled *gaijin* – 'outside people', meaning foreigners, *The Rough Guide to Tokyo* had taught me.

Japan felt like a stage set where everyone knew their part. The teenage girls that ruled the streets of Shibuya, the salarymen staggering bleary-eyed to their long-haul commute home, the fashionable Japanese couples, the sophisticated *gaijin*, too cool for a boozy night in Roppongi or Shinjuku. Everyone played their part.

And I wondered – what is your role in Japan, Tara? What part are you playing tonight?

Led Zeppelin were cranking out 'When the Levee Breaks' from the fourth album and the LP's iconic cover was displayed on the bar's cream-coloured wall – an oil painting of some old rustic geezer collecting a bale of twigs hanging on the ruins of a demolished home in the foreground as a bleak tower block loomed large in the background.

Behind the bar there was a single large black truffle under a glass case and, beyond that, a young female chef working in the steam of the small kitchen. The bartender placed a glass of Australian Shiraz in front of me and asked me if I had any musical requests. They would play anything you liked as long as it was Led Zeppelin, of course. And I grinned because this was it – a bar that served only truffle pasta, with a wine list offering only red Australian wine and a playlist where the only music was Led Zeppelin – on vinyl. It was a great bar, a bar that had good music and fine food and drink all waiting for you at the end of the universe.

Christian would have loved it.

When I arrived back at the hotel a couple of hours later, I spotted James Caine through the glass wall of the lobby, waiting in his running kit for the lift to the top – the Park Hyatt occupies the thirty-ninth to fifty-second floors of a three-stepped skyscraper, Shinjuku Towers – and I saw how fit he looked.

Not fit for his age, but fit for any age.

He saw me and waved.

And then I felt it.

It was like a train suddenly passing inches from my face. I attempted to stand stock still, yet found that I was still moving. The pavement seemed to shudder beneath my feet and it was as if the air all around me was being dislocated by something of unimaginable force. The train that I could not see continued to roar past my face.

I didn't understand what was happening. The panic flew in my heart.

Then James Caine was beside me, taking my arm, and I could smell the sweat on his running clothes.

'We have to get away from all this glass,' he said.

I made to move into the street where the traffic was slowing to a stop but the pressure of his hand tightened above my elbow.

'No, not the street,' he said. 'That's where the masonry could fall. We need to go over here. Come on, Tara!'

There was another office building next door, without the great cliffs of glass of our building, and we took shelter under the stone arch of its entrance. Japanese office workers huddled next to us, staring at their phones.

'We're going to be fine,' James Caine said, and we both looked up at the great skyscrapers of Shinjuku and I expected them to tremble and crumble and collapse. The invisible train was still rushing past my face, and the worst thing of all was not knowing how long this would last. I was sick with fear now.

'It's not the big one,' he said. 'It's bad but it's not the big one.'

'But what's happening?'

He realised that I truly didn't get it.

'It's an earthquake,' he said.

And then it was over. The invisible train had passed.

'There's an earthquake in Japan every day,' James said as we walked back to the hotel. 'Most of them, you don't even notice. Are you all right?'

Was I all right? No, I didn't feel as if I was all right at all. There was something wrong with my sense of balance. As I walked, the ground was not quite where I expected it to be when I placed my foot down, and the panic lingered in my heart, the memory of the train passing so close to my face that it felt like it would remove a layer of skin.

'Japan is the safest country in the world,' he said, trying to cheer me up.

'If Mother Nature doesn't kill you,' I said.

We both smiled.

'Are you OK?' he said as we passed through the walls of unbroken glass into our building. He was still holding my arm. 'We're safe now.'

I could not shake this feeling. My first ever earthquake made me see how fragile we all are, how there are forces at work that we never even think about, and how you can never really know what is going to happen next.

My heart was pounding so hard that I could hear the blood in my veins.

In the lift, I hit the button for the fifty-second floor. The bar.

'I need a drink,' I said.

There was no small talk this time. I sipped another glass of Shiraz in silence as James Caine rehydrated with sparkling water and the red emergency lights of the Tokyo night looked like they were putting on a show just for us. All that twinkling hard red glitter. The bartender came across and James Caine engaged him in some natural disaster conversation.

The bartender was sanguine. It wasn't the big one, the one that the forty million residents of Tokyo were all waiting for, the one that could come tomorrow morning or one hundred years from now, the one that would be the end of everything.

I drained my glass and I stood. This time I let James pay the bill as I walked uncertainly from the bar. Something had been disturbed in me. It was everything coming together, I told myself. The jet lag and the mad bar and the relief that the speech was done and had gone well and all the beer and red wine I had drunk tonight and the guitar of Jimmy Page and memory of that invisible train so close to my face. We rode the lift in silence to the club level, still full of delegates at the conference. It was real night now, though not yet late. Our rooms were on the same floor, I realised as we exited the lift and began down the long corridor. He made no attempt to touch me but I sensed that he was ready should I stumble or fall. I did not. His room was nearest the lift.

'This is me,' he said, taking out the card key for his room. 'Good night then, Tara.'

I nodded and moved on down the corridor, remembering the way it had felt when I was waiting for the world to start coming apart.

I paused outside my door, grateful that the earth was no longer moving.

He was still waiting at the other end of the corridor, as if making sure I was safe, standing there like a younger Harrison Ford just back from a run. Does Harrison Ford run?

James Caine was concerned about me. And there was something else. Of course there was something else. It was as if he was giving me time to make up my mind.

Because, you see, I still hadn't quite made up my mind.

I stood there, knowing that I should be well on the way to drunk by now, but I suddenly felt stone-cold sober and nowhere near ready to rest my eyes.

James was still waiting, the room key in his hand, watching me.

I let out a breath that I might have been holding for a few moments or several years and started back towards him.

My choice, then. My consequences.

He watched me coming all the way.

And I bought the ticket, Daddy.

4

TARA

Christian and I had shared a bed for ten years.

We were still young, and we were still crazy about each other, and the major problem that our sex life had was the eternal married challenge of scheduling. There were nights when the iced Prosecco did not flow as it perhaps should because there was a child or a dog in our bed, or because one of us – almost always me – had been exhausted by the day. And of course when you have been in a loving relationship for a few thousand nights, there is one thing that you know for certain – there is always tomorrow night. And, if it is really a frantic, energy-sapping week, the Prosecco will still be there at the weekend. And so will you.

But I loved the hard, muscled bulk of my good-looking husband, who had the kind of body that a grown man only gets when he works at it, and I loved that he knew what I wanted, and what I liked, and what I expected in bed. After those few thousand nights of sharing a bed, Christian had a PhD in my needs, preferences and what it took to make me sigh from the bottom of my soul. On the nights when Marlon was sound asleep and I was not worn out by work and we had the time and energy and appetite for each other, Christian knew exactly where the treasure was buried. And it worked the other way, of course, I knew exactly what drove him wild, although it is always far more simple with men to find the buried treasure. Christian and I had an adult life that was obliged to deal with the mundane chores of having a home and a family together. But we still had that old hunger for each other. The old hunger had not faded, not yet. Yes, it had changed but we were still at the stage where familiarity with each other's bodies was nothing but a really good thing. Sex with my husband was loving, caring and reassuringly regular – to the envy of our friends we were still managing to slot it in, as it were, a few times a week.

But there is one thing that I will not deny.

Christian and I made love.

And in Tokyo, I was fucked.

There was no love in it with James Caine.

We kissed in the hallway of his hotel room, his hands moving all over me, his mouth on my lips as though he was starving for me. It was somewhere beyond desire, or hunger, or anything resembling the healthy appetites that I was accustomed too. It was on the edge of brutal. He quickly ripped off his running clothes and then he was clawing at the nice Stella McCartney summer dress that I had worn to that mad bar – stepping back for a moment and catching his breath with his fingertips still feeling me, as I negotiated the complicated zip and clip at the back.

And then we were tumbling towards the king-size bed, hands and mouths still working, neither of us totally naked – he still had on his white Just Do It running socks and I was still in my pants and high heels. Then the pants came off and were tossed aside and he went down on me on top of the bed, far rougher than I liked for I prefer a very light touch with the tongue, and I was still wearing my shoes, the heels ripping at the pristine hotel duvet until he suddenly broke away and went to the bathroom, coming back still unfurling a condom over his erect cock. Then he turned me over, and slipped a pillow under my belly and fucked me from behind.

After, we had a few beers from the minibar, watching the winking red lights of the Tokyo night, not talking much, which was fine by me, and then when I was starting to feel sleepy, he took my hands and led me to the bed and fucked me a second time, between the sheets this time, a bit slower this time, face to face this time, both of us totally naked now apart from the white hotel bathrobes we wore after a shower, and if that second time had none of the mad urgency of that first, it was still – how can I put it? – desperate, and rough, with an edge of what felt like real spite.

I fell asleep with my back turned towards him, aware that I was on the wrong side of the bed – compared to the side that I slept on at home, I mean, the side of the bed that I was meant to be on, the side of the bed I had been on with Christian for a few thousand nights – and then there was our third and final fuck that must have been somewhere just before dawn, because first the white light of a spring morning was creeping beyond the cracks around the hotel room's black-out blinds as I came awake with my back still turned towards him, still on my side as he slowly but implacably penetrated me. I was not ready, nowhere near it, and it hurt this time and it felt like he was having me because I was there, because he could, and I felt it again, that hint of something dark and nasty in his hard, highly experienced rutting. I was several light years from coming by the time he had finished and so he wanted to go down on me but I declined, my hands under his chin, lifting him up, and when he grinned I imagined I saw a touch of relief in his face. He looked older in the almost-morning, and he was so matter-of-fact as he checked his phone – as if nothing life-wrecking had happened between us – that I wondered how many other women James Caine had fucked in rooms just like this one.

After that he started talking, as if we knew each other now, as if we were not still total strangers, and that was really when I felt the first stirrings of fear.

I had not looked in the mirror of the hotel bathroom because the guilt had been there from the start, the shame of breaking all my promises to Christian, all those promises that could never be put back together again no matter what I did. But if the guilt was kicking in, the first pulsing pain of a tumour that will never be cut out of you, it was fear I felt most of all. James Caine lay on his side running a hand over my bare shoulder and he talked of meeting again – later that day in Tokyo, because there was so much I still had to see, blah blah, and then when we were back home, because this could not end here, he said.

I was already plotting ways to avoid him in the long day ahead. Don't commit to a meeting. Don't answer the phone. Forget about all the networking opportunities around the conference. Don't show up at the conference's farewell dinner tonight. Get out of the hotel and spend the day getting lost in this city of forty million. As he talked about meeting up for breakfast, I was plotting how to shake him off. I had had enough of him. Just get through the day and go home to your life, Tara, I thought. Because James Caine scared me a bit now, and what we had done terrified me, and I quickly pulled on my clothes and went back to my room as the day was breaking.

And I was glad to get away from him.

5

CHRISTIAN

Tara cried out in her sleep.

Jet lag, I thought, rolling onto my side and placing a single kiss on her shoulder, slipping an arm around her waist and under her T-shirt, feeling the warm, long length of her, the total adorable Tara-ness of my beautiful wife.

'It's OK,' I whispered in the darkness. 'Sleep some more. It's not time yet.'

She moaned something I didn't catch and shifted, as if trying to get comfortable and failing, and I held her until she was still again and gently breathing, sliding back into that shallow restless sleep that comes after a twelve-hour flight across the planet and a body clock that is no longer still over there but not yet back over here.

Then I lay on my back and I stared at the ceiling.

Work, I thought.

It's her work.

There was an unremitting stress that came with running her own business, the pressure that comes with never really clocking off, the constant demand on her mind and body and budget.

And there was something else bothering me, too.

There was a car that came hurtling down our little street five days a week, Monday to Friday, very early and recklessly fast. A man who I felt in my heart wanted to kill my family.

Some mornings I heard him as I was getting up to walk the dog. And sometimes I saw him – screaming down our quiet residential road in his disgusting little modern car, a virtue-signalling, greeny-cleany, halo-polishing bug of a vehicle that he no doubt thought made him a morally superior person who was going to save the planet.

He always drove as if he was moments ahead of the rush hour. And he always drove as if he didn't give a damn. And one day he was going to kill someone, possibly someone I loved, and all because he wanted to keep his smug green bug five minutes ahead of the morning traffic.

From what I had glimpsed of him, he looked like an educated man, a successful man, a man at the far end of some high-flying career. There was certainly money in his life, and it had been there for decades. And there was also the casual arrogance that comes with money, the selfish disregard for the little people.

Tara stirred as I slipped from the bed.

'Sleep some more,' I whispered.

'I don't think I can.'

'Then just rest your eyes.'

I had been telling her the same thing for ten years.

We had met when we were both music journalists, back when the world was still paying young people to write about music, back when there was still music worth writing about.

Neither Tara nor I had excelled at school and so we were attracted to a job where the only qualifications required were the ability to stay up all night, look good in a leather jacket and string an overexcited sentence together. You would never guess it to look at us now – in the park at weekends with our little boy and our yellow Labrador, or supervising an Ocado delivery, or dutifully carting out our recycling bins – but we were once a pair of wild kids. Especially Tara. But we came in too late to turn hanging out with bands into a serious career. When we got our start on the music press, hip young gunslingers were already an endangered species. When the advertising revenue dried up, our inky weekly music paper became a freebie and then went online only and finally got shoved into oblivion with most of the other newspapers and magazines on the planet.

The print plunge, they called it.

We had moved on by then – at twenty-five you were menopausal in the music press – and I was writing a weekly column about music for a national newspaper, curating the dad rock canon, ruminating every Thursday in a sleepy corner of the Arts & Culture section on why U2 and Springsteen and Dylan should still matter for trad rock fans in their middle years. Meanwhile Tara, now pregnant with Marlon, picked up whatever freelance work she could find from the women's pages in the nationals and what was left of the glossy monthlies. Her speciality was think pieces on sex and romance. *When sex dies but love remains. When your friend is with the wrong guy. How to know if he's the one. Should you ever fake it?* I don't know where she got this stuff from. But we were young practitioners of a dying trade and the work was drying up fast. These were the twilight years of print journalism when there were really only two conversations being had.

One – '*You're fired.*' And two – '*How can we pay you less?*'

Time and technology meant journalists like us were not simply losing our jobs – we were losing our careers. Tara – former party girl, rock chick, wild child – was surprisingly the one who adapted to the new world order.

And I was the other kind. The kind who didn't.

As I tapped out my one thousand words on the eternal genius of *Meat is Murder* and *The Joshua Tree* and *Born to Run* and *Exile on Main Street* and *Blood on the Tracks*, I was like the optimistic blacksmith who thought – *well, people will always need horseshoes, right?* – just as a million

Model T Fords puttered over the horizon. I was that blacksmith. And the world had no further use for me.

Then, just as Marlon started walking, Tara started her business. A dating app. Angel Eyes. I didn't really understand.

'So it's an online business?' I asked, more than once.

'No, Christian,' she said, because I still didn't get it. 'All business is online business now.'

It was as if a great tide had come and picked Tara up and washed away the likes of me. For the first time, there was money in our life – our own money, I mean, not money that came from Tara's parents. Not crazy money, because what came in from Angel Eyes subscriptions and advertising went on extra staff (a guy to answer the phones) and office space (two rooms in a start-up ghetto instead of doing it all from our living room). But five years on, Tara had made her idea work in the grown-up world.

And I was so proud of her.

When we were kids at the music paper, I thought we were exactly the same. I saw now that we were very different.

Tara was driven.

And I was parked.

We sometimes talked about me returning to work but in truth I would need to do what Tara did – have a total career rethink and invent some clever new way to get a payday.

Because my old skill set was redundant. No, not redundant – dead. Print journalists like me had been left out for the bin men of history.

But there was one thing I could still do in this changed world.

I could still protect my family from those who would do us harm.

And what could ever be more important than that?

As I was pulling on my dog-walking trousers, Marlon wandered into the bedroom, more asleep than awake, and I scooped him up and placed him in bed with Tara.

I stirred Buddy from his basket and, with his tail wagging and a sleepy grin on his face, we headed out. As I closed the front door quietly behind me, a big black Merc purred up to the kerb. Tara's car to take her to the office. I realise that I have not given you the entire Tara-picture. I have made her sound as if she ploughed every hard-earned penny back into her business. Not quite. The car to whisk her to and from the Angel Eyes office was her one nod to executive luxury – although Tara thought of it as a legitimate business expense. She liked to work when she was travelling and she couldn't do it on the Tube. A face like a small moon peered at me from the Merc. Her driver was one of those fabulously obese men that look like a heart attack waiting to happen. Fat Phil.

He gave me a big grin with what I perceived as unearned intimacy. I had never cared for Fat Phil's assumption of some unspoken fraternity between us, his obvious belief that we were rather alike. As if we – Tara's no-visible-income spouse and her driver – were both on the payroll. Fat Phil grinned broadly as Buddy lifted his leg for an early wet on his favourite lamppost.

Fat Phil considered me with barely disguised hilarity.

The stay-at-home husband with the successful missus! Walking the dog! Who is taking a leak!

You can see how that would tickle the likes of Fat Phil.

Buddy and I headed off down the street on our walk, Fat Phil gave me a thumbs up and I decided not to tell him that Tara was sleeping off her jet lag and he was going to have to wait a while. Fat Phil knew the drill as well as me.

Tara did what Tara wanted to do.

Buddy and I were nearing the end of our road when I saw him.

The man who wanted to destroy my family with his driving.

The dumb bastard in the Smart car.

He took a rubber-screeching fast right into our street and slammed the accelerator to the floor. If Marlon or Tara had stepped into the street at that moment, he would not have been able to stop.

He probably thought he was a respectable man. A decent, caring man. He probably fretted about plastic in the ocean, the planet heating up. Greta Thunberg's granddad. He no doubt gave money to charity. He probably had a weakness for all those pious hashtags that bloom on social media. And yet he drove far too fast down the street where our son took my hand to walk to school.

He drove through the place where we lived like it was some kind of race track. As I watched his tail lights fade, my vision blurred with tears, and they were tears of rage that anyone would dare put my family in harm's way.

I was glad it was still dark.

I was glad our street was empty.

I was glad nobody could see me.

Because I knew I had murder in my eyes.

6

TARA

It began immediately on my return.

I had spent my last day in Tokyo avoiding James Caine, ignoring his multiple text messages asking me why I wasn't at the conference, and later the hideously matey voicemails asking if we could meet for lunch or dinner because he knew a great tempura place in Ebisu and blah blah blah, and finally the crass note pushed under my door from the hotel's message desk asking if I was up for a repeat performance of last night. But I stayed away from the hotel all day, losing myself among the teeming crowds in that infinite city, and I told myself that it was easy enough to avoid James Caine, and to keep blanking him until he got the message, and to never see him again in my life. We have grown so used to cutting people from our lives with just a push of the button. *Delete. Block. Mute. Unfollow.* That's what I was doing as I wandered alone in Tokyo, and that was the unspoken message I sent to James Caine as my pinging phone remained unanswered while I stood with Japanese office workers staring in wonder at the great pink mass of cherry blossom that was everywhere in Tokyo. *Delete. Block. Mute. Unfollow.* I returned to the hotel near midnight, and the door to his room remained mercifully closed as I silently, and quickly, walked by. I had to get up very early because flights to London leave Tokyo around dawn. I was so relieved when I finally sank into my British Airways business class seat that I had a glass of champagne before breakfast, and then another. *Delete. Block. Mute. Unfollow.* Made it! Or so I thought.

Yet here I was, back so recently that I was still half out of my mind with jet lag, and James Caine was hot on my trail, hunting me down and refusing to get the message, for all the world as though it was impossible to amputate someone from your life if they refused to be cut.

It was the day after I got home and my first day back at work. My first coffee of the day was still steaming when my phone erupted into life and I knew, somewhere in my blood and bones, that I would not be allowed to walk away from what I had done.

A voice next to me was saying, '*Not him ... not him ... not him ...*'

I ignored my phone, hoping it would go away, an inexplicable feeling of dread building. I was at my desk at Angel Eyes. My close friend and colleague, Mary, genius website designer turned dating guru, had her chair pulled up beside me as together we scrolled through the faces of smiling men, choosing next month's male lead for our home page.

'Not him ... not him ... oh, blimey, definitely not him!' Mary said.

The phone stopped ringing and started beeping with the notification of a new message.

'Not him,' Mary said, laughing as she scrolled through the smiling men.

The story I always liked to tell was that my friend Ginger made my business happen. And in a way this was true enough. But if Ginger was the inspiration, then it was Mary who did all the heavy lifting. Mary created the Angel Eyes website, Mary got our subscription service up and running, Mary always made it look as if I knew what I was doing, when I really didn't, not at the start. Mary never got the credit she deserved for Angel Eyes. Not from me – because she did not fit the story that I liked to tell – and not from the world at large. That framed magazine cover on the hallway wall of my home should, if there was any justice in the world, also feature Mary, who came to the photo shoot with me and who had had a facial and been to the hairdresser's and bought a new dress from Zara, all in anticipation of having her photo taken. But the photographer did not want Mary in the picture because she is a strong, stocky, powerful-looking woman. Mary's looks did not fit neatly into an article about finding love online. It was all a bit awkward. 'You're the babe,' the photographer told me, with Mary standing right by my side, still glowing from her facial, but Mary took it with her usual jokey grace. 'He's right, Tara! You're the babe!' She has a lovely, impossibly sweet face but, quite frankly, there are weight issues. Even as we sat working out our lead man for next month, so soon after breakfast, Mary had an emergency almond croissant by her side.

'Not him ...' she said, lighting up with delight.

The faces on our home page – the people who might love you – changed every month. We already had our woman for next month – a friendly-looking redhead, pretty rather than beautiful, who looked as if she was kind and fun and not one of those lost souls who lug around suitcases full of misery and disappointment. In the redhead's shy smile, you believed that many good years were still ahead. Now we just needed to find next month's leading man.

My phone beeped again. Mary frowned with concentration.

'Not him – gawd! – not him ...'

The faces we selected – and Mary and I always did this job together, not least because she enjoyed it so much – were very rarely the most attractive we could find. We chose the sort of faces that made you believe in the possibility of happiness. There was a knack involved, and somehow Mary the tech whiz had mastered it. Which was ironic because Mary was not, as far as I could tell, a big dater.

'A bit weird . . . not him . . . ah, he's nice . . . how about this one, Tara?'

And I finally looked at my phone.

Unknown Caller ID, it said.

And then I was staring at my phone in disbelief. Because the locked-screen preview displayed three photographs of me in a stranger's bed.

In all of them I was sleeping. In the first two images, clearly taken just moments apart, I was on my side, my face half-buried in the pillow, the hotel room of the Park Hyatt Tokyo in darkness. In the third image, which must have been taken hours later, there was the honey-coloured light of a Japanese dawn pouring into the room. Morning had broken in Tokyo and I was moments from waking up in James Caine's bed and being fucked for the third time. My stomach lurched and I tasted something bitter in my mouth.

There was a single word under the three images.

Kawaii.

Cute. *Kawaii*, I knew, is the Japanese word for cute.

Then I was standing up, the phone gripped in my hand, the sickness rising.

'Tara?'

I stared at Mary.

'How about him?' she said.

I looked at the face on the screen. A man in his early thirties, grinning with what looked like two decades of self-satisfaction. I numbly shook my head.

'Oh, I get it,' Mary smiled, leaning closer to the screen. The man looked like he had already had considerable success on dating apps. And off dating apps, come to that. 'He's too much the male model, right?' Mary said. 'Women don't want a man who looks like he cares more about his skin regime than they do!'

I turned my back to her, shielding my phone, afraid she might have already seen.

And I stared again at the photographs with dread and disbelief.

'Not your type,' Mary said.

'I didn't know I had a type,' I said sharply, turning to look at her.

Mary looked surprised.

'Of *course* you do! The sensitive hunk! *Christian*. Your husband? Isn't he your type?'

'I have to go out for a bit, Mary.'

There was a beautiful child waiting in the reception area. No, not a child I saw on second look, but a very young woman, a young adult. She swept her long hair from her face and considered me with her huge brown eyes. Michael, our receptionist, mouthed a single word to me.

'*Intern*.'

I nodded at the YA, who jumped to her feet. She was wearing some lacy, pink number that looked like a bridesmaid dress.

'What's your name?'

'Skyla.'

'You're hired, Skyla,' I said. 'Mary will take care of you.'

Our office was at the end of a mews right on the edge of Islington. Once horses had been stabled here but now it was home to small digital start-ups like Angel Eyes. At least, that had been the theory ten years ago when this micro business centre was being blessed by the local council. But now the decline of the high street had reached our little mews. Half the offices were shut and one of the spaces had been leased to an old-school business, a second-hand record shop, The Vinyl Countdown.

An elderly hippy – Wiggy – gestured at me from the window, holding up a copy of *Weird Scenes Inside the Goldmine*. Christian had been looking for a copy of the out-of-print Doors compilation for ages.

I gave Wiggy the thumbs up and kept walking until I reached the traffic crawling down Upper Street. Then I stopped, choking on the traffic fumes, suddenly feeling trapped, and I could not stop looking at the photographs on my phone. I did not know what to do. So I called the only person I could talk to. I called my best friend.

'I think I'm in trouble,' I told Ginger.

7

TARA

Ginger and I sat in a working man's cafe on the Holloway Road, a place of uncomplicated coffee and just one kind of tea, and scaffolders wolfing down their fry-ups. We let our builder's tea grow cold on the stained Formica table between us as Ginger scrolled through the photographs on my phone without comment. She was a tall, athletic woman with a wild red mane that she combed with her fingers, like a Valkyrie, if Valkyries grew up on Bondi beach.

She stared at the three images for a long time without speaking and then she briefly looked at me and bit her lower lip and looked away, staring out at the stalled traffic as if thinking of something else. I felt – I knew – I had let her down in some way that I could not explain. Ginger liked to play the big, bluff, plain-speaking Aussie girl cast adrift among the tight-lipped, cold-blooded English, but today she seemed lost for words.

When she finally looked at my face, I knew she saw it all.

'What happened? I mean – God, Tara – I can *see* what happened. But – how could you? Not you, Tara. Not you and Christian.' She stared at the phone, still getting used to the idea, shaking her head. 'This makes no sense. What the hell happened over there?'

I looked at the workmen tucking into their fried breakfasts and then back at Ginger.

'I don't know.'

'Well, you have to do better than that.'

I took a deep breath and held it for so long it became a stifled sob.

'I feel like I wandered away from my real life. Just for a little while. It felt like – what did it feel like? – it felt like *freedom*. And now I'm being punished.' Tears of self-pity flooded my eyes and I angrily blinked them away. 'And suddenly everything feels so . . . breakable.' I took a breath. 'I can't lose my family, Ginger.'

'Exactly where were these photos taken?'

'At the Park Hyatt in Tokyo.'

'And who took them?'

'The man I met over there.'

She shook her head.

'A man you met on your business trip?'

'I know it's a cliché, Ginger.'

She waited, wanting more. 'Who is this guy?' she said at last.

'James Caine.' His name sounded strange in my mouth. 'I met him at the conference. He gave me some great advice about public speaking. We talked. We bumped into each other again in the hotel bar. We had a few drinks.'

'And that's it? You risk your family – your life – for some stranger you meet in a bar?'

'We didn't meet in a bar,' I said weakly. 'And there was an earthquake.'

She looked at me as if I was lying. 'I didn't hear about any earthquake.'

'Because they happen every day! Because you only hear about the ones when lots of people die!'

Ginger pushed the phone across the table.

'Christian will kill him,' she said, and I felt the sick dread rise in me, even worse now.

'Christian's not going to kill him,' I said, snatching up my phone. 'Because Christian doesn't kill people. *And because Christian is never going to know.*'

She shook her head and sighed.

'This is the way *other people* act,' she said. 'Not *you*. Look at your life! You've got Christian, you've got Marlon, you've got your business, you've got *so much!* You've got your lovely home. You've got your bloody dog. You put all that at risk – for what? A casual shag on a business trip?'

'It was wrong,' I said. 'I know it was wrong.'

'Then *why*, Tara?'

I had thought about it non-stop. I found that I was thinking about it in my sleep, and when I woke up, and when I was looking at the faces of next month's men with Mary. And I wanted to say I was drunk, or I was tired, or I took one of those missteps that we are all capable of taking in any life, no matter how lucky, no matter how blessed. That one wrong step that takes you off the edge of the cliff and into thin air.

'It's hard to explain,' I said slowly. 'Things at home – they're good. They're great. Christian is my man forever. He is. But *that* side of it – the intimacy – has been put aside a little bit because all this other stuff keeps getting in the way. Work. Being tired. The house and all the things that go wrong with the house. And – *time*. There's not as much time for just us as there used to be. I guess I felt – if I'm honest, Ginger – like I had earned some pleasure that didn't hurt anyone.'

Ginger was unimpressed. 'And you thought you would get away with it.'

I felt my face flush with shame.

'Yes,' I said. 'And that.'

'That's why *men* are unfaithful. Because they think they've *earned* it. Because they think they *deserve* a little sugar in their bowl after eating all of life's boring vegetables. And because they think no one will ever know. Opportunity, Tara. Men have been doing it for years.' She shook her head, and I saw something soften inside her, and she reached out and touched my hand across the stained Formica tabletop. 'I guess it's our turn now.'

'I don't want my turn, Ginger.'

I was afraid she would stop liking me. I could see a world where everyone I loved would stop loving me, and think less of me, if only they knew. But Ginger nodded grimly and she patted my hand.

'We are going to get you through this,' she said, nodding at the phone. '*Kawaii?* Do me a favour. What kind of sick bastard takes photographs of a woman when *she's sleeping?* That's outrageous! There's bugger all *kawaii* about it, mate.'

Ginger's anger was making her more Australian. And I felt the first stirring of resentment. Yes – what right did he have to take my photograph when I was sleeping? Christian never took a photo of me when I was sleeping. Not in all our years together, not in all those three thousand nights.

'Do you want to see him again?' Ginger said. 'This James Caine creep?'

'See him again? What are you talking about?'

'Are you planning to have an affair with him?'

'Christ, *no*. It was one night, Ginger. And I will regret it all my life.'

'Then it's simple. If you're going to have something on the side, if you are going to sneak into hotel rooms in the afternoon, if you are going to be worried about who you bump into at restaurants, if you are going to be hiding your phone from your husband – *then* it's complicated. You know why? Because someone always falls in love and someone always finds out. And everyone – everyone – always gets hurt.'

She knew so much about it. She sounded, I thought suddenly, like the world expert on infidelity. She sounded like she could teach a masterclass in playing around. She sounded as if there were fault lines in her marriage that I had not noticed before.

'But if you don't want a repeat performance, Tara, then you need to do one thing – *get him to back off*,' Ginger said. 'You need to send him the signal that what happened ended out there and that, as far as you're concerned, it never even really began.' She indicated the phone. 'Because I have to say this makes it look like he wants more of you.'

I was shocked. 'You mean – call him?'

'Yes, call him. Text him. DM him. Whatever it takes. Whatever works. You might need to look him in the eye before he finally backs off.'

'And what if he doesn't back off?'

I wanted her to promise me that it was easy.

I wanted Ginger to say that it was as simple as pressing a button that said *Block This Caller*. But she took a sip of her builder's tea and her face flinched with distaste.

'I was going out with someone when I met Spike,' Ginger said carefully. 'Omar. Remember Omar?'

I had a vague memory of Omar. A good-looking Anglo-Lebanese guy making conversation about old rock bands with Christian in restaurants that have long since closed down. Was that Omar?

'Omar was not keen to call it a day,' Ginger said.

'You never told me that.'

'Because you were so bloody happy that I had found Spike. I didn't want to disappoint you. I didn't want to spoil the moment with my stalking problem.'

'Omar stalked you?'

'He couldn't get over the fact that it was done between us. Just wouldn't accept it. He was texting me four or five times a day. My phone beeping all the time when I was out with Spike. He was trailing me all over social media like some love-sick spaniel, liking my posts, obsessively retweeting me, all of that soft stalking. He was not a bad guy, Omar, but he would not move on.'

I waited.

'So Spike got him to back off,' Ginger said, a harder note in her voice, and it seemed absurd to me that I had ever fretted about my friend being lonely, about the lack of love and sex and romance in her life, about the absence of a good man. Because Spike was always out there waiting for her.

'And how did Spike get Omar to stop?'

Ginger sipped her tea, pulled a face. Combed her hair with her fingers.

'Spike had a word.'

Spike was a big affable Aussie and I could not imagine him becoming violent with anyone. But then I also knew that Spike had been crazy about Ginger since their eyes first met across a crowded gym and I knew – I just knew – that he would do anything to keep her safe.

'Spike threatened Omar?'

'Just talking, Tara. An honest conversation. Just a warning.'

The idea was repulsive to me. 'I don't want any threats made. I don't want even the hint of violence. I'll take care of it.'

Ginger picked up my phone.

'What are you doing?'

Ginger looked at me as if I was insane.

'If Christian sees these photos then it all falls apart immediately. Your family, your home, your marriage. All of it, Tara. Look – anyone can make a mistake, OK? But are you going to let your one mistake ruin your whole life? Are you going to let it destroy your family?'

Her thumb worked on my phone.

Delete. Delete. Delete.

Then she pushed the phone towards me, as if she was sick of it.

'They're still on *his* phone, of course,' she said. 'And he could do anything with them. The truth is, you can't really delete anything these days. Once it's out there, it's out there forever.'

'You're scaring me, Ginger.'

'Good,' she said. 'Because you need to send this sick bastard a message. And he needs to get it.'

'And what if he doesn't?'

'Then you're not in trouble,' Ginger said. 'He is.'

A quiet night at home.

'*The dominant primordial beast was strong in Buck*,' Christian read to Marlon at bedtime, their happy, familiar voices cackling through the child monitor, and I could have wept with love for them. '*And under the fierce conditions of trail life, it grew and grew.*'

Christian came into the living room with a shy smile.

'Do you know what I heard is great for jet lag?' he said. 'Prosecco!'

Our lovemaking was urgent and fierce after our time apart, and when it was done we lay breathless and grateful, tangled in each other's arms and legs, drifting easily into deep and dreamless sleep, and as my mind emptied at last, I heard Christian's laughter in the dark.

'You should go away more often,' he said.

8

CHRISTIAN

'Harder,' Spike said.

I was holding a sweat-slick medicine ball, one of those big 12-kilo babies that you have to wrap your arms around just to pick it up, trying to control my ragged breathing.

I looked up at my Personal Trainer. Spike was a big man in a proud-muscled sleeveless top with shoulder-length hair so long, blonde and silky it looked like he should be advertising hair conditioner. The only surfer dude in town. Spike wore shorts to the gym even in winter.

'Be right with you,' I gasped.

Spike chuckled with pleasure.

We were at the end of our session, and Spike had pushed me to the limit. The lactic acid was making my muscles ache, the salt of my sweat burned my eyes and I was right on the very edge of sickness.

Spike was a good trainer.

We always ended our sessions in the same way. We stood ten metres apart, the gym usually empty at this time in the early afternoon, and we threw the big medicine ball at each other. He widened his eyes at me. Amused, challenging.

'No rush, mate – but are you going to chuck it or give it a cuddle?'

I threw it at him. A good shot. He did not have to reach or move his feet. All he had to do was catch the thing. And that was tough enough. The wind whooshed out of him as he took the impact against his abdomen.

We laughed. Throwing the medicine ball at each other never felt like training. It felt like play. Spike threw it back, his aim just a bit off so it came at me slightly high and wide. I caught it on my chest, above my heart.

Spike grinned.

And then two women came into the gym, one of the young PTs and her slightly older client, half-watching us as they discussed the client's tight hamstring, and Spike and I both stopped smiling. We could both feel it.

Training was always a little less fun, and always a little more serious, when there were women watching us. I threw the medicine ball at Spike and he threw it back at me with a poker face, a touch harder than necessary.

Because when the women were watching, somehow it never felt like play.

When his working day allowed, Tara's father Leo joined me to meet Marlon from school. About once or twice a week, I would arrive at the school gates and find him waiting for going-home time.

Leo Doherty was a bull of a man, his bald head shining in the spring sunshine, and the ragged T-shirt, baggy cargo pants and old boots he wore told me he had rushed to school from some building site. Leo had doted on Tara, his only child, and now he was smitten with Marlon, the way only a grandparent can be smitten. Me, Leo was a little less keen on.

He glanced at me as I greeted him and before his natural working-class courtesy kicked in, there was the usual flash of disappointment in his eyes. Leo always looked at me as if I was a washed-up thirty-year-old music journalist who had somehow married his smart, successful, drop-dead-gorgeous daughter when she could have had anyone. Fair comment, really. Someone had once told Leo that he looked like Pablo Picasso and Leo later confirmed this was true – 'I Goggled him,' he said. Leo liked looking at pictures of Picasso, rather than Picasso's pictures, and he had exactly that sense of strength and power packed into a compact frame almost as wide as it was high. Picasso and Leo even had the same kind of unapologetic baldness.

'Christian,' Leo said. 'Any luck?'

Tara's dad and I had this ritual. Actually, it was more of a pantomime. We both acted as if my lack of gainful employment was purely temporary.

Leo talked as if my days were spent scouring the newsrooms of Fleet Street where hard-bitten old hacks in green eyeshades looked approvingly at my CV and told me to try again next week, son, and we might just have something for you. Perhaps Leo really believed that lost world still existed, and that there were still newspapers and magazines out there that were hiring, rather than firing.

'No luck,' I said, and Leo nodded as if something would turn up eventually, and his daughter would not have to be our family's principal breadwinner forever. We stood together in awkward silence, waiting for Marlon.

My father and mother, a greengrocer and a dinner lady, had both checked out early – the last generation to kill themselves with cigarettes, dying of smoking-related lung cancer within twelve months of each other soon after I started work. And when Tara had taken me home to her family's home in Bushey, I had secretly hoped that her parents might be up for some sort of informal adoption.

No chance.

Tara's mother – Jen, a serious beauty in her day and into her fifties, a compact, spectacularly pretty blonde who looked like she could have dated Rod Stewart in the Seventies – was friendly enough if distant in the English fashion.

But Leo had never warmed to me, not when Tara first took me home for tea – and to get her laundry done and to collect some cash from her dad – when I was a young music writer in a cheap leather jacket with a face white and drawn from staying up for two nights in a row, and not at any time since.

Leo was a builder. In the middle-class bubble of the music press, Tara had been very boastful about the fact. 'Yeah, my old man's a builder,' she would say, her accent suddenly more London, languidly poking a finger into a hole in the fishnet tights she wore with her Dr Marten boots. She made it sound like Leo was a working-class man who had spent a lifetime grafting in the physical world, a hard-nut manual labourer who had been born into poor but proud London-Irish stock. And Leo was indeed all of that, but he had also gone on to make serious money.

Leo was a builder who had had his own business for thirty years. He made his first real money converting multiple-occupancy Victorian terraced houses into family homes in areas that were ready for gentrification – like the one in Camden Town we lived in, a labour of love for Leo – and more recently his firm had specialised in new-build flats for downsizing, well-heeled boomers with the kids finally off their hands. Leo was where Tara got her entrepreneurial spirit from and there was enough money in the family that the first time I walked into her parents' home, I was stunned. Tara's parents lived in a mansion. Tara had grown up in the lap of luxury. After growing up in a modest, pebble-dashed semi in a quiet corner of Essex, that's how it seemed to me. Everything was white, and new, and looked expensive. There was all this *space* – big rooms, high ceilings, a kitchen with a television set. A bathroom with a television set! It smelled nice. There was a lady from Manila doing the cleaning. The only sign that all of this had been hard-earned was Leo's big white builder's van on the gravel drive, next to a couple of shiny new BMWs.

Bushey was only thirty minutes up the motorway north of London, but to me it seemed like another world. And my sense of wonder only increased as I walked deeper into all that suburban splendour and saw what was beyond the big French doors at the back of the house.

'There's a horse in your back garden,' I said.

The three of them laughed at that – Leo, Jen and Tara in perfect amused harmony – and we all stood and watched a horse amble lazily across the rolling green field that stood immediately beyond their manicured back garden, sweeping up to a single-storey brick building.

'That's Half Acre Field, not our back garden,' Tara said. 'And that's not a horse – that's Maple.'

'Mable?'

'*Maple*,' all three of them said, as if I had insulted the favourite member of the family.

'Like the leaf,' Tara said, smiling at me as she read my mind.

You never mentioned anything about a bloody horse.

'Tara's horse,' Jen said. 'She's old now.'

There were photographs all over the white room where we drank our tea and watched Maple out in Half Acre Field. They were the silver-framed photographs that proud parents always used to display before life migrated online and they were on every available surface. Above the open fireplace, on top of a piano, lining the window-sills. And most them featured Tara in all her adorable childhood, doing something with Maple. Brushing Maple. Sitting on Maple in a hard hat and jodhpurs and riding boots, proud Leo holding the reins. And Tara grinning a gummy smile, her milk teeth newly gone as she held out a palm of whatever it is that a horse eats. Oats, is it? And then older, Tara a young teenager now, and Maple suddenly bigger, Tara holding a blue rosette that she had won in some pony club competition, her arm around Maple's neck, her face growing into the Tara that I would know and love.

'Our family has always had horses,' Leo said, as if it was something I needed to understand if I was planning to stick around.

As the lemon drizzle cake came out and we watched Maple doing her languid horsey stuff in Half Acre Field, a whippet-thin old man appeared from the stable at the top of the field. The old geezer, Tara told me, was Uncle Jack – formerly Gypsy Jack – who had turned up at the front door when she was a little girl and Maple was a colt, attempting to sell the young horse for fifty quid. Leo bought the pony on the spot and put Jack on the payroll to take care of her. The building at the top of the hill was home to Uncle Jack as well as a stable for Maple. It turned out the horse stuff stretched back for generations in the Doherty family.

'My father was a lad in stables,' Leo said, and his wife and daughter fell into a kind of delighted spellbound silence, although I suspected they had heard the story many times. 'In racing stables just outside Dublin. Before my father crossed the water as a young man to work in the building trade. The Doherty family always worked with horses, all the way back to as far as anyone can remember.'

'And Granddad did his courting on a horse, didn't he?' smiled Tara. 'That's how he wooed Grandma, right? Tell Christian.'

Leo nodded his big bull head. 'Your granddad used to ride an Irish draught mare across fields to see your grandma when they were both sixteen years old.'

Was Leo's accent becoming more Irish as he told the tale of his romantic, Irish draught-riding dad? As he told his tale, I thought I could hear his London accent softening, some of the old country slipping into his vowels. We were all silent for a moment. Maple was in the field, staring into space. The old man – Uncle Jack – was walking back to the stable.

'And do you ride, Christian?' Jen said, her Debbie Harry face suddenly close to mine as she topped up my tea.

I nodded enthusiastically, and then shrugged, suddenly afraid I might be asked to saddle up.

'*Oh, you know, just a bit*,' I almost lied, anxious to ingratiate myself and my mouth full of lemon drizzle cake. But I saw a light in Leo's eyes suggesting he saw right through me and I quickly shook my head.

I got why Leo didn't love me at first sight. That was understandable. He thought I was a phase, a leftover from Tara's wild years, and not her future. In the years since that first day that Tara took me home to her folks, I had not shown Leo anything to make him change his mind and that hurt me more than I wanted it to.

All the significant moments when Leo might have warmed towards me – when I had landed a grown-up job on a national newspaper, when I married Tara, the birth of Marlon – had failed to win him over. When we first met, Leo had taken one look at me and decided I was not good enough for his daughter – and so it had proved. Leo was always painfully polite to me, but I could see that losing my job had confirmed all his worst suspicions. After leaving school at sixteen Leo had built his building business up from nothing and a stay-at-home father was an oxymoron to him.

Fathers supported their families.

That's what fathers did.

That's what fathers were for.

But although I knew that I would not have been his first choice for a son-in-law – I would not even have scraped into the top ten – there was a part of me that always liked Leo because of his unconditional devotion to his daughter and grandson.

We both loved Tara and Marlon.

And if nothing else, Leo and I would always have that in common.

Deep inside the school, the going-home bell rang. Leo straightened up with excitement as the children started coming out. And suddenly there was Marlon, walking alone, his shirt untucked, his blond mop looking like it had never been combed in his life. The most beautiful boy in the world.

His grandfather and I shouted his name together, as though we had rehearsed it.

'Marlon!'

The headmistress, Mrs Macduff, a doughty Scot in her last year before retirement, stood at the school gates shaking hands with the tiny children. Mrs Macduff knew all their names, and she had the same instruction for all of them.

'Eye contact!' she told Marlon, as she told them all. 'Eye contact!'

We walked home, Marlon chatting between us about his day, holding our hands. This is when it was easiest for my father-in-law and me, when Marlon was there, gabbing away.

Just as we reached the house, a Smart car turned into the far end of the street.

It began to hurtle towards us.

The car that wanted to kill my family.

'I'll see you inside,' I told Leo and Marlon.

Neither of them moved.

The car was getting closer, still gathering speed.

I felt a surge of anger as I stepped into the middle of the street.

The driver slammed on his brakes and the car stopped.

I saw now that the Smart car man was even older than I had thought. He must have been around Leo's age, somewhere around sixty.

'Twenty,' I said, my voice shaking with emotion.

'What?'

Just one word and I hated him even more. I heard an educated voice, and a life of privilege and money and education. It infuriated me that you could have all of that and still be so stupid, so arrogant, so careless with the safety of others.

'*Twenty*,' I said again. 'The speed limit on this street is *twenty miles an hour.* What were you doing in your stupid car? Fifty? Sixty?'

'Oh, *fuck off*,' he said, and it sounded like a second language in his mouth.

Fark orf. Even the way he cursed me got my blood up.

We glared at each other and then he drove past.

But as the car reached the end of the street, his arm appeared from the window as he raised a middle finger at me. Not two fingers, in the British style, after the fashion of our archers taunting the French at Agincourt. But the more international middle finger.

A man of the world. A global kind of guy.

Leo and Marlon had still not moved. Leo was holding Marlon close, shielding his eyes, as if he did not want his grandson to witness my total inability to keep him safe. I looked at Marlon's face.

And that is when I snapped.

The car was still idling at the end of the street.

He did not drive away.

He wanted me to see.

The middle finger was still in the air. And when he saw me watching, the finger began to slowly move up and down.

'Daddy?' Marlon said, fear and uncertainty in his voice.

I looked at Leo.

'Please take Marlon inside now,' I told him.

And they still didn't move.

There were recycling bins on the pavement ready for tomorrow's collection, one of them so full that the lid was half-open.

There was our empty bottle of Prosecco on top. I snatched it up by the neck and stepped into the street.

'No,' Leo said, coming after me. 'Christian – no!'

The bastard was still giving me the finger when the bottle left my hands.

The police arrived within the hour.

At the time, I wasn't sure if that was fast or slow. I watched them coming from the window of the living room.

Two uniformed officers. A young woman and an older man who looked too long in the tooth to be in uniform. The squad car was parked right outside, and they took their time strolling up the path. In a few windows up and down the street, our neighbours watched the show.

Leo looked up from the sofa where he was reading *The Call of the Wild* to Marlon, and shook his head in disbelief.

'But what should I have done?' I said, unable to keep the resentment out of my voice.

'Stuck one on him,' Leo said, and turned back to the book. '*There is a patience of the wild – dogged, tireless, persistent as life itself.*'

I opened the door before the police could ring the bell.

'Hello, sir,' the old cop said. 'Sergeant Cooper and this is WPC Patel.'

The young female cop muttered something.

'Oh, yes,' said Sergeant Cooper. '*PC* Patel. I keep forgetting we don't have WPCs any more!' He beamed. 'Senior moment! May we come in?'

It wasn't a question.

He was already stepping over the welcome mat.

'You could have killed someone today, sir,' the old copper said, almost conversationally.

I had to laugh at that. '*I* could have killed someone? *Me?* Do you know how fast that cretin was driving?'

PC Patel looked at my kitbag where I had dumped it in the hall. There were a pair of red 16-ounce Cleto Reyes boxing gloves on top. She picked one up and showed it to Sergeant Cooper, as if it was evidence.

'Like your combat sports, do you, sir?'

'It's just to keep fit. I don't hit anyone, if that's what you mean. I punch bags, and mitts, and thin air. Not people.'

'Well, you hit that car with a bottle, didn't you, sir? You hit that all right, sir.'

I was learning the police use *sir* as a synonym for *you fucking dickhead*.

I suddenly felt sick with shame. Sergeant Cooper was right. I was a dickhead.

Sergeant Cooper told me that the driver in the Smart car wasn't pressing charges. But they wanted to scare me. And they wanted to see me. And they wanted me on file. And they wanted to give me a warning.

Leo made tea for everyone. Marlon showed PC Patel Buddy's full repertoire of amazing tricks – slowly laying on his side at the vague promise of a treat, basically – while Leo and the old cop were soon talking man to man, the urgent fraternal whispers of two tough but wise old boys who knew how the world worked.

'The car was definitely fast,' Leo muttered in the kitchen as he and Sergeant Cooper sipped their tea. 'No need for that bottle – no, of course not. He's home all day, you see. Lost his job. Too much time on his hands. Yes. I don't know what's wrong with him.'

They were talking about me like I was some kind of mad housewife obsessed with the minutiae of life on my little street.

And maybe they were right. Maybe that is what I had become.

Sergeant Cooper chugged down his tea and came to say goodbye.

'I don't want to see you again,' the old cop told me, his voice with that sudden teak-hard tone that comes so easily to officers of the law. 'Do we understand each other, sir?'

I nodded.

Tara came home as the police were leaving. She tried to listen to all of us at once – Marlon, her dad, me and Buddy barking excitedly – as we crowded around her telling the story.

'He only chucked a bloody bottle at some motor, didn't he?' Leo said.

'Buddy did tricks for the police lady,' Marlon said.

'Sorry,' I kept saying. 'I'm so sorry to bring trouble to our home.'

'Baby,' she said, her eyes filling up. '*You're* my home. You and Marlon and this mad, flea-bitten mutt.'

Buddy took the noise up a notch.

'Listen,' Tara said, taking my arm and leading me down the corridor, until we stood under her framed magazine cover. 'I've been thinking about it – let's move.'

'Move?'

'Let's get away from this street. Get out of this house. *Start again.*'

Why would we would we want to do that, I wondered?

'All we need is each other,' she said. 'You and me and Marlon. That's all we will ever need.'

And as Tara told me that everything would be fine, and Leo and Marlon left us alone, I could taste the salt as she held my face in her hands and covered it with all those kisses that I had not earned, and all those tears that I did not deserve.

9

TARA

On the front desk first thing next morning, Michael the receptionist fluttered with concern.

'This gentleman says he's your first of the day, Tara, but there's nothing in the book ...'

James Caine was sitting in reception, his face impassive.

He looked older, and he looked like a stranger, and that was the thing that made my stomach fall away.

I do not know you.

This man I had shared a bed with, this man who had been inside me, this man who had the power to smash up my life. Who the hell was he? I walked into my office, numb with shock, blanking both of them.

Mary and our new girl-Intern – Skyla – were waiting for me.

'You need to see this right now,' Mary said.

Through the glass partition, I could see Caine saying something to Michael that made my receptionist laugh nervously. James Caine was a man, I saw, who acted as if he was at home anywhere. That's what I had liked about him, I realised, but now the supreme confidence that was indistinguishable from overbearing arrogance made my skin crawl.

'Skyla found it,' Mary said.

The girl-Intern looked at me with her huge wide eyes. She had her laptop in her arms. She had struck me as a child when I first saw her. Now I saw she was just young and nervous. But whatever she had found, I did not have time for it now. I glanced again through the glass. James Caine and Michael were laughing together. Michael was as easily charmed as a Labrador.

'Tell her,' Mary said.

'It's a blog,' Skyla said, dragging me back. 'It's called *The Accidental Dater.* A woman writing about her experiences with online dating.' She scrolled through the site. 'My date with Mr Married Man,' she read. 'My date with Mr Roving Eye. My date with Mr Thief.'

'Let me see.'

I sat at my desk and skimmed through the last one.

In the morning I told him – I have to go to work, so let yourself out. And he did. And when I got back he had gone. And so had my iPad, some cash I had in the bedroom drawer and a Tiffany frame with a photograph of my cat.

'I'm afraid it comes with the territory,' I said, leaning back in my chair, my eyes drifting back to James Caine waiting in reception. He smiled at me and I looked away. 'Tinder alone has got nearly sixty million users in 190 countries. Online dating is full of these creeps. The guy who is already in one or ten relationships. The guy who looks like Brad Pitt in his profile picture and the Elephant Man in the flesh. And the one who is a married man, the one who is always looking over your shoulder for something better to turn up and the one who steals a silver-framed photograph of your cat.'

'You're not looking, Tara,' Mary said, her voice bristling with irritation.

'It's all about us,' Skyla said.

'Look closer,' Mary said. 'Really look this time, will you, Tara?'

And so I did.

Mr Married Man – met through: Angel Eyes, I read. *Mr Roving Eye – met through: Angel Eyes. Mr Thief – met through: Angel Eyes.*

'I'm sorry,' Skyla said, her huge manga-sized eyes clouded with concern.

And I knew that this could be the end of everything we had worked to build, this could be the start of a contagion that would ruin us all. And if my business fell apart, how would my family survive?

But I did not have the space in my head to think about financial ruin. Not now. Not with James Caine sitting on the other side of the glass, grinning at me as if he knew things about me that the rest of the world would never know, not even my husband.

'No, it's OK, Skyla, you did good,' I said.

I looked at Mary for her damage assessment.

'Clearly the optics stink,' she said. 'This blog makes Angel Eyes look like a safe space for predators, and it makes us look as though our clients – or rather a lot of the men – are creeps.'

'Why us?' I said. 'Why not Tinder or Bumble? Or OkCupid or CoffeeMeetsBagel?'

Mary shrugged.

'Who would do such a thing?' Skyla said.

'Someone who wants to hurt us,' I said. 'A business rival. The big boys wouldn't bother, but it could be a rival start-up.'

'Why don't you think they're genuine?' Mary said, surprised.

I scrolled through the blog, more carefully this time.

A sixty-second trawl through his social media crowing reveals that Mr Married Man has a lovely wife and three adorable children. And I am still on the bus to the restaurant.

'They could well be genuine,' I said. 'But singling us out looks like an act of spite against this company.'

'Should I do a press release or something?' Skyla asked. 'To say – I don't know – that we do all we can with validation?'

I looked out at James Caine and I truly could not think about any of this stuff right now.

'Maybe the Accidental Dater is just unlucky in love,' I said, more flippant than I felt.

'We have to take it more *seriously*,' Mary said, and I felt her investment in this company, and how it was in some ways much greater than mine, as if she really believed deep down in her sweet-natured heart that we were selling happy endings. But the world did not work that way. I knew we provided a good service for our clients, but I do not believe that anyone finds their happy ending by going online and providing a credit card number. Mary was a tech genius and I loved her to bits but, let's face it – she did not have much real-world experience with men.

'I am going to have to ask for the room,' I said.

Usually my office was open house but Mary stood up and indicated the door to Skyla. I rapped on the glass to Michael and he sent James Caine into my office.

Immediately, he tried to take me in his arms.

I stepped back and clattered into my desk.

'Are you fucking insane?' I said, looking out at the office. Mary, Skyla and Michael were crowded around the intern's laptop, reading about the adventures of the Accidental Dater.

'I want to sign up,' he said, smiling. 'I want to meet a beautiful, incredible woman—'

I felt like slapping his face.

'How dare you?' I said. 'How dare you take those photographs of me? How dare you send them to me? How dare you come to my place of work?'

'But you looked beautiful in them.' He seemed genuinely confused. 'God knows I didn't mean to upset you, Tara.'

'Are they still on your phone? Christ almighty, what are you? Fourteen years old?'

'I would never *show* them to anyone,' Caine said, his face clouding. 'Look, I can see you're angry. You blocked me on your phone, didn't you? If you want me to, I'll delete them, of course.'

Mary looked up and waved at me, giving me a tight grin, letting me know that we would get to the other side of this mess. There were blinds on the walls of my office that I could pull down. But of course that would have made it all seem even worse.

'Do it now,' I told him. 'I want to see you do it. Delete them. Go on.'

I watched him delete the three images, the big heavy Rolex Submariner sliding up his wrist. When he was done, he held out his phone for me to inspect and I ignored it.

'What do you *want*?' I said.

'Isn't it obvious? I want you.'

He took a step towards me and stopped when he saw the warning light in my eyes. But he was still smiling, as if it was all a good joke. I wondered what it would take to wipe that smug *I've-fucked-you-good* smile off his face.

'Remember how it felt, Tara? When we were in Tokyo?'

'You can't come here. It's wrong. It's inappropriate. I want you to leave now.'

And finally his cocky smile disappeared. 'Would you prefer me to come to your home?' he said, and for the first time I really understood that it was not going to be as easy as pressing *block caller*.

There were three framed photographs on my desk and he picked them up, one by one, and studied them. I didn't like him touching them, and I didn't like him looking at them, but there was nothing I could do to stop him. He made me feel helpless and I understood that he liked making me feel totally helpless. He likes that more than he likes anything, I thought, as I watched him looking at my world.

The first photograph was of Christian alone, and younger, just a year or so out of the music press and still in the same cheap leather jacket. His hair was far longer than it was now and his smile different somehow. He seemed unburdened, young, not married yet, no child yet. The Christian who I fell in love with. And the second photograph was of Marlon, around three, hugging Buddy the puppy around the neck, our boy with a big ecstatic grin on his face, and the tiny Lab grinning gamely. And finally James Caine picked up the photograph of my family, of the four of us, including Buddy, enjoying a summer day out at Henley, the sun-dappled Thames in the background. A photograph of our life.

'Your family,' he said. 'I've enjoyed looking at you.'

'Looking at us?'

'Online.' He replaced the photograph. 'You can find out about anyone these days.'

There was something wrong with my breathing.

'I do understand,' he quietly went on. 'I've seen all the pictures on Instagram of your husband and son and that adorable dog.' His face split with a grin. 'I'm not some stalker, Tara. That's what you have to understand. I'm not some mad bunny boiler!'

I looked through the glass partition. The little party had broken up now. Michael was manning the front desk and Mary and Skyla must have drifted off to the cafe.

'I know we have to be discreet,' Caine said.

I almost laughed in his face.

'You think coming to my office is discreet? You think sending photographs of me in your hotel bed is discreet? You thinking sniffing around—'

I saw the first flash of his temper.

'I'm not *sniffing around* anything, Tara. You think I want sex? Is that why you think I'm here? Look, if that's all I wanted, there are women *everywhere*. Great women. Willing women. But I want an emotional connection. I want intelligent conversation. I want intimacy. I want friendship. I want a companion. I just want to talk and text on a regular basis. I want *to chat*.'

'To chat?'

'We had something that night in Tokyo, Tara. You know we did. And I don't want it to end so soon.'

'What about what I might want?'

'I think I know what you want.'

I took a long breath and tried to control the hammering of my heart.

'Are you threatening me?'

'I'm just saying – *you can't pretend it didn't happen*. That's all. That's the thought for the day. Is that what you're trying to do, Tara – to pretend it didn't happen? Sorry – *I will not allow it*.'

'I would like you to leave now.'

He laughed.

'Who's going to throw me out? That fruit you have working on the front desk?'

'Me,' I said. 'I'll throw you out if I have to. You think I can't do it?'

'Oh, come on! I don't want to argue.'

'Then go.'

'As you know, I live in Brighton but I stay at the Langham Hotel when I'm in London. Meet me there.'

'That's not going to happen.'

'But I don't want it to end.'

'It never *began*, James. It really didn't.'

There were tears in his eyes.

'I have a life too,' he said, nodding at the photographs on my desk. 'Or I *had* a life. I had a wife. Lost her to breast cancer. Thirty-nine. Three years ago. Our daughter was thirteen. Can you imagine what that's like? For her? For me?'

I let out a breath that was ragged and shaking.

'Listen – you're a good guy. That's why we connected. That's why ...'

Why what, Tara?

'You have to understand,' I said, trying again to make him understand. 'There's just no room in my world for whatever you're looking for. My life is already full. Sorry.'

He smiled, but there was something sour in it now, something toxic and twisted and with that hint of spite that I had felt in his bed.

'So what was it then? Tell me that and I'll be off and you never have to see me again. What was it? A bit of fun for a bored wife? A sexual thrill while you were away from home? A big mistake?'

'Christ, I don't know. Why does it matter? All of the above.'

'Well.' He sighed elaborately. 'I can't pretend I don't feel a little *used*, Tara,' he said, his mouth contorting with a spasm of spite.

'And I can't pretend I don't feel a little scared, James. You have pictures of me on your phone. You turn up at my office uninvited.'

He smiled, pleased with himself now, gaining his confidence again. No, it was always more than confidence. James Caine was only sweetness and light when he was getting what he wanted and when he wasn't, everything turned ugly as sin. I had called him a good guy but that was only because I wanted to get shot of him. He was not a good guy. He was a good-looking bad man, with a mean streak.

'May I give you a present?' he said. 'Two presents, actually. Then I'll go.'

I waited. He brought out two tickets and placed them on my desk. They were for a show at the Royal Albert Hall.

'Bryan Ferry,' he said. 'Your company is named after his song, isn't it? "Angel Eyes".'

I shook my head. He had it completely wrong. He had everything wrong about me. I thought of my father and his old vinyl record collection.

'You've got the wrong "Angel Eyes",' I said. 'We're named after the Frank Sinatra song. Two different songs, both "Angel Eyes". We're the Sinatra song.'

'Ah.' He frowned at the tickets on my desk. Then he remembered his other gift.

It was a telephone, still in the box but with the cellophane wrapper torn off, as if it had been opened and charged.

'It's in case you ever need a friend. Or something more.'

'No thank you,' I said. 'I've already got one. A friend, I mean. And a phone. Listen – James – I don't think you understand. You need to get this into your head. *I've already got a life – and you are not a part of it.*'

'And I don't think you understand, Tara. *You've got a new life now – and it includes me.*'

I watched him through the glass walls as he left. He smiled at them all – Michael and Mary and Skyla, carrying drinks from the cafe – Caine gave them his wide white smile dialled all the way up and all three of them smiled back, totally charmed.

I looked at my desk. He had taken the tickets for the wrong "Angel Eyes".

But he had left me the phone.

10

TARA

'Who was he?' I asked Ginger.

We were in the kitchen at home. She quickly shot a look back at the living room where Christian and Spike were scrolling through restaurant menus on Christian's laptop.

'The boys can't hear us,' I said. 'Who was he?'

'Who?' she said.

'The guy,' I said. 'You know, the one you had an affair with.'

We both stared at the men in the living room. Before Marlon was born, the four of us would go out to restaurants two or three times a week, but this had been reduced to one takeaway a week delivered to our place. We took turns in choosing. Tonight it was Christian's turn.

'Not Thai again,' Spike was saying.

'Tara likes Thai,' Christian said.

Marlon and Buddy sprawled on the carpet beside them, the boy's hand running through the soft fur on the dog's belly, the dog with its head thrown back in dreamy ecstasy. Ginger's voice was so soft I had to lean in close.

'You never met him,' she said.

'Somebody from the gym?'

'No, I didn't meet him at work.'

'And how did it start? How did it end?'

'Why do you want to know all this stuff?'

'Because you understand what happened to me. You've been through it. And I can't talk to anyone else.'

She sighed. 'Spike and I hit a rough patch early on. I know these things are meant to happen when a marriage has been going for years but that's not what happened to us. We had only been married for eighteen months or so. I thought at the time that maybe Spike and I were built for honeymoons. We liked all that – the passion, the drama, the excitement, the mad sex. But when the fever wore off, it took some time to adjust to marriage. Bills and bins. And there was someone I had known before.'

'Our age?'

'Older,' she said quickly. 'A bit. But he was nothing like—' She would not say James Caine's name in my house and I was grateful. 'Your one,' she said. 'My one was *kind*. Kindness is very underrated in a man. Sometimes that's all you need. And he knew me. And we talked, because we knew each other well enough to talk. And one night he said – '*You know I'm on your side*,' and I said, '*I know you are*.' And that was it – we were off.'

'How long did it go on for?'

'Too long.' She glanced toward the living room. 'We should go in to join the boys.'

'How did it end?'

'Look – it just fizzled out, OK? No big dramas. The way it fizzles out when you both understand that nobody is going to leave their family.'

'Married?'

'They're all married, Tara.'

'And Spike never knew?'

'Spike would have killed him if he knew.'

Such an easy thing to say, I thought. Such a hard thing to do.

I'll kill you.

'You can't compare what happened to me with what's happened to you,' Ginger said, and for a moment she had that wistful look when an old lover is remembered. 'As I say, he was nice.' She squeezed my hand. 'You're going to get through this and I'm going to help you.'

'He wants to own me, Ginger.'

She took both my hands in hers and held them hard until they stopped trembling with sickness and fear. She was the best friend I ever had in my life.

'And what do you want?' she said.

'I want him to go away,' I said.

And then we went to join our men.

'I can't believe it's Thai again,' Spike complained. 'Christian always chooses Thai. I'm going to turn into a vegetable spring roll. I'm going to dream about Pahd Thai noodles. I'm going to stop coming round.'

'Oh, don't stop coming round,' Marlon said desperately, looking up from stroking the dog's belly.

Christian grinned at me. There had been one spectacular Thai meal that I had loved a year ago and since then every time it was Christian's turn to choose the takeaway, my husband ordered Thai for me.

I smiled back. I knew he was thinking of me but how could I break it to him? Sometimes a girl just wants a good pizza.

Later, after we had demolished green curry, spiced fish cakes, Pahd Thai, chicken satay and, yes, vegetable spring rolls, Spike held up his palm and grinned down at Marlon.

'Go on, smack it, mate,' Spike said. 'Smack it as hard as you can.'

'Don't teach that beautiful boy to be a thug,' Ginger said. 'He's not like you, Spike.'

Spike and Ginger loved Marlon with the sense of wonder of grandparents, or childless friends who you suspect are trying, and have been trying for a while. But even if – when – they had their own child, I knew their love for Marlon would be undimmed.

Marlon's eyes gleamed with excitement. He raised his hand and very slowly and very gently touched his tiny fist against Spike's calloused open palm. Spike recoiled with mock agony, howling with theatrical pain. Marlon smiled shyly while Buddy barked and capered, excited at having visitors in the house that played such totally brilliant games.

'Enough,' Ginger said, grabbing Marlon and hugging him close. 'My Marlon's a sweet boy, a gentle boy.'

'He's a wild man!' Spike insisted. 'He's a sleeping volcano, ready to blow. Just like his dad!'

Spike had been greatly amused by Christian's brush with the law.

'I'll tell you what, mate,' Spike said approvingly, 'I bet he doesn't speed down *this* street any more.'

Christian pushed his glasses up his nose, always a sign that he was embarrassed. He looked shame-faced as he opened a second bottle of Shiraz.

'Time for bed,' I said. Marlon and Buddy were both getting overexcited.

'Five more minutes,' Marlon said. 'I implore you.'

'And I implore you to go and brush your teeth,' I said, proud of his new word.

'Want Auntie Ginger to put you to bed?' Ginger said.

Marlon was apologetic. 'My daddy reads me a story.' He picked up *The Call of the Wild* from the coffee table and showed it to Ginger.

'You know, angel,' I said, 'you're allowed to have lots and lots of different books.'

'But I like this one. It's about a dog.'

Spike looked at the cover. 'It's not about a dog called ... Buddy, is it?'

Marlon smiled politely. 'No, it's actually about a dog called Buck.'

Christian filled our glasses and then nodded at Marlon.

'Come on, kiddo,' he said. 'Let's hit the hay.'

Buddy trooped after them as they left the room. Ginger leaned back in her chair, looking at me over the rim of her wine glass. She nodded. It was time.

Spike had wandered off to the far side of the room and was flipping through Christian's extensive record collection. He pulled out a copy of *Sticky Fingers* by the Rolling Stones with the original Andy Warhol artwork on the cover – the image of the jeans with a real zip. Spike began testing the zip.

'So vinyl's coming back, is it?' he said.

'Vinyl never went away,' I said.

Ginger looked at me. I shook my head. So she started the thing herself. 'Tara has a problem,' she said.

Christian's voice came over the child monitor.

'*Buck was ravenous. The pound and a half of sun-dried salmon, which was his ration for each day, seemed to go nowhere. He never had enough, and suffered from perpetual hunger pangs.*'

Spike didn't look up from the cover of *Sticky Fingers*. 'Problem?'

'She gets these cranks,' Ginger continued. 'Because of her business.'

'Yeah, I bet!' Spike laughed. 'The Internet creaks and out come the freaks!'

'There's this anonymous blogger,' I said. 'The Accidental Dater. She writes about the dates she has had through Angel Eyes, all these dates from hell. She's got a lot of followers. *A lot*. And it could really hurt the business.'

I was babbling, and totally avoiding the subject. Ginger frowned sternly at me.

Spike was still fiddling with the Andy Warhol zip on the front of the album, trying to undo it.

'Cranks,' Ginger said. 'Total nutjobs, right, Tara?'

Spike smirked over his shoulder at us, not taking it remotely seriously.

'Dates from hell,' he chuckled. 'Well, we've all had a few of those, right?'

'And one of them – one of these cranks – *is a man*,' Ginger said. 'And he's starting to scare Tara.'

Spike finally looked up.

'To really scare her,' Ginger said.

'OK,' Spike said, paying attention at last.

'He's not leaving Tara alone,' Ginger continued. 'It's starting to worry you, right, Tara?'

They both looked at me. I nodded.

'So who's this guy?' Spike said, looking back at the *Sticky Fingers* album. But he wasn't messing about with the zip now.

I said nothing. I had no idea what to say.

'He's a disgruntled client,' Ginger said simply. 'And he's making a nuisance of himself.'

'What – online?' Spike said. 'Like – what are they called? – a troll?'

'No,' Ginger said, with married impatience. 'Not a bloody troll, Spike. This guy has turned up at Tara's *office*, all right?'

'There *was* some online harassment,' I said, thinking of the three photographs of me sleeping in a stranger's bed that appeared on my phone. 'But it's escalating now. And as Ginger says – one morning this guy turned up at the office.'

Spike was still not quite getting it. How could he?

'And what did he want?'

'He's just some random madman, all right?' Ginger said, heating up. 'Who knows what he thinks he wants?'

Spike looked at *Sticky Fingers* thoughtfully.

'Call the police,' he suggested, carefully placing the LP back in its correct spot. Christian's record collection was fanatically alphabetical.

'Are you kidding?' Ginger said. 'The police are not going to do anything, Spike! Not until it's too late.' She looked at me. 'Tara thought you might be able to help.'

And there it was at last – a direct appeal to the macho Australian male's sense of chivalry. Spike looked at me, and then his wife, and finally at the child monitor, where Buck the dog was starving in the Yukon.

I knew what he was thinking. It was a fair question. *What about your husband?*

'Christian doesn't know,' I answered. 'And I don't want to worry him.'

Spike raised his eyebrows. *Why me?*

It was another fair question.

'There's nobody else I can ask, Spike,' I said, and it felt like the one true thing that Ginger and I had told him. 'There's nobody else close enough to ask.'

I gave him the business card that James Caine had given me in Tokyo and Spike stared at it as if it was written in a language that he could not understand.

'Well,' he said quietly. 'What exactly do you want me to do?'

Ginger impatiently snatched the business card from him.

'Oh, just forget it, Spike,' she said. 'I'll do it myself. I'm going to sort this creep out. I mean it! You think I don't?'

Spike frowned at her, and gently took the business card back.

'I just want to understand what you want me to do. Tell him to leave Tara alone? Is that it?'

He stared at me. I looked at Ginger for help.

'Remember Omar?' she said.

'Omar?' Spike said, his voice neutral, as if he might not remember Omar, but below the surface, I could see that he remembered Omar very well.

'My ex-boyfriend,' Ginger said.

'Your ex-stalker,' Spike said, his tone still even. 'Yeah, I remember Omar. Good old Omar. Whatever happened to good old Omar?'

'He went away, didn't he?' Ginger said. 'Do *that* again, Spike. That's what we want. Do whatever you did with Omar to get him to go away and leave me alone. Is that too much to ask for?'

And now Spike flared with his own married impatience. 'Darling, you have no bloody idea about what happened between me and your ex-boyfriend because you weren't there, were you? And you never asked, did you? You did not want to know.'

For the first time, Ginger looked a little uncertain. 'You talked to him,' she said slowly. 'You went to his place of work, and you talked to him, and you asked him to stop contacting me.'

Spike laughed, and there was an edge to it that made me think this was all a very bad idea. 'That's it! Me and Omar had a good old chin-wag. We had an excellent conversation. We had a frank exchange of views, Omar and I. We cleared the air once and for all.' His blue eyes narrowed. 'You have no idea what happened with Omar,' he told his wife.

My stomach fell away as I wondered what Spike really did to make Omar leave Ginger alone. Now this did not seem like such a good plan. It felt like another misstep. And I was frightened.

Spike was a big friendly bear who doted on his wife and my family but there was something in the muscular bulk of him that reminded me of the police who had come to our door when Christian threw that bottle. Spike was like those cops – all smiles until you crossed some secret line that only they knew about and you knew that in one bad moment it could suddenly all be very different if that secret line was crossed.

'I know it worked,' Ginger said flatly. 'And that's all I care about.'

She crossed the room with the glass of red wine in her hand and kissed Spike on his unshaven cheek. He looked up at her with the same expectant face that Buddy got when he thought he was in line for a treat.

'I know that thanks to you Omar never contacted me again,' she said. 'I know that he never called, texted or turned up on my doorstep with a bouquet of roses and a jumbo packet of condoms. I know the problem – and it was a real problem at the time, let's be honest – ended overnight.'

'That's what I remember too,' Spike said, taking a long pull on his wine, looking pleased with himself.

Ginger leaned into him and placed a soft kiss on his mouth. He looked up at her, eyes shining. He was crazy about her. And that's why she could get him to do this thing for me. So it was perhaps a good idea after all.

On the child monitor I could hear Christian tucking in Marlon.

Spike looked at the business card and then at me.

'James Caine of Samarkand Wealth Management,' he read, and the sound of that name in my home made something choke in my heart. 'Some rich big shot who thinks he can do whatever he likes and there's never any consequences.'

I nodded. 'That's about it.'

Spike was thoughtful. 'So you'd never seen this guy until he showed up at the office? You'd never met him before?'

'What does it matter where she met him?' Ginger snapped. 'He's a problem, Spike. Last chance – you going to help or shall I do it myself?'

I could feel my anger toward James Caine rising, that anger I had felt when I saw those photographs of me on his phone, and the anger I had felt when he had appeared at my office.

'He turned up at the office and I'd never seen him before in my life until that day,' I lied, and then I paused for a little of the bitter truth, because I was learning that lies always work best when seasoned with as much of the truth as you can manage. 'And Ginger is right – he's scaring me, Spike. He's really scaring me. Because I don't know what he's going to do next.'

Ginger came to me on the sofa and put her arm around me.

'You're afraid this guy – this James Caine – might come to the house?' Spike said.

'Yes.'

'You're afraid of what he might do if he turned up here?'

'That's right.'

'And Christian doesn't know because you don't want to worry him?'

I nodded, unable to speak.

Spike slipped the business card into the back pocket of his jeans. 'No worries,' he said. 'I'll have a quiet word.'

'Good boy,' Ginger said, and blew him a kiss. She indicated the empty wine glass in his hand. 'I'll get you a cold one from the fridge, shall I, lover?'

Ginger went off to the kitchen for Spike's beer reward, and we were alone at last. Spike stared at me for a long moment and then his face split into a knowing grin as if, after all these years of being friends, we saw each other clearly at last.

He had listened very carefully to my sad story.

And he didn't believe a word of it.

11

TARA

It was my father's sixtieth birthday and just as we arrived at the party, my phone started buzzing inside my bag. I ignored it but it kept right on buzzing as Christian paid the taxi and Marlon and I stood on the pavement holding hands, the pair of us gazing up at the room above the pub that had been rented for Leo's big night. On and on my phone buzzed as Frank Sinatra sang about escaping down to Rio.

'Doesn't Mama look pretty?' Christian said.

Marlon considered me in my white strapless dress.

'She looks like an angel.'

Christian smiled proudly.

The phone was still demanding my attention and I was still pretending I couldn't hear it. Christian's warm, open smile began to dissolve.

'Do you want to get it?' he said.

'Quick work thing,' I said, slowly reaching inside my bag. 'You two go in.'

James Caine was calling more frequently now.

I had blocked his mobile number but he was using other phone lines that told the little lie – *Unknown Caller.* I knew my caller all too well. He left silent messages but sometimes I could hear him breathing on voicemail, Classic FM in the background, sounding like his patience was wearing thin. Every morning I expected to see him sitting in reception at work. Every night I expected to find him standing on our doorstep. All the time – and I do mean all the time – I was waiting for my life to fall apart.

But tonight was different because tonight there was a text message from my known caller.

It's not safe.

I felt my stomach fall away. I read it again. What wasn't safe? Did he mean that our secret wasn't safe? Or the sex wasn't safe? But the sex had been safe, I thought. He had used a condom. In fact, he had used three condoms. I remembered the self-conscious pause for protection, worth it because of the unstated promise that this would make it all cost free, pain free, that this would make it *safe*. Not safe? I remembered the two times before we slept and the third and final time in the first light of morning, and I remembered feeling desired – physically craved, as if a man was starving for me – like I had not been desired for a long time.

And I felt that way right up until I was brushing my teeth with one of the hotel's complimentary toothbrushes and I saw, next to the heavy Rolex Submariner, the green and cream packet of Cialis poking out of his washbag. I didn't even know what they were and then I read the label and I did. They were pills to make a man harder. To make a man want you more. So it was never real desire. It was the pills doing what they were made to do. Even James Caine's passion was a lie. I read his message again.

It's not safe.

'Tara?'

I shoved my phone in my bag and stared dumbly at three guests who were arriving at the party. Two men and a woman. A prosperous husband-and-wife combo and a man who could conceivably be homeless. The larger of the men, the one with the woman, had a shaven head and a good suit.

The woman with him was attractive but erring on the side of tarty, heels a touch too high for a sixtieth birthday party, the skirt way too short. The other man had a faded attraction about him, as if he had been fresh-faced once but had lost his looks to serious illness, or serious drugs, or both. I had never seen the woman before but I knew the men from my teenage years. The sight of them made me smile with real pleasure.

'The two Daves!' I said, and they grinned self-consciously. 'Big Dave and Mad Dave!'

A lot of people loved my father but Leo was especially loved by the boys who had worked for his building company in their youth. I knew that Big Dave had gone on to start his own building firm. I had no idea what had happened to Mad Dave but it was clear that he had not prospered. Whatever was wrong with him, or whatever he was taking, it was killing him.

Big Dave and Mad Dave!

I took their hands in mine, and they both blushed, like they were boys once more and we all laughed, apart from Big Dave's wife, who smiled uncertainly, as if she was being left out of a private joke. Big Dave had the air of a man who had done very well for himself in a hard and demanding world and now he took control of the situation.

'This is Tara,' Big Dave said to his wife. 'Leo's girl. And this is Suze, Tara, my missus.'

There was a diamond the size of a walnut on Suze's left-hand third finger.

'You all right, Tara?' Mad Dave said, and I realised how poleaxed I must have looked standing there reading the breaking news from James Caine.

I turned my smile up to ten. 'Fine! Let's go inside!'

I took their arms, feeling them flinch self-consciously, and I remembered the two Daves as teenage boys, already out in the working world for a couple of years at a time when I was starting to skip sixth form to watch bands, when cramming for A Levels was being replaced by staying out all night.

I remembered Big Dave was as tight-lipped as a Clint Eastwood cowboy, as if the world left him lost for words, or struck dumb by the powerful, extra-large frame that nature asked him to lug around, while Mad Dave was more confident and garrulous. But fifteen years ago both of them had blushed furiously at me from the passenger seat of my dad's builder's van as I came home from a night out and they waited for Leo on the drive, and they had stared at me with dumbstruck red faces on the nights when they had worked late on some building site and my father brought them to our dinner table to be fed by my mother. They were both tongue-tied in our big house and suspicious of sparkling mineral water and squirming with shy longing for me. The two Daves. It was a lot of fun at the time.

At least, it was for me.

I squeezed their arms now, touched that they had come to pay homage to my dad years after they had stopped working for him, and when we went inside, both my father and my mother greeted them like sons. The room was already crowded. A room above a pub was never going to be enough for my father's sixtieth birthday.

Next to the stage, Christian and Marlon were watching the band set up. Christian was pointing at a Fender

Telecaster sitting on its stand and explaining the provenance and importance of this guitar.

'Keith Richards,' Christian said. 'Joe Strummer. Bruce Springsteen. That's who plays a Fender Telecaster, Marlon. It's the working man's guitar.'

Ginger and Spike came in with a blue box tied in a white ribbon from Tiffany. I guided them across to a table already piled high with presents but Ginger always felt like she had a special relationship with my dad and began squeezing across the room to where Leo was in conversation with the two Daves.

A smooth-looking, silver-haired man in black tie and tuxedo came in and everyone cheered.

'Hank Sinatra!' I said to Spike. 'And he does look a bit like him, doesn't he?'

Spike did not reply.

He looked down at me. 'I'm not a thug,' he said. 'Whatever you might think. Whatever Ginger may have told you.'

'I never thought you were a thug, Spike. I wouldn't be friends with you if I thought you were a thug, would I?'

'I've got a sports science degree from the University of Sydney.'

'Spike—'

'No, you listen to me, Tara. I went to see that ex-boyfriend of Ginger's – bloody Omar, who I can't believe we're *still* talking about after all these years. And he was very disrespectful when I spoke to him, talking about the sex he'd had with Ginger and all this stuff a bloke really doesn't want to hear about the woman he loves. And then Omar went for me, the mad bastard, shouting about *me* stealing Ginger from *him*, and he came off worse. That's the truth. That's what happened. OK?'

'OK,' I said nervously.

'*But that was for my girlfriend*. That was for the woman who was going to be my wife.' He glanced across at Christian. 'I don't know what went on with you and this James Caine guy.'

Christian had picked up Marlon and they were making their way towards me through the crowd.

'Nothing went on,' I said quickly.

Spike shrugged. 'And I don't want to know,' he said. 'That's your affair.'

I felt my mouth going bone dry. I licked my lips.

'But I had a look at him online. This James Caine. He seems like a regular bloke. Good job in the city. Nice house in Brighton. Wife. Daughter.'

I let this settle. 'I think his wife died,' I said.

Spike shook his head. 'His wife's not dead. Whatever he may have told you.'

Christian and Marlon were getting closer.

'And how do you know all this, Spike?'

He looked at me with disbelief. 'Because you can find out about anyone these days! I looked at his bio on his firm's website. He doesn't do social media but his wife does. His missus – Sandy – she's all over it. Instagram. Twitter. Facebook. The lot. They look like a happy, normal family. And I really don't know what you and Ginger expect me to do to him, Tara.'

I felt the panic fly. 'I don't want you to do anything, Spike.'

'I mean, I can have a word with him and ask him to leave you alone, if you want.'

'Just forget it, OK?'

'And I'll do that because Ginger will kill me if I don't. But can I be straight?'

'Go ahead.'

'I think you need to be a bit more honest with your husband.'

Christian and Marlon reached me just as Hank Sinatra came on stage.

'How did all these people get into my room?' Hank Sinatra said, a direct quote from the live *Sinatra at the Sands* album with Count Basie as the band tore into 'Come Fly with Me'.

My phone began to ring.

'I'll be right back,' I told Christian, touching his arm, ignoring his concerned look. He thought I was working too hard. That's what he thought was the problem. I could have wept at my husband's innocence.

There was a staircase leading from the room for private functions down to the pub on the ground floor.

I went halfway down it and pulled out my phone.

Unknown Caller, it said. But I knew who was calling. I felt a surge of rage as I put the phone to my face.

'Never call me again,' I said.

His voice was slow and deliberate, the voice of a man adept at speaking to a tough crowd. 'What's the problem?' he said.

'The problem? Everything's a lie! I know about your wife. She didn't die, did she?'

'Is that why you're angry? We're separated but we've remained on good terms. I would recommend it to anyone. We stay together for the sake of our child. I was speaking metaphorically. She's dead to me.'

'Metaphorically? You told me *cancer.* You lied to me.'

I remembered how my heart had gone out to him when he told me about his wife dying of breast cancer. But it turned out that the wife was alive and well and living a wonderful life on social media. He was a liar and a phoney. Even his blood-gorged, three-times-a-night, fuck-you-blind passion had come out of a cream and green packet of Cialis prescribed by some Harley Street doctor.

'You're a fake,' I said. 'Everything's fake. And I want you to leave me the fuck alone now, OK? Don't call, don't text, don't leave messages on my voicemail with "Smooth Classics" on in the background. I'm warning you – *I am telling you to leave me alone.*'

His voice was very quiet. 'I am trying to do you a favour.'

'How the hell are you doing me a favour?'

'Because I have been trying to tell you, Tara – the sex we had. *It wasn't safe*.'

I took a deep breath, looking up the stairwell towards the party. I could not see Hank Sinatra but I could hear him. Hank Sinatra had finished 'Come Fly with Me' and was talking about my dad. He was asking Leo to come up on stage. People were cheering. It was a good night. Tears came to my eyes.

'Tara? Are you still there?'

I remembered again the three stops for protection. The brief transaction – pressing the pause button on passion to ensure that what happened far from home stayed far from home. I remembered the belief – even when the guilt was growing like a tumour inside me, even when I was crying in the toilet of a business class cabin on my way home – that there was one thing at least I didn't have worry about.

Because it was safe, wasn't it? The sex had been safe.

'The condom broke, Tara,' he said. 'That third time. Remember that third time? When it was light? The condom split. These things happen.'

'That's not true. You're just saying it. Why didn't you tell me then?'

'Because I didn't want to worry you. I was trying to be a gentleman. But I'm telling you now. Tara, my darling?'

My father had taken the microphone and the crowd were laughing. I felt a physical yearning to be among them with a drink in my hand and my arm around Christian's waist and with my mind free to be happy. I should not be hiding on a stairwell talking to a man I did not know about our unsafe sex.

'James,' I said. 'I know I'm not pregnant because my period started this morning.'

He chuckled, pleased with himself.

'I'm afraid there's something else,' he said. A beat of terrible silence. 'And I'm sorry to have to tell you this, Tara.' He did not sound sorry. He sounded as though he was loving it all. 'You need to get tested for HSV-2.'

I could not speak.

'Do you know what HSV-2 is, Tara?'

I was silent for a long moment, my mind racing.

'Is it an STD?' I said at last, the dunce at the back of the infidelity-for-beginners class.

'Well, *technically* it's an STI. A sexually transmitted infection as opposed to a sexually transmitted disease. HSV-2 is most contagious during an outbreak of sores but sadly it can also be transmitted when no symptoms are felt or visible. And *I* felt fine so I'm sure *you're* fine – probably – and I don't want you to worry, my darling – but do get tested at the earliest opportunity, will you? And for goodness' sake don't have unprotected sex with your husband!' His sickening little laugh. 'Or indeed anyone else.' Silence on the line. 'Wait – you haven't had sex with him already, have you?'

I remembered sharing a bottle of Prosecco with Christian. I remembered our kisses. And I remembered the old familiar hungry way we had loved each other and the way Christian had held me until we slept and beyond, and how we had both felt it without saying any words – that we had recovered something we believed to be slipping away, or already lost.

'Are you telling me the truth?' I said.

He made a sound that was something like a cackle.

My head was spinning. 'If you destroy my family, I'll kill you,' I said.

He chuckled at that.

'If anyone destroys your family, Tara, *it will be you.*'

And all at once I saw that he was not new to any of this.

'How many more of us are there?' I said. 'How many more women have you knocked off at business conferences with your wise advice on public speaking and your clever cures for jet lag? How many times have you charmed their pants off? How many times have you made this call, James?'

'I don't know,' he said, as if he was seriously calculating the number. 'Dozens? It's certainly not three figures.'

'You rotten, rotten bastard.'

He sighed. 'It's so easy. Some sexually frustrated wife a long way from home who doesn't get fucked as regularly as she used to. Some bored old bird, not as young as she used to be, not as firm as ten years ago, looking for a bit of love action with no comeback. Someone just like you, Tara.'

My heart was attempting to burst out of my chest.

'But listen – you're special to me, Tara, and I want you to come to my room at the Langham because we need to talk this over face to face.'

'Stay away from me,' I whispered. 'Stay away from my life.'

'Look, I'm sorry I said those things. You're the first, OK? Is that what you want to hear? Then I'll say it. This has never happened to me before.' He was laughing at me now. 'I only said it to hurt you because I'm very upset that you've been avoiding me. Acting as if nothing happened between us.'

His voice was cold now, as if he might truly hate me. 'And you can't ignore me. *Because I will not allow it.* Because I will not permit you to use me for one night and then toss me aside. I'm not a piece of meat, Tara. I'm not a sex toy you can stick in a bottom drawer when you have had enough – or when you get scared that your darling hubby is going to find out the truth. *I'm in your life now and I am not going away.* One way or another. If you wanted to just fuck me and throw me aside, then we should have used better condoms.'

I wanted to beg him to tell me that it was not true. But I could not speak. And somehow, deep in my blood and bones, I knew it was all true. I believed him.

Finally, at long last, James Caine was telling the truth.

'Tara? I think you're breaking up?'

He was right. I was breaking up. I was hot, I was dizzy, I could no longer think or breathe. The sweat was sliding down my bare back and under my white party dress. I bent over, as if I had been punched in the stomach and as I straightened up a wave of sickness swept over me and all at once my legs could no longer support me.

And then there was only the blackness.

When I woke I was lying on the stairs, surrounded by what felt like everyone I had ever known. Christian and Marlon. My parents. The two Daves. Ginger and Spike. Hank Sinatra. The music had stopped.

'Christian?' I said, and he came towards me with Marlon in his arms, and looked at me with such concern that it tore my heart out because I knew he would not look at me that way when he knew what had happened in Tokyo. Then Marlon was crying with fear and Christian took him away, my mother fluttering off with them, and suddenly Ginger was crouching by my side, smoothing down my strapless white dress where it had ridden high above my thighs.

'Oh, Tara,' she said.

'Fresh air,' my dad ordered. 'Where are the boys?'

The Daves stepped forward.

And one of his boys – he still called them his boys, these grown men with lives of their own, with triumphs and disasters that we knew nothing about – scooped me up as if I weighed nothing.

I looked into the worried face of Big Dave. Mad Dave went ahead of us, clearing a way through the party guests who had crowded onto the stairwell to gawp, getting the door as I was carried into the street.

Spike caught my eye and looked away with what might have been shame.

You big pussy, I thought. For all your bulging biceps! For all your cardiovascular workouts! Look at all these real hard men, Spike. Not gym-hard. Real-world hard. Look at the two Daves, Spike.

They would do anything for my father. I bet they would die for him, I thought, and I bet they would kill for him.

Then we were on the street and the night was cool and Big Dave gently parked me on a bench by a bus stop. My father knelt before me, the streetlights shining on his big bald Pablo Picasso skull.

'Sorry, Dad,' I said.

'Ah, it's OK, angel face.'

'I'm spoiling your party.'

'You're not spoiling anything.' Leo looked up and down the streets. 'We can have the party out here! Hank Sinatra can sing "Angel Eyes" at the bus stop! You like that song, right?'

We smiled and then his face grew serious.

'You work too hard, Tara. You try to do it all for your family. You push yourself and you push yourself and in the end your body tells you to stop. Believe me, I know what it's like.'

There were tears in my father's eyes and I felt terrible. He should not have tears in his eyes on his sixtieth birthday party. He touched my face and smiled with his infinite tenderness.

'You really bought the ticket this time, didn't you?' he said.

12

CHRISTIAN

This was how I knew my wife was having an affair.

The same way that everyone knows.

The same way that you will know.

It's the phone, stupid.

Tara's phone was a dead giveaway. And my wife's phone had, I saw now, been giving her away for quite a while.

Tara's phone was no longer left lying around our home – casually dropped on the coffee table or dumped on some random kitchen surface or on the table where we sat down as a family to eat, or stuffed half-forgotten in a bag or coat, or dropped on the dressing table by the side of our bed. At some point – *how had I missed it?* – Tara had started guarding her phone in a way that she had never done before. Her phone was suddenly under close personal protection. There was never a moment when I could mistake it for my own phone – an identical

Apple iPhone X – and pick it up by accident, and not know that I had the wrong one until I saw the photo on the home page (Marlon and me and Buddy smiling on Tara's phone).

That just didn't happen any more.

And so there was never a moment when I could covertly pick it up and start scrolling through my wife's secrets. But why would I want to do that? I could see that Tara had secrets she did not wish to share. And I did not want to know. I turned my face away. I told myself that it was the imagination of a sexually jealous, stay-at-home dad with too much time on his hands and a knockout, high-flying wife who was constantly out in the world, the eyes of men on her everywhere. My attitude to Tara's phone changed too. I stared at it clutched in her fist like it was an unexploded device.

And I didn't want it near me.

But it wasn't just her phone. There were other ways that I knew something precious had – somewhere, somehow – been damaged.

This cool, calm, supremely confident woman – scared of nothing, my wife – now visibly flinched at the sound of the doorbell or the land line ringing or footsteps coming up the driveway.

What was out there that was so terrifying to Tara?

What did she imagine was coming for her?

And for us?

Then we came home from Leo's sixtieth birthday party and she realised that she had lost her phone when she fainted.

And that was even worse.

Leo's party ended earlier than planned. When we were back at home, I was getting ready for bed while listening to Tara's frantic voice on the landline in the living room, calling the pub again and again and again, asking if anyone had found her phone yet, calling until they had all gone home or decided to put on the answer machine. She came into the bedroom with her beautiful face drawn tight with anxiety.

'Fancy a bottle of Prosecco?' I asked, thinking that there was still a way to save the night.

She smiled and nodded, glancing away.

Eye contact, I thought, like Marlon's headmistress saying hello and goodbye to the children every day. *Eye contact!*

But when I came back with the open bottle and two glasses, Tara was sitting on the edge of the bed, one palm resting against her head, still woozy and unwell from passing out.

So of course I told her that it didn't matter, that there would be another bottle when she felt better.

'I could use a cuddle,' she said.

But she held me too tight, making the moment bigger than it should have been, and I felt this new feeling again, the sinking dread that there were parts of Tara's life that I knew nothing about.

And when I woke up the next morning she was already calling the pub where Leo had had his party, asking a cleaner who clearly did not speak much English about the missing phone. I brushed my teeth and went to the kitchen and poured the undrunk bottle of Prosecco down the sink.

And as those flat bubbles went down the drain, I thought – *Oh Tara, what have you done?*

And what will it do to us?

Later that morning I was stretching at the gym, my right foot lifted up on the windowsill, feeling the pull in my hamstring, waiting for Spike.

He was talking to one of the new trainers, a stunning young Korean woman, the gym's new yoga teacher. When she went off to the locker room, Spike picked up a 12-kilo medicine ball and lobbed it to me with a knowing grin. I caught it against my abs, feeling the whoosh of breath.

'How would you like to see her downward dog?' he said.

I smiled politely. I always gave Spike a pass on the harmless sexual banter. That was just him. Spike being Spike. He seemed to think it was required of him. That's what I always believed. But perhaps that was another thing I was wrong about. I threw the medicine ball at him, putting my weight into it, and he chucked it back to me at half-velocity.

'Listen, Christian,' he said. 'I need you to cover for me tonight.'

We paused as the Korean woman emerged from the locker room, shouldering her kitbag as she smiled at Spike and headed for the exit.

I said nothing. Spike watched her go, unable to tear his eyes away.

He turned back to me just in time to receive the medicine ball.

'There's something I've got to do,' he said, wrapping his arms around the ball, holding it close, caressing it.

The gym was filling up now, the morning rush hour of people trying to get in a session before work, and he took a step towards me, smiling as if we understood each other.

'Come on, mate. You're out with me tonight, OK? Even if you're not really. I mean, Ginger is not going to ask you. She's not. But just in case she does.'

I shook my head. 'Maybe not.'

He stepped away, offended.

'I'd do the same for you, Christian.'

'But I don't *need* you to do the same for me, Spike. I don't need you to lie for me.'

He tossed the ball at me and I felt it slam against my chest. I threw it back and he caught it neatly in his big meaty hands.

'I'm not asking you to *lie* for me,' he said.

He threw the ball at me, slightly harder than necessary. It was already slick with our sweat.

'Sorry but I don't think so, Spike. I wouldn't want to lie to Ginger. She's been Tara's friend for a long time. And my friend, too.'

'Yeah, all mates together. Not going to rat me out, are you, mate?'

I threw the ball at him. 'I'm not going to rat you out. You do what you like, Spike, but I'm not going to lie for you.'

'You don't even know what you're covering for.'

'I've a pretty good idea.'

'No, mate. Believe me, you haven't a clue. You think I want to bang the little yoga teacher? Is that what you think?'

He went to say more but then shook his head.

'Go ahead,' I told him. 'Say what you want to say.'

And so he did.

'*You* don't get to lecture *me* about loyalty, Christian,' he said.

'I'm not lecturing you about anything. You do what you want. But just leave me out of it.'

'And you don't get to lecture about being faithful.'

Now I was offended.

I had never been unfaithful to Tara. Not even in the early days, when we started seeing each other at the paper, and we were not even officially together yet. I didn't care. From the moment I saw her, she was the only one I ever wanted.

Spike threw the ball at me so hard that it spun me sideways.

I dropped the ball.

People were staring at us now.

'Look to your own family, mate.'

I laughed in his face.

'You know nothing about my family,' I told him. 'Mate.'

I picked up the medicine ball. I threw it at him.

And then I got it.

When Spike talked about being faithful, he didn't mean me.

And this was how I knew that my wife was *not* having an affair.

Because when it was time for Marlon to go to bed that night, Tara placed her fingertip in his dimple and said, 'I'm going to kiss you *right there*,' and our boy placed his fingertip against her face.

'And I am going to kiss you *right there*,' he echoed, and their smiles came up like the sun.

That was the exact moment when I knew it was all in my head.

Because I trusted her.

Because I knew her.

Because I loved her.

Marlon trooped off to his room, Buddy padding behind him.

I stood in the doorway, looking back at her, *The Call of the Wild* in my hand.

'Love you,' I said.

'Love you, too,' she said, and I went back to place a quick kiss on her mouth, feeling my body flood with relief.

I knew. I just knew. Nothing and no one could ever break what Tara and I had together.

Because it was stronger than death.

TARA

The bedtime story of Buck's adventures in the Yukon was coming through the child monitor when the doorbell rang. My heart leapt to my throat as I went to answer it but I found Big Dave standing there. On the kerb there was a brand-new Range Rover Discovery with its engine idling and Big Dave's tarty wife – Suze? – in the passenger seat. Suze was watching me with her wary, unfriendly eyes.

'You dropped this,' Big Dave said. 'When – you know – you weren't feeling very well.'

My phone. Oh thank God. I grabbed it.

'Thank you, David,' I said.

'Suze found it. She picked it up. Stuck it in her bag. Forgot to tell me until we were back at our gaff.'

Suze was still looking at me, as if she knew things about me, as if she saw right through me. But Suze could not have opened my phone, and she could not have seen any messages, and she could not have wandered at will through my other life, could she? My phone opened with facial recognition and, quite frankly, Suze and I could not look more different.

But she still looked at me as if *she knew*.

I waved to Suze in a friendly, thankful fashion.

She nodded coolly, the stuck-up cow.

I licked my lips and stared at the phone in my hand. I was holding it so tightly my knuckles were white.

'Tara?'

I looked at Big Dave.

'Is there something wrong?'

I bit my lower lip. Grief choked in my throat.

But as I gripped my phone, I realised that I knew nothing about Big Dave or Mad Dave, not any more.

My memories of them were when we were all in our mid-teens, when my wild years were just getting started and they were young apprentices working for my father, embarrassed and intimidated when they were taken to the big house. I was no longer that teenage girl and the two Daves were no longer blushing boys.

'Tara?'

I looked up and somehow I was not surprised to see that Big Dave was staring at me as if his feelings for me had never died.

'Yes, David?'

'Do you need some help with anything?'

I took another breath.

'There might be one small thing,' I said.

13

CHRISTIAN

On Saturday Tara announced she was taking Marlon up to visit her parents in Bushey and so it was just me and Buddy in Camden, our presence at the big white house surplus to requirements. The dog and I were arriving home from our walk when a car turned into our street. I tensed, tightening my grip on Buddy's lead, expecting the green bug to come screaming towards us. But the car that appeared was a big gas-guzzling black Mercedes, ambling down the road, very slowly, as if looking for an address.

It came to a halt beside us.

A man got out of the driver's seat. He was maybe ten years older than me, a rich-looking man in a blue suit with a wide white smile – warm, friendly, reassuring.

A nice man.

A teenage girl emerged from the passenger seat and as the man approached me she turned her head to look at me, frowning before she looked away, dipping her long face to the phone that she gripped in her fist.

But the man was charming enough for both of them.

So it was really happening, I thought.

Tara had put the house on the market, strangely passionate about our family starting again somewhere else, maybe even moving out of the city, and she had told me the estate agent had already arranged for some potential buyers to come round. I was surprised that Tara hadn't mentioned this viewing but then she had had a lot on her mind recently.

The man held out his hand and I shook it.

A good handshake.

You could trust this man, I thought.

'James Caine,' he said.

TARA

I dropped Marlon off at my parents' house and told them that something had come up at work and I needed to drive back into town immediately. The pair of them were so crazy about Marlon, the smiles never wavered. They were probably delighted to have their grandson all to themselves. So I kissed my beautiful boy goodbye, got back on the motorway and put my foot down, anxious to keep my appointment with the doctor.

*

In the hush of the close, faintly scented air of the waiting room, I felt an unexpected pang of sympathy for the Accidental Dater, who was still busily blogging against us.

'Mr Angry Man – met through: Angel Eyes,' I read on my phone.

> *It is over before it really begins with Mr Angry Man. Because he is quite obviously disappointed in what he sees when he looks at me for the first time. He has been drinking for a while when I arrive at the restaurant. I have a couple of glasses at the table to settle my nerves but he is clearly pissed off with me for being so disappointingly ordinary so I tell him thanks so much for meeting but I am texting a friend to pick me up now. He simmers silently at the table until my friend arrives and that's when he really loses it. As my friend and I leave the restaurant, he follows us into the street. First he calls us dykes. And then we are whores. He tells me it's not over between us until he says it is over and bangs once, very hard, on the windscreen of my friend's VW Beetle until we fear for our lives. And only then does he go away. For this is what you have to understand – it's not about sex with Mr Angry Man. It's about control. It's about humiliation. Revenge. Power. That's what it's all about with Mr Angry Man.*

It all had the horrible ring of truth, I thought. The Accidental Dater was no jealous business rival trying to harm my company. She was a woman who had been misused by the men that we had matched her with, and my heart sank because I knew that this one blogger with a grudge had it within her power to end everything for me, all the hard work and the grand dreams and the million setbacks and anxieties and occasional triumphs that come with building your own business in a world that owes you nothing. And who would support my family then?

The Accidental Dater could quite easily wreck my life. Assuming, that is, that I had not wrecked it already, all by myself.

'Mrs Carver?' the receptionist said. 'The doctor will see you now.'

CHRISTIAN

I showed James Caine into our home.

His daughter – Amy, he told me, because she didn't say a word when I introduced myself – trailed behind us, a gawky overgrown child with apparently no interest in the world beyond the screen she clutched, totally immune to the charms of Buddy as he tagged along with a big grin, Lab-happy to have a young stranger come to visit.

'Are you guys local?' I said.

'No, we're down in Brighton,' Caine said, his eyes drifting to the framed magazine cover of Tara in our hallway. I moved towards the stairs but he remained where he was, gazing up at the picture.

'My wife,' I said proudly.

He nodded, not taking his eyes off her. She did look great in that photograph. But he stared at Tara smiling in her short black dress until I had to clear my throat to snap him out of it.

'Shall we start upstairs?' I said.

The pair of them followed me to the top of the house and I felt my love for this place, our big, beautiful Victorian pile in this quiet corner of Camden Town. Did we really need to leave? What was so great about starting again? Why did we need to start again somewhere else? This house had been our only real home and I felt a surge of sadness at the thought of moving out. I wanted things to stay exactly the way they were.

James Caine was silent as I gave him the big tour, his expression totally blank as he took in Marlon's bedroom and the upstairs bathroom, and he only lingered when we came to the master bedroom. He stood at the end of our bed, taking it all in, almost as if he were inhaling the room.

Tara, I saw, had left a nightdress on the back of a chair.

This slim slip of silky stuff that slid up and came off so easily.

Date-night kit. Prosecco wear.

I waited for Caine to break the silence with some comments or questions about the house. But he just stood there, staring at the nightdress. It seemed to fascinate him. The silence grew between us. It didn't seem to bother him. He could be as mute as his teenage daughter when he wanted to be.

'So you're moving to the city?' I said.

He started at my voice, turning his smile on and the awkward moment was over.

'Well, we might. With our family home down in Brighton, I have to stay up in town when my work demands it. For my sins! I'm here in town, as a matter of fact. At the Langham – do you know it?'

I nodded.

'Opposite the BBC in Portland Place. It's a grand old hotel. A lot of history. Amy's school has kept us down on the south coast but she is off to university next year so everything will change.'

Amy leaned against the doorway, unsmiling and unimpressed. Caine gave the bedroom one last look before turning away.

'Coffee?' I said, hoping he would decline, hoping he would make his excuses and leave, hoping that he could not imagine his family living in our house.

'Cheers,' he said.

We went downstairs and as I made coffee, his daughter drifted off to the car while he went into the living room. When I brought in two cups and a cafetière he was examining my record collection, his fingertip carefully tracing the cracked spines of my old LPs.

'Quite a collection,' Caine said. 'How much is it worth?'

The thought had never crossed my mind.

'I don't know,' I said. 'It's priceless.'

He chuckled as if that was my little joke. As if everything had a price.

He selected an LP and pulled it out. On the cover a beautiful young man with tangled long hair and a sad face stared from a window at autumn's falling leaves.

'Nick Drake,' James Caine read, as though the name was new to him. 'He's a sensitive-looking fellow.'

'Nick Drake was a brilliant singer-songwriter,' I said. 'Back in the Seventies. Died very young.' I hesitated. 'My wife's first love,' I said.

James Caine laughed.

'Really? Her first love?' He smiled at the cover. 'He looks like some sort of hippy. She was keen on this Nick Drake character?'

'Crazy about him. Although he died long before she was born. Lucky for me.'

'The romantic kind!' he said.

'That's my wife!' I agreed.

'Tara,' he said, almost smiling, and then there was just the long silence of the room as we stared at each other and I felt my stomach fill with a feeling that I could not name.

I had not told him her name.

'Who the hell are you?' I asked him.

I caught up with him on the street.

Now he wanted to go. Now he wanted to get away from me. Now he could see that he had pushed me too far with whatever sick game he was playing.

'Thanks for showing us the house,' he said quickly, not quite so cool any more, opening the car door, his daughter already in the passenger seat, the girl looking up at me for the first time as though I might actually exist.

'Wait,' I said, stepping into the street. 'I'm not done with you.'

The front door was wide open and Buddy sniffed the welcome mat, unsure if he should step out into the world.

I grabbed James Caine by his arm.

'I want to know what you're doing here,' I said.

He shook my hand off.

'I'm thinking about making you an offer. For your house, I mean. Not your wife.'

I could not work it out. I could not put together the pieces.

But I could feel the threat that this man posed to everything I loved.

'Just stay away from my family,' I said. 'And stay away from my home.'

And he nodded, as though he would comply, but his mouth tightened and he looked at me with one last surge of defiance.

'Or what?' he said.

'I'll kill you,' I said.

TARA

When I got back to Bushey, my parents and Marlon were out in Half Acre Field with the horse and Uncle Jack. I could not believe what I was seeing. Marlon was dressed head-to-toe in riding gear. Marlon, who had never shown the faintest interest in riding, and who had always regarded Maple with a kind of quiet terror, was suddenly the pony club poster boy in shiny new riding boots, breeches, a padded body protector and a riding hat that was slightly too big and kept slipping over his eyes. From the French windows at the back of the living room, I watched with mounting disbelief as my parents attempted to get him onto Maple's back.

My dad crouched before Marlon, giving my five-year-old son what was no doubt a manly pep talk and then an encouraging pat on the shoulder. Then Uncle Jack steadied Maple, soothing her snow-white muzzle and holding her on short, tight reins while my mum patted her blond helmet of hair into place and then, with great effort, hoisted Marlon up, swinging him through the air in the vague direction of the saddle. As he came in for landing in the saddle, Marlon's breeches-clad legs went ramrod straight and he began to cry.

Maple – my lovely Maple, always the most sensitive of horses – trotted nervously on the spot, snorting with anxiety. Maple knew that this tiny rider was reluctant to sit on her back. She could feel it in her blood and bones. My mother aborted the attempt, placing Marlon gently on the grass, pushing back his oversized riding hat so she could wipe his eyes.

'There's something wrong with that bloody horse today,' my father was saying as I reached them. Uncle Jack was down on his knees examining one of Maple's rear hooves with a tool that looked like a cross between a small hammer and a miniature pickaxe – a nailing hammer, is what we call it in the riding world, used for the healthy maintenance of your horse's hooves. If you want to dig out a stone that is trapped between hoof and horseshoe, or remove a bent nail, or fix a loose shoe, you use a nailing hammer.

Uncle Jack held up a tiny pebble for my father's examination.

'That could be the problem,' Uncle Jack said. 'Old Maple might not be so skittish now.'

'It's not Maple's fault,' I said. '*He doesn't want to do it, Dad.*'

I picked up Marlon and held him tight, his snotty little nose pressed against my shoulder. I shook my head at my father.

'Dad, Marlon doesn't *want* to ride a horse,' I said, pulling off the brand-new riding hat and handing it to my mother. 'And you can't make him.'

'Your father's not *making* him!' my mother said angrily, always ludicrously quick to leap to my father's defence.

Marlon sighed against my neck, his breath warm. He buried his face deep into my shoulder. After his hectic morning of almost horse-riding, he seemed suddenly ready to fall asleep.

'We all ride in this family!' my father said, red-faced with frustration, making it sound like an order, and I thought he was going to reminisce about coming from a long line of stable lads in the old country, bejeebers. But he did not have the heart for it today.

'He can't sit inside all the time,' he said, 'just looking at a book.'

I held out my hand for Maple's reins and Uncle Jack passed them to me, the nailing hammer hanging limp by his side.

'I know you're trying to be kind,' I said to my dad, because I saw that he was not angry or frustrated, not really. He was *hurt*.

This was meant to be a big day, a happy day, the day that Marlon fell in love with horses the way I had, a love that would last a lifetime, and it had all gone wrong. 'I know you want Marlon to love riding the way you did and the way I did,' I said. 'But maybe it's not his thing.'

My dad laughed shortly, as if he had never heard such an outrageous suggestion, and he turned back to the house, my mother soon catching him up.

'Thanks for trying, Uncle Jack,' I said.

He nodded as, deep inside my bag, my phone began to vibrate. I ignored it and started up to the stable at the top of Half Acre Field, leading my horse by my side and holding my son in my arms. The phone stopped and then immediately started again, one of those callers who simply refuses to be ignored. Maple looked at me askance, the way that a horse will, that furtive sidelong glance they give you, exhaling with nerves and nothing showing in her huge eyes except equal measures of love and panic. I stroked her face, more for my own reassurance than hers, for I had never quite lost the feeling, my last souvenir from childhood, that nothing could ever really harm me if I was with Maple.

As we reached her stable at the top of the field, I answered my phone.

'I just came from your home,' James Caine said.

14

TARA

The long spring day was growing dark when I sat in my car with Ginger, parked outside her home, feeling so exhausted that I could have happily slept for a lifetime. Through the big bay front windows, I could see Spike moving around the living room of their ground-floor flat, chomping on what remained of the takeaway pizza that had been their dinner. My stomach rumbled and I was suddenly aware that I had had no time to eat anything today. I had dropped Marlon home with Christian and now it would be time for the brushing of teeth, and putting on pyjamas and a story before bedtime, all the sweet rituals of late in the evening with your five-year-old. I felt the ache for my home and my family and it gnawed at me like hunger.

'You have to end it now,' Ginger said. 'Are you listening to me? Jesus Christ – the bastard has been to your *house*, Tara. He's been *inside your home*. If this guy doesn't stop, if you allow this to go on, then you're going to lose *everything*. Your family. Your home. Your life. *And your fucking mind, Tara*. And why? Because some creepy guy you don't even know will not leave you alone. *So stop it!*' She slapped my arm. 'Are you listening to me?'

'I don't know what to do, Ginger.'

'Go to that hotel he shacks up in. He's there now, right?'

'*I can't*.'

The thought terrified me.

'You can.'

I exhaled, my breath ragged. 'And do *what* exactly?'

'Tell him to back off! Tell him it's done!' She squeezed my arm until I could feel her fingers pressing into bone.

I pulled away from her, suddenly desperate.

'No, Ginger. *Please*. I don't want to. I just want to go home and sleep.'

'You *have* to tell him he has to stop contacting you. Final warning. Tell the bastard to leave you alone. I'm coming with you, OK? You're not going to be alone. I'll be right by your side.'

And for the first time, I thought about it.

'Maybe,' I said quietly. 'Maybe it's the best thing to do, Ginger.'

'It's the only thing to do, Tara. And you make it very clear that if you ever have to tell him again, it will be on the doorstep of his lovely home in Brighton – in front of his wife and their brat and their cat and all the next-door neighbours.' Ginger's mouth twisted with disgust. 'That usually works,' she said.

It was dark by the time we got to the hotel.

There was a homeless man sitting on the pavement outside the Langham Hotel. He was set up with an old Staffie and his cardboard sign and his backpack, only a short way from the main doors where the wall of the grand hotel curved elegantly away from Portland Place towards Oxford Street, but conveniently out of sight from the top-hatted doormen. The Staffie huddled against the homeless man with naked adoration in the cool spring evening.

A British soldier, his cardboard sign said.

'This is a bad idea,' I said. 'It's late. Let's go home. There has to be some other way.'

'You tried the other ways,' Ginger said. 'They didn't work. He came to your office, Tara. He came to your home.'

I nodded. Oh, he was just some crank, I had told Christian when I arrived home with Marlon in the early afternoon, the story meticulously rehearsed in my head on the drive home. That's who James Caine was, I said, even managing a wry smile. Sorry he bothered you, Christian, but he is just one of those sickos who sees a woman online and thinks they have some sort of connection. The Internet creaks and out come the freaks, I said, quoting Spike. That had apparently been enough to calm my husband. Perhaps it was exactly what he hoped to hear. At least, there had been no suspicion in Christian's eyes, no indication that he thought that I could ever do something that could destroy our life.

'I've seen his type before,' Ginger was saying. 'The world is full of creeps like James fucking Caine. And this particular creep is never going to be happy until he breaks you and your family in pieces.'

I knew it was true. I remembered the gloating look in his eyes when he came to the office.

I fucked you three times, that look said. *And your husband hasn't got a clue, has he? And I can have you again any time I want, can't I?*

'Stop,' I said, and Ginger put her arm around my shoulder as I bent double, my stomach heaving. I retched once, and then again, my stomach muscles cramping, but nothing came up. I straightened, tasting the bitter bile in my mouth.

'Done?' Ginger said.

I nodded.

She patted my back. 'Good girl.'

The homeless man – the British soldier – was watching us. For the first time, I saw how young he was. He saluted us with a small smile.

'Have a good evening, ladies,' he said.

'Thank you very much,' Ginger said. 'You too.'

We kept moving.

'You know the room number?' Ginger said.

'He sent me a text.'

Three innocuous numbers. That was all. Numbers that would mean nothing to someone who saw them by accident. He had it all worked out, the rotten bastard.

Ginger began heading towards the main entrance but I stopped her. The Langham has a side door for the hotel restaurant and bar, and that's the one we took. It is much more private. No top-hatted doormen, fewer guests coming and going. But the bar was crowded. We crossed the lobby where a security guard in a dark suit hovered by the lift, his eyes evaluating us for a poker-faced professional beat – me in my Stella McCartney jacket and Ginger in her casual-but-chic Sweaty Betty active wear – before he smiled deferentially and held the lift door open for us.

'Ladies,' he said. 'Have a good night.'

We went up to the top floor.

The lift door closed behind us and the noise and bustle of the ground floor suddenly felt light years away. The corridor on the top floor was empty apart from room service trolleys and dinner trays that had been left outside some of the doors. We started down the corridor and, as we turned a corner, a shadow disappeared into the service lift. We paused for a moment, listening to the hotel hush, and then walked to James Caine's door.

A piano sonata was playing softly inside. *Do not disturb*, red LED lights said on the frame of the door.

Ginger rang the bell.

No reply.

'He's probably got some woman in there.' Ginger said. 'Open up, creep!'

She banged on the door.

'He's not in there,' I said. 'Let's go home, Ginger.'

'Oh, he's in there,' she said, giving the door a sharp kick.

And it opened. By no more than an inch, but the piano sonata was suddenly much louder. Ginger and I stared at each other and then she very gently pushed the door open as far as it would go.

'Hey!' she called, but not quite so bold now.

No response. Ginger hesitated for a moment and then went inside.

I glanced up and down the empty corridor, and then I followed her.

The room was pristine in its fussy neatness, as if the maid had only just done her evening rounds, turning the sheets back on the bed, placing a complimentary chocolate on the pillow, replenishing the fruit bowl of a favoured guest. The sound of Ludovico Einaudi tinkling the ivories came from the massive HDTV.

The bathroom door was open, all lights blazing, and there were fresh white towels that had never been touched.

It was as if the room was still waiting for its occupant.

And then Ginger cried out. Not loud. Hardly a sound at all. More of a sharp inhalation of total and dumbfounded disbelief.

She stood with her hands over her mouth as I went to her side and stared down at the space between the sofa and the big HDTV where the dead man was lying on his back.

James Caine.

He had been dressed for seduction, in some kind of silk bathrobe, wantonly open now, nothing underneath apart from tight white Hugo Boss briefs, his penis a modest indentation against the cotton, and although his face was unmarked there was a black halo of blood staining the carpet around his head.

The back of his skull had been smashed in.

He looked very debonair and very dead, like Hugh Hefner if some rabid Bunny had beaten Hef to death with a sharp object.

James Caine stared up and beyond me with his lifeless blue eyes, apparently totally fascinated by some fixed point in the ceiling, and as I moved a step closer I saw the sickening dent where his skull had been caved in just above his right ear. That side of his head was a mess. He had been hit more than once, clearly, and he had been hit when he was down, and he had been hit even as he was drawing his last breath. He had been killed in a frenzy.

Ginger found her voice. 'Is he … ?'

'Oh yes,' I said.

Then I was aware of the chaos around him. The room was not so neat after all. There was an ice bucket by his side, melting ice cubes scattered all around his silky bathrobe, and a bottle of Dom Perignon between bare hairy legs that were bent at an unnatural angle. The bottle was unbroken but its shield-shaped label was smeared with something. Hair, bone, blood. Maybe a little brain. I could not stop staring at the smeared label.

Ginger was on the phone.

I heard the voice at the other end, and it was as if I was waking up.

'*Emergency services? Which service do you require?*'

I grabbed at Ginger's wrist and pulled the phone away from her mouth. We could still hear the operator asking which service we required. I snatched Ginger's phone and turned it off.

'*Are you fucking crazy, Tara?*'

I prised the phone from her fingers. 'Ginger? Listen to me. Please?'

'Are you *insane*?'

She tried to take back her phone but I held it away from her.

We wrestled for a bit but she was far stronger than me and quickly reclaimed it, and then she stared at me, both of us gasping for air.

'We have to tell them, Tara. You know we do. You're in shock.'

'Yes. Of course we do! I understand. But before we tell them, I have to tell Christian everything. Because the police, Ginger – *they will want to know why we are here*. It's all going to come out now, isn't it?'

She shook her head. She could not understand why we had to wait. I placed my hands on her phone, stopping her making the call.

'Before we tell anyone, I have to tell Christian what happened in Tokyo. He's going to find out now, Ginger. I know I can't stop it all coming out. So I have to tell him about Caine, and how really sorry I am, and how much I love him. *Please, Ginger!*'

She exploded. 'The man's been murdered, for Christ's sake! We have to tell the police *now!* We have to tell the hotel *now!*'

'Yes, but first let me explain. Just let me tell Christian. I don't want him—'

Ginger was crying with rage.

'No!' she shouted, shoving me away as she punched in 999. 'No, Tara, no. I'm sorry. But just *no*.'

She was already speaking to the operator as I ran for home.

15

TARA

Christian was still getting ready to put Marlon to bed when I burst through the front door. It was way past Marlon's bedtime, even for a Saturday night, even for a day when he had shed a lot of tears and needed some cheering up, and the pair of them were immediately on me, smothering me in kisses, and I felt sure they would see that I was soaked in the sweat of panic and dread. But they did not notice and I envied them their over-excited, ready-for-bed innocence, and their open-hearted smiles, and their good lives. Buddy scrambled up my legs with the Labrador's simple and eternal message:

I love you, I love you, I love you!

Their welcoming faces, the simple decency, their unquestioning trust – it all broke my heart.

'Say it,' Marlon ordered. 'Say our special words!'

I placed my index finger in the dimple of his chubby cheek.

My hand was trembling and nobody noticed. Marlon and Christian grinned with happy anticipation.

'I'm going to kiss you *right there*,' I said, my voice trembling, sounding strange to me, like the voice of someone else, someone I did not know, someone I had never expected to be. I looked at my husband and I could not believe that he could not see it all in my face, the whole sorry mess, the terrible truth.

'Christian?' I said quietly.

'Be right back,' he said. 'Put a couple of glasses in the freezer, would you? It feels like a Prosecco night. We've all had a rough day.'

I sank into the sofa as the three of them – husband, son and dog – went off to brush teeth and put on pyjamas and get ready for a bedtime story.

Christian's phone had been left on the coffee table and I stared at it dumbfounded, knowing that I could never leave my phone lying about like that. Not any more. Never again.

I picked it up and began scrolling through his text messages and email and WhatsApp, looking at his life, searching for the secrets that he kept.

Shopping for pain. That's what I was doing. Because I deserved some pain tonight. I deserved a lot of pain.

But Christian's life was good. And he kept no secrets from me.

And soon, punch-drunk with exhaustion, soon I was losing myself in his Instagram account and in the happy images of our family, and all the spectacular sunrises he had loved, and the skateboarding, squashed-faced French bulldogs that made him smile, and the Fender Telecaster guitars he craved. And I could have begun sobbing and never stopped for all that I had so stupidly thrown away.

His voice, the voice I loved, came through the child monitor.

'*Buck was neither house-dog nor kennel-dog,*' he read. '*The whole realm was his ...*'

I looked at my own phone, for a message from Ginger, for a sign that it had all been a terrible mistake and nobody was dead and the police were not coming.

But there was nothing. Ginger had made her call. Of course she had. A man had been murdered.

'*He plunged into the swimming tank or went hunting with the Judge's sons. He escorted Mollie and Alice, the Judge's daughters, on long twilight or early morning rambles. On wintry nights he lay at the Judge's feet before the roaring library fire.*'

When Christian came back into the living room, holding the Puffin Classic edition of *The Call of the Wild*, Buddy padding behind him, he saw that I was holding his phone. And he didn't even flinch.

How many men can you say that about? How many women?

Christian was smiling as he placed *The Call of the Wild* on the coffee table.

I carefully placed his phone on top of the book. Then I went to him and found his mouth with my mouth, my perfect fit.

He laughed when I squeezed him as hard as I could. He hugged me back, with none of my damaged, desperate madness in his embrace, and I snuggled there in his arms, enjoying his sweet warmth and hard bulk, as familiar to me as my own face.

'Love you,' I whispered, dislodging his glasses with the top of my head.

'Love you too,' he said, adjusting his specs.

And I wanted him inside me.

And I wanted him to hold me.

I wanted him to tell me all those things about loving me forever, all those priceless promises that I had been so careless with, all those treasures I had taken for granted, all that love I had betrayed. I wanted to wake up in the middle of the night and discover – and it always felt like a small miracle to me – that we had been holding hands in our sleep.

I never did that with anyone else, I wanted him to know. *I never held hands in my sleep with any other man. Nothing meant anything apart from you.*

But it was too late for all that now.

That was all over. That time was done.

Christian's smile finally faded when he saw my eyes were bright with tears.

And I knew I must tell him now that everything he thinks he knows about his life is wrong.

His phone began to ring.

'Don't answer it,' I said, and something rough in my voice froze him.

He held me at arm's length, all smiles long gone.

'Tara?'

His phone stopped ringing.

'What? Tell me. Come on, I want to know.'

No, I thought. You really don't. But I looked at his face and I took a breath.

Then I heard the sirens and I felt my husband pulling away from me, as if he was pulling away forever, and there was a look on his gorgeous face that tore me apart, because it showed that he did not understand what I had brought to our family's door, and into our home, and into our marriage, and into our bed.

The blue lights of the police cars filled the room. And I knew they had come for me.

We seemed paralysed, Christian and I, too frightened to move as we waited for the knock at the door.

When it came – the gentle rap of knuckles on wood, perversely ignoring the doorbell – I was the first to react.

'I'll get it,' I said. And then I stopped. 'Christian?'

'What?'

'I mean it, you know. I really do. I love you.'

'But what do you think they want?'

'Say it again.'

'Love you too,' he said, but he was distracted now, and worried, and scared, and he still didn't know, and he still didn't suspect that everything was about to come crashing down.

There were two policemen at the door. A young female officer and an older man, too old to still be in uniform. The sergeant who was here once before.

But they had not come for me.

'Mrs Carver, is it?' the old cop said, as if there might be some doubt about my marital status. 'We're here for your husband.'

HAVING

16

TARA

'The bitch is still there,' Mary said, staring out into the bright early morning, taking an angry bite out of her apricot croissant.

We huddled inside the smoked glass doors of Angel Eyes, watching the woman who haunted the only way in and out of our mews.

'Bloody journalists,' Mary said.

'But – the thing is – she doesn't *look* like a journalist,' Skyla said.

Our young intern was right.

The woman keeping guard at the end of our mews looked too old and too rich to be a journalist. She was a tall, lean fifty-something in a neat Chanel suit with a Stella McCartney bag and a phone the size of a dinner plate. All the journalists I had ever known looked young and poor. I rubbed my eyes, sticky from a sleepless night spent staring at my phone for messages that never came

– from Christian, from Ginger, from the police, from anyone who would tell me that the world was unchanged. I had walked the dog before Marlon was awake, and then taken him to school in a kind of fever, nauseous with exhaustion and fear, terrified that Christian must know by now what I had done, and all the while my heart was aching with the knowledge that he would never look at me in the same way ever again.

I was also worried sick that the police actually believed he had something to do with the death of James Caine.

Why the hell else would they come for him?

I had got to work early and my staff were already there with multiple messages to call the same persistent journalist. Mary, Skyla and Michael had convinced each other that this journalist wanted to write some kind of 'My Dating App Hell' feature on Angel Eyes, pegged to the Accidental Dater's latest courting misery. If only! I knew – I just knew – that the woman at the end of our mews was there because of Christian's arrest. She wasn't there because my business was falling apart. She was there because my life was falling apart.

Had some tame cop called his contact in the tabloid press? Was that how they – the journalist who kept calling and calling, the smart older woman waiting patiently at the end of the street, who was almost certainly one and the same – knew that James Caine had been murdered and that the police had already come for

Christian? I had no idea. I had been a journalist myself until the great print plunge. But not that kind of journalist.

Christian, Christian.

I was agonised by the thought of him. The night he had spent, the day he was facing and this ugly new world that I had dragged into our lives. And of course I was tormented by what he must think of me now. That most of all. I wished I could say that it felt unreal – *surreal*, as the tired old cliché has it – but there was nothing remotely surreal about it. It felt like a new and terrible reality, undeniable and hard. It seemed like the world that I had earned, the world I deserved.

'Want me to get shot of her?' Mary asked, brushing the last of the apricot croissant crumbs off her fingers. 'It's harassment.'

'It's because the dates are getting worse,' Skyla said. 'The latest one was particularly bad – Mr Angry. The one who followed the Accidental Dater into the street, screaming abuse, calling her names. It is starting to get dangerous out there. Did you see that one?'

'Can't you just tell her – you know – no comment?' Michael said.

'I'll tell the bitch to bog right off!' Mary said. 'Shall I, Tara?'

I shook my head, my mouth too tight to speak, the tears suddenly burning my eyes. Mary gave me a quick hug and, leaving Skyla and Michael guarding the door, we went into our office. I watched her as she fired up the Lavazza.

'Mary?'

'Huh?' She was concentrating on the coffee.

'It's got nothing to do with the blogger,' I said. 'It's nothing to do with the Accidental Dater. There's something else. Something worse.'

The machine began to steam. A thick stream of espresso came from a silver spout. Mary adjusted a tiny cup.

'Sorry?'

'That journalist at the end of the street? There will be more like her before the day is out.'

Now she looked at me. 'Why?'

'There was a man,' I said. 'On my business trip.'

'A man?'

I nodded. 'In Tokyo. At the conference I went to. There was a man I met there, Mary.'

She shook her head, trying to understand. My friend had always been crazy about Christian. Girls like her – the sweet-natured, home-loving, romantic girls who give their hearts away too easily – always fell for Christian. The good girls. I was never typical for Christian.

'This man in Tokyo,' Mary said. 'You didn't … you didn't have *sex* with him, did you?' There was a long moment while she adjusted to this new knowledge about me. I saw a flare of something like resentment in her eyes. 'But what about *Christian*, Tara?'

'Christian didn't really come into it.'

She shook her head with disbelief. 'But – how could your husband not come into it?'

'I'm not proud of any of it, OK? Look, I was nervous and he was kind and I was drunk and he was there. There was an earthquake.' I shrugged, aware of how pathetic the gesture must seem to Mary's unflinching eyes. 'I can't explain it to you because I can't explain it to myself.'

But I could hear Ginger's voice. From the start, my best friend had understood it better than I did.

And you thought you would get away with it, Tara.

And you thought you had earned it.

Yes, I thought.

All of that.

'The man – you saw him, Mary,' I said. 'The one who came to the office that morning. Remember him? He was not quite as nice as he seemed. He was a rotten bastard, Mary. He took photographs of me sleeping in his hotel room. He threatened to tell Christian. Then it all got worse.'

She looked appalled. 'How could it get any worse?'

'I tried to cut him off but he wouldn't let me go. He wouldn't let me act like it had never happened.' How much should I tell her? The alleged broken condom? No, I thought, too much information. 'He came to my house when I wasn't there. He went inside and looked around. He spoke to Christian. He was a bastard, Mary. The bastard of a lifetime. And that journalist who is calling – that must be her waiting at the end of the street – is there because last night someone killed him.'

'Killed him? That man who was here?'

I nodded. 'And the police came late last night and took Christian away.'

She was shaking her head. It was too much. 'But … Christian would never *hurt* anyone,' she said. 'Would he?'

'Christian didn't know anything about what happened in Tokyo,' I said, looking at my watch. My husband had been in police custody for ten hours. The shame stabbed me, opened me up, made me sick of myself. 'But I guess he does now,' I said.

Mary sagged into a seat, the coffee forgotten, watching me blankly as I headed for the door.

'Where are you going?' she said, and I could see my father shaking his head.

You bought the ticket, Tara!

'I'm sick of hiding away,' I said.

As I approached the woman waiting for me at the end of the mews, I realised that I had seen her face before, in the happy, carefully curated world of social media where families are always unbroken and lives are forever happy and the days are all fulfilled and enviable and fun, and at last I understood why this woman was waiting for me.

'Don't you know me?' she said. 'I'm James Caine's wife.'

17

CHRISTIAN

'Did you know?' the detective asked me.

What could I tell her?

You always know, don't you?

You look away. You – quite literally! – don't want to know.

But somewhere down in your blood and bones, you always know.

There are just too many clues, you see. They rub your stupid, unsuspecting face in the clues. They stuff the clues down your throat until you feel like you are choking. They bury you all in the evidence until you feel like screaming because the evidence is so overwhelming.

The unknown lover is always there, I understood now, even if you don't see them, even if you don't touch them, even if you don't know their name or what they look like or quite how long they have been sniffing around. You know that they are there.

That third person in your bed.

Do you *know?* How the hell can you not know?

My body ached from a sleepless night in a high white room with a low blue bed stained with bodily fluids that I did not like to think about. Does anyone ever sleep in a police custody suite? For even one second? The bed was almost on the ground. So that the hopelessly drunk do not have to fall very far, I assume. And I was pierced to my core by a grief that was worse than any pain in the world.

I wanted my Tara back.

'Mr Carver?'

Detective Inspector Gillian Ure was with the Major Crime Unit. She was a copper-haired young woman in glasses that took the edge off her pale beauty. There was a faint West Country burr in her accent that a few years at university and a job in the big city had not been able to completely expunge. She seemed young for the job, I thought. My age. Our age.

DI Ure had not been there when I had checked in – is checking in what you call it? The paperwork of going into police custody felt like checking into the worst hotel in the world. The mind-numbing bureaucracy of getting banged up, all those details they have to get right at the very moment when you are more terrified than you have ever been in your life. Arrival at station. Time of arrest. Offence under investigation. They write it all down. It was only when I heard the name of the offence that any of it began to seem horribly real.

'You have declined your right to free legal advice from the police station's duty solicitor,' DI Ure said. 'Is that correct, Mr Carver?'

I stared at my hands and they seemed strange to me.

'You can change your mind at any time about legal advice,' she continued. 'You can also instruct us to contact your own solicitor. But we have the right to question you about the crime you are suspected of without a legal representative present. As custody officers we are not allowed to disclose to anyone over the phone that you are under arrest and in custody. However, you have a right to what we call a notified person. Meaning you have the right to nominate someone likely to have an interest in your welfare. Can you think of anyone?'

I attempted a smile. I did not want to call Tara. I did not want to talk to her. I was not that brave.

'Not off the top of my head. Why am I here?'

'Motive,' she said.

It was always that simple for the police.

He went to bed with your wife and so you killed him.

'And someone must have pointed a finger at you.'

'Who?'

'I'm not at liberty to say.'

Someone who loved him, I thought. *Someone who loved the bastard.*

'Do you have any questions, Mr Carver?'

'I was wondering – do you know if my son went to school today?'

For the first time DI Ure lost patience with me. 'Mr Carver, do you understand what is happening to you? *You have been arrested on suspicion of murder.* What do you have to say about that allegation?'

What was happening at home? I thought of Marlon and I was gripped by a panic that threatened to consume me.

'Please look at me, Mr Carver.'

In front of the detective was a file filled with forms, photographs.

'Do you know this man?'

She pushed across the table a photograph of a successful businessman in his expense-account, executive-class prime. Some kind of official corporate headshot. A handsome man, craggy but well groomed. No stranger to the male moisturiser. The last of the great suit and ties. Nice smile.

I shook my head.

'Can you answer for the tape?'

I stared stupidly at the tape recorder, remembering it was there. 'No.'

'Look again.'

And I saw it was James Caine.

I knew it was James Caine all along.

'I met him. Yesterday.' Yesterday? It felt like a thousand years ago. 'He said he wanted to buy our house.

He came with his daughter. Amy. He looked at my records.'

'Your records?'

'Albums. LPs. Vinyl. My music. And he acted as if he knew her – Tara – my wife.'

Did I know? That was when I knew. That was when the fog lifted and I saw it all, as plain as the blood on your face. I mean the *nose* on your face.

'He talked about her as if he *knew* her,' I said, my voice tangled up with pain.

'James Caine died sometime last night in his suite at the Langham Hotel,' DI Ure said. 'And we believe it was murder.'

'Why do you think it was murder?'

'Someone had caved in his head with a blunt instrument, Mr Carver. That was our first clue.'

We both waited. I was glad he was dead. I didn't say it, but I think it showed in my face.

'Our forensic people have lifted prints and DNA from the crime scene. We are still waiting for them to be processed. Are any of those prints likely to belong to you, Mr Carver?'

I had to think about it. To lie awake all night in a police cell leaves you with a special kind of exhaustion.

'I don't think so.'

'But you're not sure? Were you aware that James Caine was intimate with your wife, Mr Carver?'

I feel something rise in me.

It was kin to the feeling I had when my parents died. It was the grief of bereavement. Something had been taken away from me before I was ready to let it go. The words were hard to say.

'No,' I said, denying it all. 'That's not us. That's not who we are.'

'A straight yes or no will suffice, Mr Carver. Were you aware that James Caine was intimate with your wife?'

'Tara,' I said. 'Her name is Tara.'

There was more that I could not find the words to say.

She is faithful, she is true, she is the love of my life. But it was all clogged up inside me. I leaned forward, as if I had been kicked in the solar plexus. A strange animal whimper escaped from my mouth. It was the crying you do when you are trying so hard to stop yourself from crying. I choked it down. I was not going to cry in front of these people.

'I am pausing the interview,' DI Ure said, watching me with something like shock as the grief bent me double.

I was too numb for tears. Too tired. Too proud.

The older cop in uniform came into the room.

Sergeant Cooper.

'Hello, son,' he said.

'Mr Carver,' DI Ure said to me while looking at him. 'Would you like a break to think things through?'

Deep down, I already knew that the worst had happened. The sense of bereavement weighed heavy on me now. But the death – the actual death of what I loved – was already in the past.

Her phone, I thought. Our lovemaking. The tears that came too easily. The sudden impossibility of eye contact, eye contact. The radical change in the weather in her head.

The way that James Caine looked at the framed picture of Tara in the hallway of our house.

As if he knew everything about her. As if she would never have secrets from him. As if he owned her.

How could I not know?

'Lose your rag, don't you, son?' Sergeant Cooper said, not unkindly.

I shook my head. 'Not really.'

The old sergeant glanced at DI Ure. He wanted to impress her. He had that air of amused desperation that men get when they want to impress a woman, no matter the age difference.

'Chucked a bottle at a bloke because he came down your street a bit sharpish,' he said. 'That's not losing your rag?'

DI Ure shuffled the papers in front of her. The police were different when the tape was turned off. You felt like anything could happen.

'Bit of a temper,' Sergeant Cooper said, like an understanding doctor asking you where your malignant tumour hurts. 'Would that be a reasonable assumption, son?'

There was another photograph that DI Ure had not shown me. She saw me looking at it upside down and she pushed it across the table to me, as if it might jog my wayward memory. In this one James Caine was no longer smiling for the camera. In this one he had the top of his head caved in.

How fragile we are, I thought. How simple to rip something apart.

A marriage, a skull.

It all comes apart so easily. It is all so simple to destroy.

'We have you on CCTV at the hotel,' DI Ure said, gently retrieving the photograph of the dead man, as if saving it for later. 'You were at the Langham on the day that James Caine died. Isn't that true, Mr Carver?'

I licked my lips.

'We know it's true, son,' the old sergeant smiled. 'The CCTV doesn't lie. Sometimes it misses the odd thing, but it never lies. You went up there to have a word with him, didn't you?'

'Is that right, Mr Carver?' DI Ure said. 'Do you have a short fuse?'

It was time to tell them the truth.

'Only when someone threatens my family,' I said. 'Are you going to turn on your tape?'

The young detective exchanged a quick look with the old sergeant.

'My boss is about to get here,' she said. 'We'll wait for him.'

And that is when I understood.

DI Ure was the warm-up act.

The police were just getting started on me.

18

TARA

'I've seen you before,' James Caine's wife said in my office.

'I don't think so.'

'I've seen you sleeping. On Jim's phone.'

Jim. He was Jim, was he? Not to me, never to me.

'Jim wasn't one of these men who attempted to hide his affairs,' his wife – his widow – said. 'They are not all men, of course! I think he was proud that he could get so many women to spread their legs for him after knowing him for five minutes. Or bend over the minibar. Excuse my vulgarity. I have been up all night. I had to identify the body, you see. And my daughter has not gone to school today. She has exams that will shape her life coming up. But she can't leave her bedroom. And she can't stop crying.'

We stared at each other. 'I'm sorry for your loss,' I said at last.

There was a kind of deep-frozen politeness about her. 'Oh no you're not, if you don't mind me saying. You must be glad Jim's dead. If you are anything like the rest of them. The ones who turned up at the house – always shocked – so shocked! – to discover that they were not the first whore to turn up ranting and raving on our doorstep! That we get it all the time! Always so pathetically surprised to learn that there was nothing remotely special about them, that we'd had Jim's whores at the door before.'

We can threaten to go to his home, Ginger had said, as if no one had ever thought of that move before, as if it would solve everything.

'My daughter grew up with the whores at the door,' Sandy Caine said.

'I'm not a whore, Mrs Caine.'

'Sorry. It's just a figure of speech. You have to understand – Jim was an addict. Not addicted to the sex. I always thought that it wasn't much to do with the sex. He could take it or leave the sex. But the romance! The newness of it all! And the *control.* He loved the control. Perhaps you noticed the way he enjoyed taking over some unsuspecting woman's life. And falling in love again. Or kidding himself he was in love, even if he didn't know the woman. And he didn't, did he, dear?' She made a noise, somewhere between a laugh and a snort of incredulous disbelief. '*He didn't even fucking know you.*'

'I'm sorry about your daughter.'

'All Amy's classmates still have their fathers. Nothing like Jim, of course. All those podgy, balding middle-aged men. Nothing like my Jim. But they are still alive and he is gone and there is so much that he is going to miss, all those good years. That's all gone now he's dead. Did you ever think about my daughter when you were in bed with my husband? Did she ever cross your mind when Jim was fucking you blind? Are you *really* sorry for *her* loss? You're glad. I know you. Don't think I don't know you.'

'Look,' I said. 'I'm not glad your husband is dead because the police came and took my husband away last night. So how can I possibly be glad he is dead?'

'But your husband didn't kill Jim, did he?'

'He didn't know about me and your husband,' I said.

Was that true? It must be true. Even having James Caine wandering around our home had not made Christian suspicious, had it? Because if Christian had known, he would have said something. Wouldn't he?

Sandy Caine touched me across the table and it was like an electric shock. I cried out loud, pulling away from her, but she took my hands and she held them and she would not let them go.

'I know who did it,' she whispered. 'I know who killed Jim. I know who went to that hotel room and beat out his brains.'

She was still holding my hands.

'No,' I said, struggling to pull away. I could smell the sweat on her. It was the smell of her sleepless night. The call at home in Brighton, the rush to the city, the body on the slab as they pulled back the single white sheet. And waiting for me to show my face this morning, standing at the end of the mews as if she was prepared to wait there forever.

Her mouth was a hard line now, almost smiling but with no trace of anything but loathing.

'I know it was you,' she said, a hiss as soft as a prayer.

My hands were still in her hands.

I stood up, abruptly pulling away, and someone's coffee cup went flying across the desk as I backed away with her accusation ringing in my brain, and she stared at me as if I represented all the women who had ever turned up on the doorstep of her family home while her bewildered daughter grew up watching the scene from the top of the stairs, and I didn't know if she spoke again or if it was only inside my head.

I know it was you!

19

CHRISTIAN

DI Ure, I saw now, was only the support act. I had liked DI Ure. She was diligent in ensuring that, even in my shattered state, I understood my rights and obligations, her watery eyes dead serious behind her thick specs as she brushed a strand of copper hair from her face. DI Ure had seemed like someone who would listen to me, and even believe me.

But Detective Chief Inspector John Stoner was different.

DCI Stoner was a naturally big man grown even larger with time, and all of the empty calories of his fifty years. His repeatedly broken nose gave his face a rakish look, and his bulk seemed squeezed into everything – his dark blue suit, glossy at the elbows, the interview room, and the chair across the table from me. Around his nose and his eyes was a map of little red lines, the broken capillaries of the dedicated drinker. He placed his giant paws on the table between us and on the third finger of his left hand, his thick golden wedding band strained angrily against his flesh. Introducing himself, DCI Stoner was friendly, sympathetic even, but it was like having the school bully on your side in the playground. There was the feeling that, no matter how smiley they were, it could all change in a moment.

And it was when DCI Stoner appeared in the interview room that I understood the police believed I had killed James Caine.

What was the worst night of my life was for him just another day at the office.

DCI Stoner had seen it all before. I was nothing new to DCI Stoner.

'So you confronted James Caine about your wife,' he said, the very first thing he said, still squeezing himself into the chair on the other side of the table. 'I don't blame you. I would have confronted him too.'

'As I told DI Ure—'

He silenced me with a small lift of his chin, grinning to take the edge off the gesture.

'And now you have to tell me,' he said.

So I did.

'I thought this guy – this man – he was someone who had come to look at my house,' I said. 'That's what he pretended. And then I started to think maybe he was sick in the head. I don't know what I thought. Some kind of stalker. He talked about Tara – my wife – as if he knew her. And so when they left the house – Caine and his daughter – I followed him into the street.'

'And what did you say to him?'

'I waited until the girl got into the car and closed the door. And then I asked him – who are you? What do you want?'

Is that what I had said or was that only in my head? I did not remember the exact words. What I remembered was the threat, the sense of real dread, the feeling that this man was a danger to all that I loved.

'What did he do?' DCI Stoner said.

'He smiled, as if he knew things that I would never know. Secrets.'

'So you told him what any man would tell him,' DCI Stoner said, prompting me.

'I just told him – *stay away from my family.*'

'And what did he say?

'He laughed at me. I felt like he had come there to laugh at me. But I knew something had happened between him and Tara. *Because he acted as if he knew her.* I thought – I don't know what I thought. I thought maybe he was someone who had seen her online or an old boyfriend or something. But from the past. The distant past.'

'Not the recent past. Not Tokyo.'

So DCI Stoner knew about Tokyo. How many people knew about Tokyo now?

'No,' I said. 'Not Tokyo. Not now. That didn't even cross my mind.'

I remembered Tara's phone call from Tokyo. I recalled being distracted, Marlon trying to kiss the dog and

Buddy not having it. Did it happen before or after that phone call? Was he in the room with her? Was he watching her as she spoke to me? Had they just made love?

'So he was laughing at you,' DCI Stoner said, unsmiling now.

'Yes. There was a parking fine on the windscreen of his big Merc. They're very strict on our street. The traffic wardens. He took it off and threw it away. He struck me as a man who thought the rules didn't apply to him. Then he was getting in the car, starting the ignition. And I didn't know what else I could do. And I don't know what I thought. I thought he was *disrespectful*. No. More than that. I could see they had been together, and I could tell that he wanted more of her.'

'And that he wasn't taking you seriously.'

DCI Stoner was easy to talk to. I felt that he understood. It was good to have the playground bully on your side.

He was encouraging me to get it all straight in my mind.

He was implying that all of my actions were completely understandable and even reasonable.

'He thought I didn't count,' I said. 'He thought I was a fucking joke.'

'And you said something before he drove away, I bet. When you confronted him outside your home, I bet you gave him a warning, didn't you? That's only natural.'

It was all only natural to DCI Stoner. That a man should want another man's wife. That her husband would object. That confrontation was inevitable. What could be more natural?

'Didn't you?' DCI Stoner prompted, a harder note in his voice now.

I nodded. But I was very tired now. They can hold you for twenty-four hours without charging you and I was halfway there. It is long enough to totally wear you out when you are dirty and scared and you have not slept, when you feel that you are losing everything you ever loved. It is a long day and night.

'For the tape, please,' DI Ure said.

'I told him – stay away from my wife.'

Stoner waited.

I hesitated.

But just for a second.

'Or I'll kill you,' I said.

DCI Stoner leaned his bulk back in the too-small chair. His wedding ring glinted in the harsh white lights of the interview room.

'Then you went to his hotel, didn't you?'

'Yes.'

'To beat the shit out of him.'

'No – to get him to leave my wife alone.'

'And you lost that famous temper of yours, didn't you, Christian?'

I looked across at DI Ure.

Her serious eyes blinked at me behind her spectacles.

'I want that lawyer now,' I told her.

20

TARA

Our house was in chaos.

My mother was crying in the kitchen, loudly declaring that I had finally succeeded in destroying her life. My father was pacing the living room, a phone pressed to each ear, trying to reach his lawyer so we could find the proper legal representation – a criminal lawyer – for Christian. Out on the street there were more than a dozen journalists milling all over the pavement, real old-fashioned journalists who kept stuffing notes through our letterbox and ringing the landline – how the hell did they get the number? – as Skyla did her best to fend them off.

And I was having an argument with Marlon.

I took a breath as I sat on his bed, hearing the baying mob outside our front gate, jabbering excitedly among themselves, and my mum weeping and wailing downstairs. Marlon folded his arms across his chest and scowled. On the bed between us was his dog-eared copy of *The Call of the Wild*.

'Listen – you can't go through your childhood and read just one book, Marlon.'

'But I love this dog! I love Buck! I love him!'

At the foot of the bed, Buddy bobbed his head and looked as forlorn as a Lab could ever look. Buck *is* kind of great, Buddy seemed to say.

'Baby,' I said. 'Marlon. Look, I know you love this book—'

'I implore you!'

I placed the tip of my finger against his solitary dimple.

'I'm going to kiss you right there,' I smiled, but he pulled away furiously.

'Well, actually I don't *want* to be kissed there! I don't want to be kissed *anywhere*!'

My mother came into the room, dabbing at the smudged mascara around her huge blue eyes. She sat on the edge of her grandson's bed, tugging at the hem of her miniskirt.

'Goodness,' she said to Marlon. 'What a fuss about nothing. Here.'

She picked up Marlon's favourite book and began to read at random with all the emotion of a speaking clock. '*But especially he loved to run in the dim twilight of the summer midnights, reading signs and sounds as a man may read a book, and seeking for the mysterious something that called – called, waking or sleeping, at all times, for him to come …'*

Marlon grinned triumphantly. I stood up to go. 'You can't have just one book,' I said.

My mother turned on me with a viciousness that shocked me.

'Oh, why don't you leave us alone!' she said. 'You cause *so* much trouble, Tara!'

The tears started up again as she settled to reading her grandson his bedtime story, her voice finally showing some emotion, even if it was only for herself. Her mouth tightened into a thin straight line, a facial expression I remembered from the worst times of our relationship, those years when I was entering my teens just as my hot mum was reluctantly entering the end of her reproductive years, the great eternal and bitter divide between mothers and daughters. It was all coming back to me now.

'You always did this to us, Tara!' my mother said. '*So* much trouble!'

'Think about Christian, can't you?' I said. 'He's the one who's suffering.'

'Unbelievable,' she said. 'Did *you* think about Christian?'

Downstairs in the living room, my father had finally reached his lawyer and Skyla was answering the landline. My young intern had been great. Mary had not been quite so helpful, switching off after our conversation, as if stunned and repulsed by my business-trip behaviour, and then ducking out of the office without saying goodbye. But Skyla had accompanied me home and was now single-handedly holding back the massed ranks of the media. It was perfect, of course – the digital matchmaker whose own marriage was a train wreck. The irony was not lost on me.

'You should talk to this one,' Skyla said, covering the mouthpiece. 'It's not another journalist. It's Sophie Sherman. The vlogger. The POI. Person of influence.'

'I know who Sophie Sherman is.'

And what a POI is, I thought. I'm not old yet.

Sophie Sherman had made her name by breaking a couple of big sexual abuse stories. A handsome Shakespearean actor in his sixties and a children's entertainer who had grinned gamely with stuffed animals from one end of my childhood to the other. Sophie Sherman had outed them both as sexual bullies, serial molesters and congenital creeps. With meticulous research and a refusal to be intimidated, she had taken them down.

'I'm not interested,' I told her, taking the phone from Skyla.

'So hang up now,' Sophie Sherman said. 'And then you can take your chances with the hyenas who I bet are already on your doorstep. And who will – I can guarantee – paint you as the Whore of Babylon.'

She breathed out, as if relieved that I was still there.

'But I can get you through this, Tara,' she said.

I said nothing. But I did not hang up. And I was listening.

Sophie Sherman spoke more quickly now.

'James Caine has a history of coercive control. He has been abusing women for years. You're not the first. Rather incredibly, I don't think you were even the last. There was a sexual harassment case that was settled out of court and there was a young woman on the fringes of his business – someone he was involved with, someone who would not let go, a young woman of junior status – who killed herself.'

My father was talking urgently with his lawyer. My mother's voice came through the child monitor. Skyla was in the hallway, collecting the notes that the press kept pushing through the letterbox.

And Christian, my Christian, was sitting in some cell, seeing me clearly for the first time.

Sophie Sherman kept talking, offering me a way out.

'This is what you have to understand, Tara,' she said. 'James Caine is not the victim here – *you are*.'

She kept talking as my father hung up his phone, giving me a wide, reassuring grin and a big double thumbs up and I smiled back at him, my eyes burning with sudden tears, for the world was always a much better, far kinder place when my dad was smiling at me.

21

CHRISTIAN

We waited for my new lawyer to show, and it was not a long wait, because my father-in-law would have stopped at nothing to make it happen, and to make it happen quickly.

Kevin Steel, the criminal lawyer that Leo's regular lawyer had found for me, had never met my father-in-law because Kevin, apparently the rising star at Hunter, Butterfield and Ash, was not the kind of lawyer that Leo had ever needed. Kevin – he insisted on Kevin rather than Mr Steel – was a working-class Geordie, nowhere near as posh as I was expecting, but reportedly very good and very expensive.

Leo was taking care of all that.

DCI Stoner looked me in the eye and I saw with a sickening clarity that he had no doubt that I had caved in James Caine's skull.

'And so you went to the hotel,' he said conversationally.

'Yes,' I said. 'But nothing happened.'

DCI Stoner smirked, as if we were enjoying a joke together. He glanced at DI Ure and then back at me.

Kevin Steel silently took notes by my side.

DCI Stoner's friendly voice dripped with disbelief.

'You didn't confront Caine? What? You went all the way from your home in Camden Town to his hotel in Portland Place and then you – what?'

I sighed and rubbed my eyes. It sounded pathetic, I knew.

'I went home. I didn't go inside. I just thought – I was frightened. I was scared of what I might do if I asked for his room number and they let me go up there. Or if I told them I wanted to see him and he came down to the lobby. I was terrified of what I might do to him. And I was even more terrified of what he might say to me.' I swallowed something down. 'I was scared of what he might tell me.'

DCI Stoner was smiling as if he really liked me, and he understood my fears, but he did not believe a word I was saying.

'You ... just ... went ... home.'

'Yes. Because when I got there, it all felt like a bad idea. It felt like nothing good could come of it.'

And so I went back home, feeling ashamed and relieved at all once, and wanting my loving world restored, wanting my wife back. And then Tara came home from the day at her parents' place and when I told her that some weirdo called James Caine had been round to look at the house she said that he was one of the sad bastards who trailed her all over social media because they had maybe seen a picture of her somewhere.

It was exactly what I wanted to hear.

'So – just to be clear – absolutely no contact with James Caine at the hotel?'

'No.'

'How about this?' DCI Stoner said reasonably, the playground bully explaining why he is about to take your dinner money and flush your head down the boys' toilet and why it is a perfectly rational course of action. 'I think you *did* see him at the hotel and you went up to his room because neither of you wanted a scene in public and then you lost that famous temper. You didn't mean to murder him. You just wanted to teach him a lesson. But things got right out of hand. Is that what happened, Christian?'

DCI Stoner made murder seem like the most natural thing in the world.

'That's what most men would do, right?' he said. 'That's what *I* would do. When you spoke to him outside your home, did he make any reference to what had happened with your wife? I mean – was he specific? Did he taunt you? Did he talk about the sex? Did he try to provoke you? Christian, mate, I'm trying to help you out here.'

'And we are going to pause right there,' my lawyer said in his Newcastle accent.

Kevin and I went to a consultation room down the corridor.

It was nicer than the interview room. Airier, lighter, cooler.

'They're working out the charge now,' Kevin told me.

I felt like sleeping. A short power nap to recover my strength.

'Christian, did you hear what I said?'

'The charge?'

'What the police are going to charge you with at the end of twenty-four hours in custody,' Kevin said with a trace of impatience, as if I should be keeping up better than this. 'Stoner is working out if the charge against you is going to be murder or manslaughter.'

We both let that sink in. There were footsteps in the corridor outside the consultation room. Voices, laughter, moving away. Kevin took a step closer to me, his voice very soft now.

'They're deciding which charge is most likely to result in a successful prosecution. If you went to the hotel with the full intention of murdering James Caine, or if his death at your hands was accidental. We can reduce a charge of murder to voluntary manslaughter if we can establish loss of control or diminished responsibility. But by your own admission you threatened to kill him some time before you went to confront him at his hotel.'

I felt the sickness rising.

'No,' I said. 'That's not what happened.'

'They have you on CCTV outside the hotel. They have a motive. And they have your own taped admission that you threatened to kill him. This is already some way advanced, Christian. You have to understand that they really like you for this.'

'This man – James Caine – he looked at my wife as if she was nothing. He acted as if he *knew* her. And whatever had happened between them – even if they had been to bed – *he didn't*. He could never know her.'

Kevin Steel shook his head.

'That doesn't help you, I'm afraid. The more you talk about what a nasty piece of work this James Caine was, the more Stoner likes a murder charge. Right now he is trying to establish if we are going to claim that there was a qualifying trigger.'

'What's a qualifying trigger?'

'Something that set you off. Something that pushed you over the edge. A spark, a provocation, a moment when it all got out of hand. A qualifying trigger is a defence that is used in a voluntary manslaughter case. It could be something that James Caine said – some sexual taunt, some offensive reference to your wife – that caused a loss of control in you, a defendant with an ordinary level of tolerance and self-restraint. Although I think Stoner fancies his chances of saying that you do *not* have ordinary levels of tolerance and self-restraint.'

He grimaced. 'He will be raising that unfortunate event with the Prosecco bottle and the car. They are going to get a lot of mileage out of that Prosecco bottle, believe me.'

'But I didn't even see Caine at the hotel.'

'They don't believe you,' said my lawyer.

DCI Stoner was angry when we returned.

I had not seen him angry before. They didn't turn on the tape, and they didn't tell me to sit down. DCI Stoner glared furiously at DI Ure.

She shrugged and then he laughed, as if you win some and you lose some.

'It's your lucky day,' Detective Chief Inspector Stoner told me.

Kevin touched my arm, his face splitting into a grin, and then I moved quickly, suddenly understanding that I was free to go home, and anxious to get out of there before they changed their minds.

And as they were checking me out of police custody – signing their forms to say that I had been given my wallet, my watch and my shoelaces – a homeless man was being checked in.

Alfred Oakley, the papers would later reveal.

A British soldier.

A veteran of Iraq and Afghanistan.

A veteran stoically enduring the fussy bureaucracy of entering police custody. Noting arrival at station, time of arrest and offence under investigation. Being told his rights before being photographed and fingerprinted. Before the screaming claustrophobia of the cell door slamming locked behind you.

Alfred Oakley caught my eye and held it for a long moment.

He may have smiled.

Because there he was – a homeless British soldier with James Caine's Rolex Submariner still hanging on his wrist.

22

TARA

Christian came home.

Almost exactly twenty-four hours after he had been spirited away, there was the diesel rumble of a black cab in the street and when I went to the window I saw him being hugged by Spike. Then Spike got back into the cab and it pulled away, Spike's concerned face at the window staring back at Christian, who just stood outside our home, looking lost.

No, it was more than lost. My husband looked totally unlike himself, as if he had been robbed of something by the night and day in police custody. And by me.

'He's back!' my mother shrieked, with her genius for stating the bloody obvious, and then she was running to get the front door while my father stayed with me in the living room. My dad glanced at me and then looked away. He knew this was not going to be easy.

We had known Christian was coming home because Kevin Steel had called my father an hour ago and told him the police had someone else for the murder of James Caine.

'Got him bang to rights!' my father had said with grim satisfaction.

But there was no joy in Christian. There was not even a sign of relief. My mother led him into the living room, chattering mindlessly as Christian stared at his home as if seeing it for the first time. He seemed shattered by his experience. His eyes met mine and then slid away. I went to him and hugged him. He did not pull away but he did not hug me back. The dog got a better response. Buddy padded up to him, tail wagging, big dopey grin, and one listless hand reached out to gently scratch the dog's head.

Christian looked at me again.

'Is Marlon OK?' he said.

'Sleeping,' I said.

'I read him his bedtime story,' my mother boasted, glancing at me, her red lips pursing with triumph. 'That book that he loves. You know the one.'

Skyla was still with us, manning the phones, making tea, and the presence of this helpful, eager-to-please young outsider somehow made my mother and I more civil around each other. Skyla had never seen Christian before and she stared at him now with something like awe. He was a handsome man, even in his current state, a guy who had just spent a night without sleep and no doubt been more frightened than he had ever been in his life. To me he looked like a man who had been shipwrecked and crawled ashore, dumbfounded to discover that he had somehow survived.

Our guests drifted away. First Skyla, refusing my father's offer to drive her home or get her a cab. Then my parents. And then there was just us. The same old us.

'Christian?' I said. 'The lawyer called. Kevin? Apparently, the police have picked someone up and have already charged him with murder.'

It felt like small talk. He did not react beyond a weary shrug to indicate that this was already old news.

'Can I make you something to eat? Can I …'

He was staring down at Buddy. The dog stared back up at Christian, looking sad. I went to him then, standing directly in front of him, but terrified to touch him.

'Christian,' I said. 'Please look at me.'

But he slumped down on the sofa and covered his face with his hands. It took me a moment to realise that he was crying. He cried soundlessly, his hands over his face all the while, as if he could not bear to see me watching him weep. I waited until he had finished. He wiped his face with the palm of his hand and sniffed.

The dog jumped onto the sofa next to him, looking mournful. Dogs read your mood, and Buddy knew that Christian had been broken.

The sofa was a state. It was the first good piece of furniture we ever bought after my business turned a profit, the white Italian leather now had that chewed-up, lived-in look known only to homes with big dogs and small children.

And finally my husband stared at me and did not look away.

I expected him to say that he was hurt and furious. Or that he had spent the night in a police cell because of my stupidity. Or that he had nothing to do with the death of James Caine. I don't know what I expected him to say. Anything but the terrible words he said.

'Did you love him?'

He reached out and touched the dog, waiting for an answer.

And now I was crying too, a different kind of crying, not trying to hide it, because I wanted him to see what his words did to me.

'No!' I said, the word choking in my throat. 'No, of course not. No, no, no. I love you. Only you. Always you.'

He stood up, not looking at me now. As if he had had enough of looking at me to last him for a while.

'I love *you*,' I said, the tears streaming now, as I spoke our secret married language. 'I love *you*, kiddo! Say it, Christian. *I love you, kiddo*.'

He sighed.

'I need a shower, Tara,' he said. 'I'm really filthy.'

'Say it, say it, say it.'

I grabbed his arm but he gently took my hand away.

Then he went off to the shower, taking his time, as if there was a lot of dirt to wash off, and then he collected a spare duvet from a cupboard in our bedroom and slowly carried it back to the sofa. And then I understood that he was not going to sleep with me, and we were not going to try to mend what had been smashed, and he was not going to speak to me in our secret married language.

Not tonight.

And perhaps never again.

CHRISTIAN

The night crawled.

I tossed and turned on the sofa, tormented by all the toxic feelings of the one who has been betrayed. Hurt, humiliation and resentment. Funnily enough, resentment above all.

Because I had my own chances to stray. There were plenty of times that I could have been somewhere else with someone else.

We spend our youth looking for love and sex and then we spend our married lives trying to avoid it.

Did Tara think I didn't have my own chances?

And I suddenly I wanted her to know – do you think I didn't have my opportunities? There was a woman at the school gates. I thought she was one of the younger mothers but she turned out to be one of the older au pairs. We got chatting – she was friendlier than the average mother at the school gates, less burdened by family chores, less wary of random male contact.

We had a cup of coffee. It turned out she was Spanish, although she was as fair as a Scandinavian from central casting. Friendly, smart. And a knockout, in an understated sort of way. Funky but sweet. The kind of woman I always liked before I gave myself to Tara who was – strangely enough – never my type at all. Tara was not funky or sweet. Tara was always the head-turner, the kind of woman – still a girl, really, when we first met – who was noticed the second she walked into any room. And Tara was always the wild one. I should have known, shouldn't I? I should have guessed how it would all end. And we had got talking, the funky-but-sweet Spanish woman and I, and we talked easily, and we got on, and by the second coffee I knew we were both aware of the great unspoken truth of human relationships.

There are a lot of people in the world who you could love.

And so we both took a step back, the funky-but-sweet Spanish knockout and I, because the alternative was chaos.

We would always talk when we saw each other at the school gates but you could feel that dangerous little spark being allowed to fade and die – there was no more coffee, no more looks that lingered for a moment too long. And then she moved away with her family and I never saw her again. So nobody got hurt, when for a moment there was the opportunity of everyone getting hurt.

And as I lay sleepless on the sofa, I thought how Tara would sneer at my platonic flirtation at the school gates. How tame it would seem to her. How pathetically timid. What was the great insult when we were two kids running wild on the music press, Tara?

Lightweight!

That was what we said about those who declined a hit on a joint at the editorial meeting, or who balked at staying up all night, or who showed the first symptoms of wanting to give up sex and drugs and rock and roll – going home at midnight, not getting off your face, keeping your underpants firmly on – and go to that small death called growing up, settling down, getting old.

Lightweights!

I was a lightweight now. I had had my chance for a different life – a good chance with a great woman who was worthy of love – but I didn't take it. Because I loved my wife and I thought – no, I knew – we were going to spend our lives together. That's how naïve I was, that's how stupid.

And when I stopped thinking about the Spanish woman, that's when I was right there, with Tara and James Caine in that hotel room. *His hands on you.* I could not close my eyes to that hotel room in Tokyo. *His hands on you. His hands on you. His mouth on you.* I could see them together. I closed my eyes, I tossed and twisted, but it would not leave me alone. *His hands on you. His mouth on you. His tongue on you.* The kisses and the clothes coming off, easing himself inside her, the noises of pleasure that she made. The unasked, unanswered questions so obvious, so banal, and so very much like having your skin ripped off.

And was he better?

And did you like him more?

And did you love him, kiddo?

And I was beyond hurt. I was wrecked.

And I wanted to tell her – to tell her to her face – *do you think I didn't have my fucking chances, Tara?*

I kicked off the duvet.

Buddy protested with a low canine groan as I got up and went off to our bedroom. Suddenly it was the most important thing in the world – to tell her that I could have been other places too. And they would have been better places than this wretched place I had found with her.

And I didn't, because I love our family.

And I didn't, because it would not have been worth risking everything.

And I didn't, because the only one for me was you.

That's how stupid I am, Tara.

That's the kind of lightweight I am.

But I did not get to tell Tara these things because my wife was sleeping the sleep of total and utter exhaustion.

I realised with a start that she had been awake for twenty-four hours too.

But it had not occurred to me that she would be sleeping on this night. I had assumed that neither of us would ever sleep again in this broken home.

Tara had kicked off the sheets and now she shivered in her sleep in the cold spring night wearing just T-shirt and pants.

And even now – I loved her. And I wanted that love to stop, to turn it off, because it would never do anything but hurt me.

I reached for the sheets and went to cover her and then, angry at myself now for my Labrador-like devotion, I dropped them and turned away without covering her.

And so we wear down love, I thought, and so we chip away at it, and so we reduce something precious, something priceless, to nothing much at all.

23

CHRISTIAN

Have you ever noticed this really weird thing about life?

It goes on, even when life is changed, damaged, diminished.

Normal life!

It goes right on, even when there is nothing normal about it.

When my parents died I wanted the world to stop, just for a day or two, just until I could adjust my head to this new and unimaginable reality. But the world doesn't stop. That's what you learn when life kicks you in the teeth and then stomps on your face. Life goes on and doesn't give a damn about your sleepless night, or your aching heart, or your breaking home.

The first milky light of dawn was creeping into the room when Buddy appeared in the doorway, blinking at me. Marlon would not wake for another hour or so and then he would need breakfast, coaxing to clean his teeth and his hand held as we walked to school. Even in the ruins, there it was, the never-ending routine of family life, even as your family is falling apart.

I hauled my aching body from the sofa. Buddy and I headed for the hallway where his collar and lead were waiting.

There was nobody around outside.

The photographers and journalists had all gone home at some point in the night. Would they come back during office hours? Perhaps it wasn't enough of a story to stay out all night. *The dating guru and her murdered lover.* Perhaps the news agenda had changed now they had picked up the guy who they believed really did it.

Perhaps he was the story now.

The British soldier.

Buddy and I turned right, the pair of us so accustomed to our route that there was no pull on the lead.

The Smart car turned into our road and it proceeded down our road at a responsible speed. And as the car passed us, I saw the pure terror in the man's eyes. How quickly the word gets around.

Killer!

He looked quickly away, licking lips that went dry at the sight of me.

And I enjoyed his fear.

I relished it. I bloody loved it. I loved what I saw in his eyes.

It made me feel better than I had felt in ages.

TARA

Ginger called. Jolted from a shallow sleep, a wretched dream-filled excuse of a sleep, I scrambled for my phone, sensing the quiet in the house, knowing that Marlon must be still sleeping and Christian must be walking Buddy. Ginger and I had not spoken since the night we went to the hotel. There had been no message from her, no text of remorse for calling the police as I fled for home, no hint of apology for doing exactly what I had begged her not to do, no sorrowful justification for not waiting until I had a chance to talk to Christian, until I could prepare him for what was to come.

And there was none now.

'The police just came round,' Ginger said.

I felt my stomach lurch.

'What did the police want?'

'Some little copper-haired slip of a girl and some big thug who was pretending to be all matey. The guy gave me his bloody card. *DCI Stoner*.'

'But they've already got someone, haven't they? They arrested someone and charged him with murder.'

The soldier, I thought. That poor bastard sleeping on the street with his Staffie.

'It was more questions,' Ginger said. 'Because we're *witnesses*, Tara.'

She spoke to me with a kind of brittle impatience that was new to our relationship, as if I did not understand the seriousness of the situation, as if I was always thinking about myself.

'We found the body,' she said, as if I might need reminding. 'And this detective – DCI Stoner – he's the – what is it? – Senior Investigating Officer. So it's his murder case and he told me he's going to talk to you very soon.'

'But I spoke to the police already. That's all done, Ginger.'

I had talked to them two miserable nights ago after they took Christian away. A uniformed officer had asked me about what Ginger and I had found on the floor of the Langham, wanting to know why I had left the scene before speaking to the authorities, all prune-lipped with disapproval because I let Ginger handle the formalities. I told him straight with as much authority as I could muster.

My family needed me home.

I was in shock.

My friend was handling it.

Please leave me alone, please.

'That was only the start,' Ginger sighed. 'What did this redheaded copper call it? *An initial brief account.* The top guy, the big cop – DCI Stoner – said that you and me are what they call significant witnesses. We are going to have to tape interviews, and we are going to have to go to court,

Tara, when this comes to trial.' A pause, but I could hear her breathing. *'And so we need to get our story straight.'*

'What are you talking about? Why do we need to get our story straight? We just tell them what happened. We just tell them the truth.'

'But they will want to hear the truth again and again and again. So we have to be sure that we keep telling them exactly the same thing. I've realised how they work, Tara. They keep asking you the same questions so they can see if the answers always stay the same. They were asking me about a watch. Was James Caine wearing a watch when we found him?'

I thought of Caine's big Rolex. Was he wearing it? I had no idea. To be honest, you don't notice a man's expensive timepiece when the top of his skull has been bashed in.

'I don't know anything about a bloody watch, Ginger.'

'Look – don't get snippy – I'm not even meant to be *talking* to you, OK? I'm not meant to be talking to *anyone* about it. I'm only calling to say – don't mention Spike to them, all right?'

'Why would I mention Spike?'

'You know why, Tara! Because the plan was that Spike would get this James Caine guy to back off the same way he got Omar to back off. My ex? Remember?'

'But Spike never talked to James Caine.' I hesitated. 'Did he?'

'No – of course not! So don't mention Spike, OK? There's no need. If they start digging into what Spike did to Omar, then it might not look so good for him.'

'But I don't like the idea of keeping anything back from the police.'

'Jesus Christ – you can tell them whatever you like, Tara! But leave Spike right out of it, OK?'

And then she was gone.

Christian came back with Buddy. There were the familiar sounds of the Lab being carted off to the ground floor bathroom for a quick hose down in the tub and then Christian's soothing voice as he dried Buddy off with his own dog towel.

They came into the kitchen and in the early morning Christian and I crept around each other with the heart-breaking formality of total strangers who had somehow found themselves living under the same roof. I offered Christian coffee. He politely accepted. We both looked at the dog. We had not had the argument yet.

But the big awful row was coming in, it was building, like a storm that was about to break. It was waiting for us, just beyond the strained good manners, the moment when we said all the things that, sooner or later, could not avoid being said. And I knew it was going to be horrible.

But for now there was a ceasefire.

My father – one of those late-twentieth-century men who felt that he had missed something by never fighting in a war – had once told me about the British and German soldiers who had played football on the first Christmas Day of the First World War. My dad said – *they only ever did it on that first Christmas*. He thought that was very significant. That was the only time, the first Christmas of the war, because after that they hated each other too much to have a kickabout in no-man's-land on Christmas Day.

Christian and I were like that now, I felt. We were keeping it polite, having a nice final kickabout in no-man's-land, because soon it would be far too late for being nice. We both looked to the window as a car pulled up outside.

'It's Fat Phil,' Christian said, his voice neutral.

He knew I hated it when he called my driver by that name. I drained my coffee cup. This morning I had an appointment with Sophie Sherman, best known for smiting justice on powerful men who had abused vulnerable women. I thought I would not mention it to Christian.

'I'm going to work now,' was all I told him.

He nodded, visibly relieved, reaching to scratch the dog between the ears, and for the first time in the long history of us, my husband looked like he was glad to see the back of me.

24

TARA

'Did he tell you a condom broke?' Sophie Sherman said.

I stared at her.

When she had arrived at the office, Mary, Michael and Skyla had treated Sophie Sherman as visiting royalty. This was the activist who had broken two of the great sex scandals of recent years – the children's entertainer known as Uncle Norman in my childhood, a laughing, avuncular banterer with a gaudy tribe of stuffed toys, and the knighted Shakespearean actor who the tabloids were now calling King Leer. Uncle Norman and King Leer had more in common than was at first apparent. They had both used their positions of power to torment women and girls. It had gone on for decades in their dressing rooms and they had got away with it until Sophie Sherman – not yet thirty, whippet thin, dressed all in black like some hanging judge – had shone a spotlight on their crimes. Sherman had painstakingly collected evidence from victims, she had stood up to the bullying threats of legal action and never working again in her life, and she had been there in court when Uncle Norman and King Leer were put away. Then she had appeared on *Newsnight*, giving notice that this kind of sexual abuse was being put out for history's bin men. But she could do nothing for me, I thought. I didn't want James Caine exposed. It was too late to send him to jail for whatever he had done to me or anybody else. I just wanted it to all go away. Agreeing to meet Sophie Sherman had been a mistake. And then she dropped the bomb about the broken condom.

'He did, didn't he?' she said, taking my stunned silence for affirmation.

I finally nodded. She was not surprised.

'It was Caine's standard MO,' she continued. 'I've heard his broken condom line from a few women already. There's a kind of sick genius to it, really. It's a great way to torment a woman, a great way to control her, a wonderful way to take away her marriage, her family, her life.' She sipped the espresso that Mary had made. 'Her sanity.'

I glanced beyond my office window at my staff, collected around the front door, watching the journalists and photographers who were gathering at the end of our mews, and I still did not want to be a part of the next Sophie Sherman sex scandal, and I still did not want to be a part of her next worthy project. But I could talk to Sophie Sherman, and talking was a relief.

'After he told me about the broken condom, he told me to not have sex with my husband because I might have a sexually transmitted infection,' I said. I bit my lower lip. 'HSV-2, he said. I had never even heard of HSV-2. It sounds like a fucking highspeed rail network.'

'Caine told a number of women there was a problem with protection. You have to wonder where he was buying his condoms from. Once you believed in the condom malfunction, everything else was credible. He liked women to think that they were possibly infected, or pregnant, or both. He enjoyed their fear. I think he enjoyed it more than the sex.' She did not pat my hand – she was not the type for patting hands – but it felt like it. 'Your test results were clear, Tara?'

I nodded, my eyes filling with tears of relief and rage.

'But once he tells you that, you just don't *know*,' I said angrily, remembering how petrified I had been sitting in the Harley Street waiting room, going to see an expensive private doctor because she would give me the results immediately, and also because I was far too ashamed to see our local GP, the gentle old man who cared for my family's minor ailments. 'And until you get the results from the doctor, you can never know.'

'James Caine had a PhD in coercive control,' Sophie said. 'It wasn't only women he met on business trips. A co-worker in his office brought a sexual harassment case and got paid off to keep quiet, and a young woman who delivered lunch boxes to his office took her own life.'

'A woman committed suicide because of Caine?'

Sophie Sherman took a deep breath.

'Some things are difficult to prove. But other women are coming forward. Other women are contacting me. Women who were abused by James Caine. Women he tortured. Women like you.'

'Women like me?'

'Women like you,' she repeated. 'Women he met on a business trip and then had a brief affair with.'

'It wasn't an affair.'

'What would you call it?' she said sharply. 'A one-night stand?'

I didn't want to call it anything. I wanted to forget all about it, but the vultures were gathering at the end of our mews and I could hear them even from my office, waiting for their pictures and their quote and to shine their spotlights in every corner of my life.

'I'm not like the other women you've helped.'

'You're exactly like them, Tara. And you need to get ahead of this story. And more than that, *you need to get justice*.'

I thought of the women who had turned up at the Caine family home in Brighton. The whores at the door, his wife had called them. The women who did not realise that it was a well-trodden path and that taking it would impress no one and change nothing. The whores at the door. Women like me.

'James Caine was a bastard,' Sophie Sherman said. 'And now you have to own your story. Because if you don't, somebody else will. Those people at the end of the mews are going to eat you up if you let them. *The dating expert whose secret lover wound up dead.*' She raised her eyebrows. 'I have been reading about your company for some time. This anonymous blogger – the Accidental Dater – seems to have it in for you.'

I felt my defences rise. The Accidental Dater was doing my business real harm. Subscriptions were down, advertising was down and so our revenue stream was drying up. If the money stopped coming in then soon I was going to have to ask the bank for an overdraft or my father for a loan, or both, to buy some time to try turning things around. At any other time, these money worries would have consumed my every waking hour, and quite a few of my sleeping hours too. But right now it felt like I had a bigger fire to fight.

'Every business like ours has the same problem,' I said. 'How do we keep a distance from the liars, the bullies, the sadists, the sickos and the controlling creeps? It's the same problem for every dating app in the world.'

Sophie Sherman smiled for the first time, and I realised I liked her.

'And every woman,' she said.

CHRISTIAN

I watched Tara online, standing in the bright spring sunshine outside the Angel Eyes office, reading a prepared statement, the thin young woman in black by her side.

'I made a mistake,' Tara said. 'And I will regret it for the rest of my life. I have let down my family, myself and most of all my husband. I send my condolences to the family of James Caine, who have lost a husband and a father.' She lifted her face to the media pack and the cameras clicked. '*But*,' she said, and let it hang there for a while, 'James Caine made my life a misery.'

Then the press were shouting their questions at Tara and Sophie Sherman, sensing another big scalp to put up there with King Leer and Uncle Norman, another juicy exposé that would run and run. Tara bent her head, and for the first time I saw the pain in my wife, and I saw the weight she carried, and my heart clenched with feeling for her.

'For the victims of abuse,' Sophie Sherman said, without the need of prepared notes, 'it is never over. They live with the wounds inflicted by their abuser every day of their lives and they carry those wounds to their grave. Long after your headlines have faded, those wounds will impact on every corner of the lives of the victims and the lives of their loved ones. And this is true even when the abuser – like James Caine – is dead.'

I could not tear my eyes from Tara's face.

How could you?

Was he better than me?

Did you love him?

So quickly the mind adjusts to the previously unimaginable.

And then the questions change.

Do you still love me?

I wiped my eyes with the back of my hands, knowing what I wanted to do as soon as my wife came home.

25

TARA

Christian wanted to have sex with me. The sex light was in his eyes, and I guessed the bottle of bubbles was in the fridge and two flutes were in the freezer. More than me, perhaps, my husband craved routine. When I returned home in the early afternoon, he was waiting, all ready for love action, and I could tell he had seen my speech because he had the red-eyed and snotty look of someone who has been crying.

Christian was not a big weeper. He had cried the first time he told me about the death of his parents, and again when Marlon was born, and then when Buddy had pancreatitis and we thought we might lose him. All good reasons. But now he had been crying about me, and he swallowed down some of that leftover grief and he took me in his arms and I huddled into his hard bulk and it felt good, being held. No, it was a bit more than that – being held felt like it was enough for me right now. I felt wrung out by all those strangers staring at me, shouting questions at me, wanting to rip apart my life and feed it into the gormless maws of the great unwashed.

'This feels nice,' I said.

'I miss us,' he said. 'I miss when it is just us.'

He found my mouth with his mouth, and that felt good too, but I felt the first flutter of panic because I knew how Christian thought he could start healing our wounds and I was not in the mood for penetration.

'I haven't got to pick up Marlon for an hour,' Christian said and kissed me long and deep, and I kissed him back, but dialling the passion down a notch. 'Prosecco?' he said.

And I sighed. Sorry, I just couldn't help it.

'Don't you ever get a wee bit *tired* of Prosecco, Christian?'

He pulled away, clearly offended, and then all at once it broke without warning, the storm that had to break, the row that had been coming for us, the argument that we could not avoid, and I saw that the afternoon sex would only have been a way to defer the confrontation, it would have been one last pretence that we were the same, that we were unbreakable, and unbroken, *and it just was not true,* no matter how much we both wanted it to be.

I turned away and he seized my wrist.

'You loved him, didn't you? Why don't you just say it?'

'Christ. We had this conversation already, didn't we? *I love you.*'

'Then why did you sleep with someone else?'

'I was stupid. I was scared. I was drunk.' A beat. 'I was flattered.'

'Flattered? Fucking *flattered*?'

I pulled away from his grip. 'I'm only telling you the truth.'

'First time for everything.'

'And I wanted ...'

'Go on!'

'All I wanted was to be wanted.'

He went into the living room, Buddy padding happily behind him, and began furiously looking through his collection of vinyl, pulling out old favourites and looking at the cover, all those twelve-by-twelve-inch comfort blankets, then skimming them across the floor.

'I want to be wanted, too,' he said, looking at the records and not at me. 'You know what stopped me ever acting on it? The thought of losing you and Marlon. Only that. The opportunity was there, Tara. The women were there – fabulous women. At the gym. At the school gates. And online.'

'Christian,' I said, trying to calm him down. 'Look, just because someone "likes" your photograph of a sunset on Instagram, it doesn't necessarily mean they want to have sex with you.'

'Maybe it does! But I couldn't risk losing you and so I did nothing. And then I lost you anyway. So what was the point?'

'I'm sorry. I really am.'

He wasn't listening. You get to apology overload, I suspect. He put on some music. *Some Girls* by the Rolling Stones, turned up to ten. The Stones' late-Seventies response to punk and New Wave, I thought, the music journalist in me kicking in. Their last great album, quite rough on women as I recalled. Very loud. Loud enough to bother the neighbours, loud enough to make them want to move to the country. I felt a sudden burst of anger with him. Sometimes Christian seemed stuck in late adolescence, lost in music and never really having to worry about tax, bills, life, the money running out – *and then what? How do we live?* The thought that hits you at 4 a.m. in the middle of your dreams, the thought that you are living a way of life that very soon you will not be able to afford. He was happy to leave all of that to me.

He turned to look at me.

'You're so spoilt, Tara,' he said. 'Always so spoilt. What child grows up with a *horse* in their back garden?'

'Leave Maple out of it, will you?'

He shook his head and adjusted his spectacles.

'I don't know you,' he said.

'Oh, you know me. You've always known me, Christian. Remember? You didn't want the girl next door, you wanted the wild one – and you got her. Well – this is what she looks like and now you're stuck with her.'

'And now you've ruined everything.'

I couldn't argue with that.

'What were you *doing* out there anyway?' he said, as if it could all be undone if we both saw how senseless it was. 'What were you *doing* all those thousands of miles away?'

'It's called earning a living. You should try it sometime. It's much harder than I make it look.'

He recoiled as if he had been slapped in the face.

And I was suddenly disappointed in both of us. For the cruel truth was that my husband was in decline. Not physically – he looked far better than he ever did when he was that pale, skinny twenty-something going on the road with bands getting up to God knows what in cheap hotels around the world. But Christian's horizons had shrunk. He was a great dad, a loving husband – even if the sex had been somewhat sidelined, something else to be squeezed into a busy schedule. But Christian, I suddenly saw, was a man who *needed* to work, a man who was made *better* by work, for his own sense of self-worth, if nothing else. And I suspected all men were like that, and all women too, of course.

I knew Christian could never physically hurt me, but I also knew that there was a violence in him, and I could feel it coming. He got up from the floor, stepping all over his beloved vinyl as he picked the nearest thing – the ice bucket, filled to the brim with cubes, for he had the healing, Prosecco-fuelled rumpy-pumpy all meticulously planned – and hurled it with full force at the wall.

'Oh, smash the place up, Christian!' I shouted, raising my voice above the Stones cranking out 'Respectable'.

'You make me laugh,' he shouted back.

'Good!' I said. 'I'm glad you still get some pleasure out of me because I was starting to think that side of things was all over.'

What had James Caine called married sex? One-and-you're-done.

'No, I get a lot of pleasure out of you because you make me bloody laugh, Tara – the idea that your company was some adorable accident – set up to help your lonely friend – poor old Ginger! It's all bullshit, Tara. You were always as hard as nails. You were never going to wither away and die after the journalism folded. You're just like your old man.'

'You make that sound like a bad thing.'

'So *stupid,*' he said, suddenly on the verge of bitter tears again. 'Stupid! Stupid! Stupid!'

He pounded his forehead with his fists and I tried to put my arms around him.

'I know. I know. I know.'

He shook me off.

'Not you, Tara. *Me*. I'm the stupid one. I've been the stupid one all along. But I'll tell you what – I'm glad that bastard is dead! He deserved to have his head smashed in! That evil fucker deserved to die!'

We must have been shouting at each other for a while because we did not hear that someone was banging on the door until Mick Jagger took it down a notch and was crooning 'Far Away Eyes'.

When I opened the door, the police were exactly as Ginger had described them – the copper-haired slip of a girl and, behind her, the affable thug. Detective Chief Inspector Stoner grinned at me and I saw they must have been outside for a while, the music drowning out the doorbell.

And they had heard it all.

26

TARA

The big detective, Detective Chief Inspector Stoner, sat on what was usually my sofa with a cup of tea and his legs apart, a smile on his face, affable and terrifying in equal measures. Buddy gave his calves a quick inquisitive sniff and DCI Stoner's meaty features lit up with an expression of pure delight. Tea, dog, dead lover. *Isn't this nice?*

The other one, the frosty-faced young redhead in glasses, Detective Inspector Ure, stood by the window with her arms folded across her chest, squinting at me with a combination of lifelong myopia and instant dislike. I sat at right angles to DCI Stoner, on what was usually Christian's sofa, and my mouth was very dry.

We were all in the wrong places. When I spoke I hated the sound of my voice, the flutter of nerves, the giveaway tell-tale sign of fear.

'I gave a statement. The night ...'

The night the body was found.

The night I fled the scene.

The night you took my husband away.

The night it all came out.

DI Ure looked me up and down and I realised that it was considerably more than dislike. It was loathing at first sight. I had been spoilt by Sophie Sherman. I thought that all women were my sisters now and they would rally around in my hour of need. But not this one. The short-sighted copper looked at me as if I was a crack whore who had somehow conned her way into a nice house.

'That first interview was what we call an initial brief account, Mrs Carver,' DI Ure said briskly. 'That's not the end of the process.' Her mean little mouth pursed with disgust. 'Only the start.'

'You're very important, Mrs Carver,' DCI Stoner, his patronising, pub bore matey-ness turned all the way up to ten. 'You and your friend – Mrs Ginger Sallis – found the body of the deceased. You are both significant witnesses.'

DI Ure watched me through her specs. She saw me as a spoilt rich bitch who thought she could get away with a quick fling on a business trip. Fair comment, really.

I licked my lips. I was going to have to stop licking my lips.

'Please don't be apprehensive, Mrs Carver,' DCI Stoner said, and I hated that he could see I was frightened. 'This is just to tie up some loose ends. Nothing to worry about. But some new evidence has come to light.'

'What new evidence?'

They ignored me. The police, I would learn, had the secret power of selective deafness. They did not say – *we ask the questions*. They didn't have to. Events proceeded at their pace and nobody else's. DCI Stoner smiled, and he did not stop smiling until Christian – leaning against the doorjamb, neither in nor out of the living room – asked a question.

'Does my wife need a lawyer?'

DCI Stoner stared at him, pressing the pause button on his hideous friendliness.

'Tara hasn't done anything wrong,' Christian said.

'She fled a crime scene for starters,' DI Ure said.

Bitch.

DCI Stoner smiled pleasantly. 'Why would your wife need a lawyer, sir?' Silence. 'Mrs Carver is a significant witness,' Stoner said. '*A witness*. Witnesses don't need lawyers. Only suspects.' He turned back to me. 'We appreciate your time, Mrs Carver. The criminal justice system can't work without the cooperation of witnesses.'

'So I don't need a lawyer?'

He seemed genuinely amused. 'I'll let you know if you need a lawyer, Mrs Carver! But I can assure you now that you don't need one to make a witness statement.'

'What new evidence?' I asked again.

'Theft of a significant item of property from the deceased,' DI Ure said.

'A twenty-nine-year-old man has been charged with the murder of James Caine,' DCI Stoner said. 'Did you see this man begging outside the Langham Hotel?'

He looked at Ure and she crossed the living room with her phone in her hand and held it out to me, displaying a police mug shot of the man Ginger and I had seen on the pavement outside the Langham.

'The British soldier,' I said. 'That's what his sign said. He had a little cardboard sign. *A British soldier.*'

'And did you speak to him?'

'No.'

'Did he speak to you or Mrs Sallis?'

'No. That is – yes.'

I glanced over at DI Ure, caught her shaking head, stifling a theatrical sigh.

'And which one is it?' asked DCI Stoner, very gently.

'He told us – have a nice night,' I said. 'Enjoy your evening. Something like that. I don't remember exactly.'

'Was he wearing a watch?' DCI Stoner said.

I thought about it.

'Mrs Carver? Was James Caine wearing a watch when you and Mrs Sallis discovered the body?'

I realised then that I should have asked Ginger exactly what she had told them, and that she was dead right. We should have got our stories straight.

'I don't know,' I said. 'I don't know if he was wearing a watch.'

'Do you ever think about the amount of food we throw away in this country?' DCI Stoner said. 'It's obscene.' He sipped his tea, his eyes clouding with disbelieving rage. 'That's what our suspect, Alfred Oakley, was doing in that five-star hotel, Mrs Carver. This – er – gentleman who served in the armed forces. He was scavenging for food that was being thrown out. All the food that people in the hotel ordered from room service, and put on their credit card, or their expense account, and then leave on the side of the plate to be thrown away.'

I stared at him.

'That's how our suspect fed himself, by scavenging in hotel corridors,' DCI Stoner said. 'I've got the CCTV of Alfred Oakley going in through the service entrance at the back of the hotel. God knows he would never have made it through the front door! Or even the side door. Apparently, he's done it before. He calls it "the leftovers run", if you can believe that. Our suspect would go in and wander the floors and help himself to what was on the trays outside the rooms. And it was working out quite well for him until he took a shine to James Caine's Rolex.'

'So he did it?' Christian said, still lurking in the doorway.

DCI Stoner did not look at him, or acknowledge that he had even heard. 'How much is a watch like that worth?' he mused. 'A Rolex Submariner 6536?'

'More than I earn in a year,' DI Ure said.

DCI Stoner chuckled good-naturedly. 'Above my pay grade too!' Finally he looked at Christian, his smile fading. 'Did our suspect – his name is Alfred Oakley – kill James Caine? Is that what you're asking me, sir?'

Christian nodded.

'That's for the court to decide,' DCI Stoner said primly. 'A man is innocent until proven guilty in this country. But let's see – we've got James Caine's watch on Alfred Oakley's wrist. And we've got Oakley's prints all over the room service trolley. And we've got James Caine's DNA all over Oakley. But here's the thing – *Oakley claims he never entered the hotel room*. He claims that this watch – this ridiculously expensive watch – was carelessly left on a room service trolley and that's where he found it.'

'But that's ... insane,' I said. 'Isn't it?'

'The thing is – hotel guests *do* accidentally leave all sorts of things on room service trolleys. Remote controls for the TV, their wallets, their passports. Even – please forgive my vulgarity, Mrs Carver – vibrators.'

A short mirthless laugh from DI Ure.

'And then – the silly things – they shove the trolley out in the corridor for collection,' DCI Stoner went on. 'And later in the evening they wonder whatever happened to the remote control, or their wallet, or their watch.'

'Or their vibrator,' DI Ure said to herself.

A silence settled over us and then DCI Stoner shrugged his broad shoulders. 'Who knows what really happened between James Caine and Alfred Oakley?' he said. 'On the face of it, a jury might decide it looks like a robbery that went too far. It might be just about believable to a jury that a man could accidentally leave his expensive watch on a room service trolley, but we are also asked to believe that the same man ended up murdered – and it had nothing to do with the homeless chap who took his watch. Everything says Alfred Oakley did it,' DCI Stoner said.

He paused dramatically, enjoying his power.

'Apart from one thing,' he said.

DCI Stoner sipped his tea, smiled, stared down at Buddy sleeping at my feet. Taking his time. He looked up from the dog, staring over at Christian and then at me.

'My gut,' he said. 'My gut tells me this former British soldier did not murder James Caine.'

He thinks we did it, I thought, my heart pounding.

He thinks Christian and I did it together.

Or he thinks we hired this poor bastard they've got locked up.

DI Ure laughed.

'Your famous gut,' she said, truly amused.

'So if you don't think he did it,' Christian said, 'who did?'

Shut up, I thought. *Shut up shut up shut up.*

'As I say, that's for a jury to decide, sir.'

Christian smiled. It was *sir* now.

'The evidence against Alfred Oakley is considerable,' DCI Stoner said. 'But I imagine his defence will make something of his right arm.'

I licked my lips again, my mouth feeling like it was made out of cotton.

'What about his right arm?' Christian said.

'It's not there,' DCI Stoner said. 'Alfred Oakley has a prosthetic arm. He lost his right arm, below the shoulder joint, to an IED in Helmand.'

I shook my head. 'IUD?'

DI Ure looked disgusted. 'Not *IUD*. An IED. An improvised explosive device. A bomb.'

DCI Stoner smiled appreciatively. 'IUD! That's very good, Mrs Carver!' And then all serious. 'When Alfred Oakley was serving in the armed forces, he was hit by a roadside bomb in Afghanistan. The bomb killed the rest of his patrol and took off Oakley's right arm just below the shoulder joint.' With his left hand, DCI Stoner made a chopping motion at the top of his right arm. 'There,' he said softly.

'Must have been his lucky day,' DI Ure said. 'Or his unlucky day.'

'James Caine was killed with some force,' DCI Stoner said, thinking aloud now. 'The forensic post-mortem will obviously give us more detail, but it's clear his head was caved in with some kind of sharp instrument, and that he was struck multiple times. When you are right-handed – as Alfred Oakley was before his injury – how do you do that with one good left arm?'

I was going to be sick.

'Excuse me,' I said, walking quickly from the room.

On my knees in the bathroom, the water running so they could not hear me retching, I heard their voices in the living room, Stoner making small talk about Christian's record collection, sounding interested. How do you do that? Talk about someone's brains being smashed in one minute and the timeless glory of vinyl the next? I heaved and heaved until it hurt but nothing came out, just a bitter trickle of yellow bile. The sweat was slick on my face. I dabbed cold water on my forehead, shivered as though someone had stepped on my grave, and went back and joined them.

'You all right?' Christian said.

I ignored him. I sat on the sofa, all business.

'So I don't see how Alfred Oakley could have beat him to death with that arm,' DCI Stoner said, looking at me.

'Maybe he was desperate,' DI Ure said.

Stoner smiled pleasantly. 'Not my concern,' he said. 'Did you ever come across a man by the name of . . .'

He looked across at DI Ure who had her notebook in her hands as she stared at me.

'Omar Haddad,' she said.

'Thank you, Gillian,' DCI Stoner said. 'Omar Haddad – ring any bells?'

Keep Spike out of it, Ginger had said, and that was all she had said, I recalled, fighting off my hurt feelings. I suppose in the end all we care about is protecting our own family. No friendship in the world can be more important than your family. I made a show of thinking about the name and then I shook my head.

'Omar Haddad?' Christian said.

Shut up shut up shut up!

'He used to go out with a friend of ours. Years ago.' He looked at me and I nodded, miming my memory being jogged. 'Ginger . . .' And then he realised that – of course – Detectives Stoner and Ure had already met Ginger. 'But what's Omar Haddad got to do with it?' he asked.

DCI Stoner totally ignored him, drained his tea and smacked his lips. He slapped his big hands on his thighs, as if preparing to take his leave.

'One final thing,' he said. 'We always say – *find out how a murder victim lived and you will find out how he died*. James Caine – we know – was sexually promiscuous, and it is quite possible that he was not killed because he had a nice watch but because of the way he lived.'

'I don't understand,' Christian said, but I was afraid I did.

'James Caine had the habit of giving his women a second phone,' DCI Stoner said.

I felt Christian flinch, and I felt his flesh crawl, or perhaps it was my own flesh crawling.

His women.

DCI Stoner was shaking his head as if this was just an annoying administrative detail that needed clearing up. 'And I was wondering if James Caine ever gave you a second phone, Mrs Carver.'

I stared at him blankly.

'I think I am correct in saying there was no mention of a second phone in your statement.'

He looked over at DI Ure.

'There was no mention of a second phone in Mrs Carver's statement,' she confirmed.

'Now think very carefully,' Stoner said, as if it may have slipped my mind. 'Did James Caine ever give you a phone?'

I remembered the day James Caine came to my office. I remembered the tickets he placed on my desk for Bryan Ferry at the Royal Albert Hall – how he got the wrong "Angel Eyes", how he thought the company was named after the Roxy Music song and not the Frank Sinatra classic, and I remembered that brand-new phone, still in the box but with the cellophane wrapper torn off, as if it had been opened, charged up and was ready to go.

'It's in case you ever need a friend,' Caine had said. *'Or something more.'*

And I remembered telling him that I already had a friend, and I already had a phone, and I already had a fucking life. And I remembered that he took the concert tickets and left the phone.

And I remembered where I had put it.

'Mrs Carver?' Stoner said. 'I'm asking you again – did James Caine give you a phone?'

I looked him in the eye. 'No,' I said.

CHRISTIAN

We were the happy family waiting at the school gates, the stay-at-home dad, the beautiful, high-achieving mum and the adorable dog. Waiting for their beautiful boy to appear at going-home time. But that afternoon there were looks, and muttered asides, because the gossip was already on the grapevine and you were certainly not innocent until proven guilty at the school gates.

You were guilty right from the start at that place.

That's the one who shagged that murdered guy.

And that's the husband who they thought did it.

It turns out it was some mad homeless squaddie with PTSD.

'He scares me, Christian,' Tara said. 'That policeman. Stoner. He scares the daylights out of me.'

I did not reply. I did not know what to say to her any more. I was afraid that anything I said might open up wounds that would never heal.

Wounds in her, wounds in me. So I kept my mouth shut.

'Stoner thinks we're involved in this, Christian. You and me. Maybe he thinks we did it together? Maybe he thinks we hired that poor one-armed bastard they've got locked up. I don't know what he thinks but I do know he doesn't care if our family comes apart. He doesn't care about Marlon. Christian? *Please*. We have to stick together now. Because if we don't, then they're going to take everything away from us. We can't let that happen.'

And I stared at the school where the bell would ring soon and I pondered the final mystery of all couples.

Are you enough for me?

And am I enough for you?

It was not such a mystery any more for us.

We knew, didn't we?

Tara was fighting back the tears now. And I was aware that mothers were looking at her differently now, and that fathers were looking at her too, in a way they had not looked at her before.

As if Tara was an option now. As if she was available.

The bell rang and Marlon appeared, just one face in a sea of faces, but the face that held my heart, the face that felt like the centre of the universe, and my reason for living, and the loveliest face in the world.

Buddy began to bark wildly.

Our beautiful boy smiled and waved and began running towards us.

I took Tara's hand in mine.

'He scares me too,' I whispered.

27

TARA

'Sorry,' I told Sophie Sherman, 'but I can't do this.'

After a sleepless night thinking about what it would mean to really share my story with the world, I found my feet were stone cold. The interview with DCI Stoner had badly shaken me and I had no appetite at all for the scrutiny that would come with facing the press. But Sophie Sherman was not listening to me. It was early afternoon and she had no time for anyone's cold feet as she watched the assorted journalists, photographers, bloggers, podcasters, broadcasters and cameramen cramming into the Angel Eyes office, chatting happily among themselves, getting the light right on the faces of the three women who had already taken their place behind a table at the end of our open-plan office.

And as I watched them – the three women waiting to tell their stories of horror at the hands of James Caine, the indifferent media pack preparing for the latest breaking news of sexual abuse, and Mary, Skyla and Michael looking bewildered at what our once happy place of work had come to – I knew that I wanted no part of it. I didn't want the attention and, try as I might, I could not muster the self-pity. Because as much as I hoped that James Caine was burning in hell right now, I did not feel like his victim. He was *dead*, wasn't he? Somebody had given him exactly what he deserved, hadn't they? He had died and I lived. And to be frank, I was expecting a bigger turn-out of victims. I had imagined that there would be an army of women who had been tormented by James Caine, that we would find strength, and some sweet anonymity, in our numbers. Listening to Sophie Sherman, I had assumed that I would look like one among the many women that Caine had tortured. But it wasn't like that.

There were just five of us at the press conference, and even that modest handful included the dead girl, Nora, a lunch-box delivery driver who had met Caine at his office and later taken her own life. Above the three women sitting at a makeshift table at the far end of the office, nervously waiting to tell their stories, Nora's shyly smiling face looked down from a big HDTV screen. Poor Nora. She had been so young that she was still having trouble with her skin. I wondered what exactly James Caine had done to her. I wondered if he had used the same cruel playbook on young Nora that he had used on me.

The rest of us were older. Two of them were women in business suits who had once worked at Caine's firm, Samarkand Wealth Management. One of them was a shockingly beautiful Anglo-Indian woman of around forty – Rani, it said on the little laminated ID badge she wore on her jacket – and the other a woman in her middle-twenties, pretty but rather washed out. Marta, said her badge. I felt a flutter of apprehension. Sophie Sherman didn't seriously expect *me* to wear a badge, did she?

'Here's your badge,' she said as we hovered by the side of the little table. 'Helps them get the names straight.'

Rani and Marta were a team, acting as if they had known each other for years, whispering urgently among themselves and totally ignoring the third woman – a pale young thing with pink streaks in her white-blonde hair and some kind of complicated ethnic wrap – Peruvian, was it? – wrapped around her bare shoulders. All I knew about her – *Wendy*, her badge revealed helpfully – was that she had started a pet care app and bumped into James Caine at a conference in Helsinki. Perhaps Caine gave Wendy a few tips about public speaking.

Be sincere, be brief and be seated.

And that was us – five victims of James Caine's coercion, control and abuse, five women – one dead, four living – whose lives were made a misery by the man. But if he was truly a monster, rather than just a lying scumbag, then it felt like there should be many more.

I glanced over at my staff. Mary looked close to tears. I knew how she felt today. When we started the business, we had honestly believed there was a huge market for bringing men and women together and it had never crossed our minds that there were men like James Caine out there. I fingered my badge, still delaying the moment when I put it on.

'Sophie?' I said again.

'What can't you do?' she snapped, checking her watch. So she had heard me after all.

'I'm not doing this,' I said. 'I'm really sorry. But I can't be somebody's anecdote.'

And finally she looked at me.

'Fine,' she said. 'But you're not letting me down. You're letting *them* down.' She gestured at the women waiting at the table. 'And you're letting down Nora, who killed herself because she thought that James Caine was in love with her and was going to leave his wife. And you're letting down Rani, whose marriage broke up after she confessed everything to her husband after believing James Caine's broken-condom lies. And you're letting down Marta, who lost her job after she started self-harming. Don't let the business suit fool you – Marta has been unemployed for two years. All of them went from a short stay in Caine's bed to years and years under the heel of his Gucci loafers. And now you don't want to do it, Tara? No problem! I understand. Sometimes husbands and boyfriends and partners are not as supportive as we would wish, especially when they find out some other man has dominated your life.'

'Caine never dominated—'

She held up her hand.

'You want to be one more person that lets them down?' She gestured at the women waiting, their faces tight with nerves. 'Then go now.'

But it's my office, I wanted to say. But of course I said nothing. Instead I meekly put on the laminated badge that said *Tara* and I took my place at the table with the others, the three women and the smiling dead girl.

'This is your office?' Rani said, her accent mid-Atlantic.

I nodded. 'Angel Eyes, the dating app. I don't know if you've heard of us.'

'You bet I have! Home of the crazies!' Marta said.

So she had been reading about us too.

'The Accidental Dater?' she prompted me. 'Isn't she one of your clients?'

'Whooh,' I said. 'Angel Eyes doesn't have a monopoly on crazies. Do you know how many police call-outs the average dating app gets?'

'I imagine it's rather a lot,' Marta said. 'Christ, I need a smoke.'

Wendy was trembling under her Peruvian wrap.

'Are you OK?' I said.

'I thought I would feel like I was taking control today,' she whispered in a strong West Country accent. She laughed. 'But I just feel nervous.'

I squeezed her hand.

'Me too,' I said.

Sophie stood up and spoke for all of us.

'Abuse does not end with the death of the abuser,' she began. 'The abuse goes on and its wounds last for a lifetime.' A searching pause. She was good. 'James Caine was a grandmaster of coercive control. He was a groomer. He was a sexual predator. Above all, he was a man who loved to inflict psychic pain on women. He was a virtuoso of mental cruelty. He was—'

'James Caine was a *husband*, a *father* and a *beloved friend!*' shouted a well-spoken female voice from the back of the room. 'James Caine was a decent man!'

The press pack turned its attention to an elegant woman in her middle years trailed by a lanky teenage girl.

'Oh Christ,' muttered Marta. 'Not that mad cow.'

The angry widow had gatecrashed our press conference. Sandy Caine began walking around the perimeter of the media, their ranks shuffling back to give her space even as they pointed their phones and cameras at her. She was heading straight for us, her gawky daughter trying to keep up with her grimly determined mother, but around the halfway mark they got stuck in the crush of the crowd. The press pack had all turned towards her now, and we were suddenly forgotten, but Sandy Caine had not forgotten us and she jabbed a furious finger in our direction.

'Any sex that my late husband had with these women was *consensual*, and if Jim was unfaithful,' she said, and as her voice broke there was a flurry of action among the photographers, 'then that is a matter for me and my husband.'

She glared at us defiantly.

'Our marriage was *strong*. Our marriage was *good*. And' – her face twisted with loathing – 'I *know* these women! I know you all, don't I?'

Sophie turned to look at us. 'I can handle this,' she said.

'*We are a bereaved family*,' Sandy Caine cried, and the struggle she had maintaining her voice made her grief all the more raw. 'I have lost a husband. My daughter has lost a father.'

Sophie turned to us, maintaining an executive calm. 'Let's take a short break and then we can get started again.'

We slowly rose from our chairs, realising that the moment we had all primed ourselves for was not going to happen until Sandy Caine had stopped shouting, and that was not going to happen any time soon.

'These women – these women! – they are *not* feminist icons! They are home wreckers! They are whores! And I have seen them all before! They came to our family home!'

We were hurrying away now from Sandy Caine's invasion, heading for a service door at the back of the office.

'The whores on the door!' Sandy Caine said. 'Those three!' She meant Marta and Rani from Samarkand Wealth Management and Wendy from the conference in Helsinki. '*They came to my house!* They spoke to my daughter when she was tiny! *They* tried to intimidate *us*! And you gullible fools turn them into heroes!'

Marta and Rani exchanged awkward glances. Wendy stumbled into them, almost fell to her knees. I helped her to stand up. Her ethnic wrap was dragging on the floor like the flag of a defeated army.

'And *her!* The dating app bitch! She's the worst of the lot!'

'Out the back door,' I said. 'Keep going!'

But James Caine's widow was pointing at me and I felt a chill in my blood as she began a chant that was taken up by her daughter.

'Kill her! Kill her! Kill her!'

I fled with the others, Marta and Rani staggering in their tailored business suits and high heels, one of my arms wrapped around the shoulder of poor Wendy, her eyes streaming with tears, with Sophie behind us attempting to address the press as if this was just a bad day at the office and normal service would be resumed as soon as possible. Fat chance, I thought.

'Kill her! Kill her! Kill her!'

We burst out of the back door and stood in the shocking daylight by the recycling bins, sweating and trembling and glad to be out of it.

'Sandy was always a lunatic,' said Marta, pulling out a pack of low-tar Marlboro.

'That's why Jim was always so keen to get out of the house,' said Rani, accepting a cigarette. 'What man wouldn't want to get away from that crazy old bat?'

'Their happy home was wrecked long before any of us came along,' Marta said.

Wendy smiled weakly at me. 'I couldn't believe what they were shouting at you,' she said.

'We're OK now,' I said. 'But – yeah – it's not pleasant, is it? *Kill her, kill her!* Jesus Christ.'

Rani and Marta laughed, exchanging a knowing glance. Rani sucked hungrily on her low-tar cigarette and narrowed her eyes at me.

'They weren't shouting *kill her!*' she said. 'It was a bit worse than that, dear!'

Suddenly I understood that I had misheard the angry widow and her daughter.

What they had actually screamed at me was, '*Killer!*'

I felt the smoke from the cigarettes curdling in my fluttering stomach, stinging my eyes and choking my throat.

'*Killer! Killer! Killer!*'

28

CHRISTIAN

I arrived early at the school gates for going-home time, so early that nobody else was around, and I watched the press conference on my phone with the sound coming through crisp and clear on my Apple AirPods.

'*Killer! Killer! Killer!*'

The woman facing the cameras and microphones did not look like Tara.

Is this what it would be like now, I wondered?

This public sifting through our dirty secrets?

You think you know someone so well and then one day you realise that you are a fool.

Because you do not know them at all.

The brute fact of Tara's cheating was bad enough.

But as I watched that farce of a press conference, I felt like I had lost my best friend.

And the thought made me sadder than I had ever felt in my life.

I watched until it all started to fall apart after James Caine's widow showed up, pointing and shouting and refusing to go quietly, and I was glad to turn my phone off when Tara and the other women got up and fled.

More parents and carers were arriving at the school gates. I stood apart from them and tried to avoid eye contact. But there was a woman who smiled at me, and who did not look away, and who drew my gaze.

And I could not tell if she was an older childminder or a younger mother but, in her smile, there was that thing we all seek, that look of recognition in the eyes of a perfect stranger.

You see a glimpse of another life you might lead.

A fleeting hint of a way out.

She smiled at me and from somewhere far away, a bell began to ring. It was only the bell for going-home time, but it felt like more.

A wake-up call.

Then the children were coming out, and Marlon was brandishing a red paperback in his paint-stained hands.

'I've got a new story,' he said. 'Look.'

And I looked. *White Fang* by Jack London. A Puffin Classic. A wolf on the cover, showing his gnashers.

'*Born in the wilds of the freezing-cold Yukon, the wolf-cub White Fang soon learns the harsh laws of nature, growing fiercer and more independent in his struggle to survive*,' I read aloud. '*Yet buried deep inside him are distant memories of affection and love. Can he learn to trust man again?*'

'Another book by Jack,' Marlon said. 'Jack wrote more than one book, you know.'

'That's great, kiddo. There are lots of great stories in the world.'

The woman was collecting a girl who was not her own child.

She smiled again, and said, 'Bye then – it was nice almost talking to you!' And – again – there was that look of recognition in the lovely face of a woman who I had never seen before in my life, and like White Fang, her smile stirred distant memories of affection and love.

You did that to me, Tara.

You made me see that there is more than one great story.

TARA

I opened the last bottle of Prosecco in the house as I listened to Christian's voice coming through the child monitor. A new story tonight. Somehow Marlon had broken his *Call of the Wild* addiction. And I realised how much I loved Christian's voice – deep, calm, kind, the words coming out warm and honey-smooth, and in some secret chamber of my heart, I believed that hearing my husband reading to our son was perhaps my favourite thing in the world.

'The pale light of the short sunless day was beginning to fade when a faint cry arose on the still air. It soared upward with a swift rush, till it reached its topmost note, where it persisted, palpitant and tense, and then slowly died away.'

'What?' Marlon said. 'That bit before dying.'

'Palpitant means – a bit shaky. The cry was a bit shaky. OK?'

'OK.'

Christian continued. '*It might have been a lost soul wailing*,' he read, '*had it not been invested with a certain sad fierceness and hungry eagerness*.'

I sipped the sweet Italian bubbles and enjoyed the reading. Then I poured myself another glass. My cunning plan was reconciliation sex. I had showered, shaved my legs and changed into a little black dress. I thought about a chemise but the little black dress was better, wasn't it? More of an invitation and less of a command, a little black dress is always fun to pull up and pull down and take off. Christian would like all of that, he would like it very much, and one of the really good things about spending years with someone is that you know exactly what they like. Tonight my husband and I would start putting together the broken pieces of our marriage.

More nervous than I thought I would be, I took a long pull on my drink as I heard the familiar sounds of Marlon growing sleepy, of Christian thumbing the pages for a good place to stop for the night and finally Buddy being stirred from the end of Marlon's bed and goodnight kisses all round.

I tried to look casual, I tried to make sitting there with a bottle and two chilled glasses and a black dress not quite covering my thighs look like the most natural thing in the world.

Christian came into the room, Buddy padding behind him.

'New book?' I said. 'I'm impressed.'

Christian frowned at the red paperback in his hand, absent-mindedly shoving his specs further up the bridge of his nose. He looked at the Puffin more than he looked at his hot and willing wife.

'His teacher gave it to him. It's no great stretch. It's all Jack London. It's all wolf-dogs in the freezing Yukon and hairy-arsed trappers.'

I poured him a glass, feeling a little foolish as he flipped through the book. Frankly, I thought he would have his mouth on mine by now, and the little black dress up over my ass, or possibly down around my ankles. There was nothing but a thong like dental floss under there. Come on, Christian! Man up! But he plopped down with a sigh on the opposite sofa and stared at the dog, and I began to feel underdressed, over eager and unimaginably stupid.

We sipped our drinks in miserable silence. I was a bit ahead of Christian, having knocked back a couple while he lingered with White Fang in the snowy wastelands of the frozen north, but I didn't realise quite how drunk I was until I went over and sat next to him and aimed my mouth at his Clark Kent face.

He turned away and I ended up kissing the side of his head above his ear. I felt my face burning with alcohol and humiliation.

'You really think we can just pick up where we left off, Tara?'

'We can try, can't we? What else can we do?'

'I don't know.'

'I am yours and you are mine, Christian. And I'm sorry – so sorry! – to make you think that I'm not yours. But you're my guy, Christian, and I love only you.'

He was unconvinced.

'You are, you are, you are!' I said, ploughing on, refusing to let him deny it. 'I want to grow old with you – still. I want to spend my life with you – still. You *saw* me.'

He shook his head. He really didn't know what I was talking about.

'When we were young,' I said, determined not to cry, not to soil the moment with tears. 'When we were at the paper. You saw me for who I am, and you were the only one who saw me. Everyone else saw – I don't know – some wild child. But you saw me and you loved me, Christian. I know you did! You can't say you didn't! You loved me!'

He looked at me. Say it, I thought. Go on, just say, *I still do*.

But he said nothing, and so I went on. 'We have to stick together now, Christian. A lot of people want us to go down. That detective, DCI Stoner. That speccy bitch, his sidekick. The angry widow and the weird daughter. We have to face it – they all want to see us suffer. They don't give a damn about Marlon.'

He sipped his drink as if Italian sparkling wine had no special meaning for us. But he was thinking, and I knew he was trying to get it right, and to say what he felt without rancour or regret or bitterness, and I loved him all the more for it, that we meant so much to him, that he wanted to get it right even if I had ruined it forever.

'You were the one for me,' he said quietly. 'And there was never going to be anyone else for either of us.' He stared at me. 'But then there was.'

'I know. And I'm—'

'Stop telling me you're sorry, will you?'

'All right. Sorry. Ah! Sorry! But we're not a couple, Christian. We're a *family*. And we can't just do what we want any more. Do you hear me? We're not over.'

'I'm not saying we're over,' he said. 'Do you think I would ever leave Marlon? How could I ever do that?'

He bolted his drink like it was medicine to be forced down, and then he shook his head.

'But you broke my heart,' he said.

*

We went to bed early now.

I lay there on my side of the bed with the other half empty, the house in darkness, waiting until nothing was coming from the living room but the sound of Christian sleeping on the sofa, a soft wheeze that was more like rhythmic breathing than snoring, and when I was quite sure that the house was sleeping I got up and went to the kitchen to check my second phone.

Buddy was in his basket and grunted in his sleep as with a murmured apology, I felt deep inside his cushion and retrieved the phone that James Caine had given me. Crouching by the basket, I turned it on.

You have one missed call.

I went to *contacts*. There were only two numbers on there – the number for a dead man and the number that I had added. When I called I expected it to go straight to voicemail, but it was answered after one ring.

'Don't call again,' I whispered. 'Please. We're done.'

There was a moment of silence and then I hung up. The only light in the kitchen was the screen shining on my face. It died as I turned off the phone. Buddy opened his eyes and stared at me, black eyes shining in the darkness, wondering if he was having a dream, as I slipped the phone back deep inside his cushion.

'Mama?'

Christian was standing in the doorway with Marlon in his arms. He turned away with a look of disgust and

I went to the corridor, listening to him settling Marlon down, licking the lips of my cotton mouth.

He brushed past me and went back to his living room. I waited for a moment and then I followed him. Our home seemed to howl with a terrible silence.

He was back on his sofa, staring at the ceiling with his hands behind his head, as if he knew that there would be no sleep tonight.

'Can I explain to you why I have that phone, Christian?'

He did not speak.

'James Caine gave me that phone because he gave all of us phones,' I said. 'You know. His women. His girls.'

Christian winced as if he had been slapped.

'And I never used it – not once – for any of the reasons he wanted me to use it,' I said. 'Not for setting up secret meetings with him in hotel rooms. Not for dopey little love messages. Not for sex texts. Not for sending him pictures of myself.'

Christian's eyes flicked towards me.

'But I used it for something else,' I said. *Tell him now,* I thought. Tell him everything if there's going to be any chance of holding this family together.

'I used the phone Caine gave me to see how much it would cost to have him killed,' I said. 'And to find out if there were any takers.'

Christian sat up, the blood draining from his face. 'Oh, God.'

'I didn't go through with it,' I said quickly. 'I swear on Marlon's life that I didn't pay anyone to have James Caine killed. It didn't go that far. It was purely academic, of course, and strictly in the interests of research, and a nod to poetic justice. But I thought about it – a lot. When things were at their worst, their very worst, I could not stop thinking about it. I was obsessed with the idea. I was desperate, Christian. I thought I was going mad.'

When I thought James Caine had given me a disease that I might have passed on to my blameless husband, when Caine had made my life a living hell, when he made me want to kill myself. Yes, I wanted the rotten bastard dead then and I was willing to pay above the going rate, whatever that might be.

'That's enough to get you locked up, Tara. That's enough to get you sent to jail. That's enough to smash this family to pieces.'

'I know! But I was at the end of everything and I was *scared* and I thought I was going to lose you and Marlon and everything I love.'

I wanted him to take me in his arms and to tell me that he understood, I wanted him to tell me that he loved me still, I wanted to hear – *I am yours and you are mine*.

'You brought all of this into our home,' he said instead.

And he meant more than the phone. He meant all of it.

'Get rid of it,' Christian said.

29

TARA

'I have to ask you – is the Accidental Dater for real?' Sophie Sherman asked me the following morning. 'Or is it someone making up these things to hurt you?'

Mr Flat Share – met through: Angel Eyes, I read on my phone, as Phil watched me carefully in his rear-view mirror, the early rush-hour traffic crawling on the Camden Road.

In the restaurant, Mr Flat Share is all charm. And in the cab back to his place, he is all old-world courtesy, even with his tongue down your throat. It is only when you accept his invitation to go back to his shabby rooms that Mr Flat Share shows his true colours. Because his friends are there, and they have had a few drinks, and they are waiting for you.

I lifted my head and sighed. Sophie Sherman was worried what the Accidental Dater's anonymous blogs were doing to my image and, let's be honest here, also what they were doing to Sophie's brand, because it became much harder to present me as another blameless victim of toxic masculinity when my dating app was busy setting up unsuspecting women with toxic males.

And at first it does not seem possible that they are waiting for you, that this has all been planned, that you are their dollop of porn for the evening,

I read, my spirits sinking. I felt for this woman, whoever she was, I truly did, but I couldn't deny that I also felt for myself, and what her horrible experiences meant for my world, and my family, and everything that I had worked for. But as I read the words of the Accidental Dater, I saw how what I had built could all come crashing down.

Fear paralyses you for long painful, desperate, terrifying minutes but you fight – literally fight – your way out of that hellish room and by the time you are out on the street – an unfamiliar neighbourhood, too late for the Tube, no cabs to be had – there are these marks on your skin. On your arm and the top of your thighs and the back of your neck where one of them held you down with your face in a carpet that smelled of sweat and beer and weed and pizza. The marks on your skin are brown, yellow and black, as round as freshly minted coins. They are bruises that are left by fingertips.

'I have to say that it has the ring of horrible truth,' I told Sophie. 'Sadly.'

I heard her curse quietly. 'You see the problem?' she said. 'We are meant to be *helping* women, Tara – not enabling their tormentors!'

'Oh, yes, I get it,' I said, although I felt that Sophie and I had very different problems now. Sophie's problem was negative stories about my company appearing online, while my problem was feeding my family if my business went under. Sophie was worried about angry hashtags on social media and I was worried – worried sick, to tell you the truth, worried sleepless, so worried that I thought I might be getting an ulcer – about how Christian and I were going to pay our mortgage if there was no money coming in. Sophie was concerned about image, and I was rather more concerned about how my family would pay the bills if my business fell to bits. Sophie cared about me – I don't doubt it for a second – but we had very different priorities now.

'I'll be in touch,' Sophie said, hanging up, although I have to say it didn't feel like she would be in touch again any time soon. Angel Eyes and I were both toxic now.

Phil was still watching me in the rear-view mirror. He looked at me a bit differently these days, perhaps wondering if he would have a job by the end of the week.

We were arriving at our destination but the entrance to the mews was deserted.

'Nobody here today,' Phil said cheerily, meaning the press, with some of the old avuncular Phil style.

'Maybe they've had enough of me,' I said.

Outside the front door of the office there was a recycling bin that shouldn't have been there because all of our bins were out the back, a small green food waste caddy with ISLINGTON in white letters on the front. I looked back at the end of the mews to confirm that Phil was gone and then I opened up the waste caddy. Inside there was a fat brown envelope, designed for A4 paper, that had been folded in half. I took it out and let myself into Angel Eyes, turning off the burglar alarm, and then I went into my office and placed the brown envelope on my desk. I already knew what was in there but I peeled it open anyway.

There had been £10,000 in twenty-pound notes and it looked like it was still all there. I had told myself that I would no longer look at the second phone again but now I took it out, powered it up and read the one new message waiting for me.

Refunde

I sighed and shook my head, thinking – there's no bloody second *e* in refund, dummy. I took the phone and the envelope into the staff restroom and climbed onto the toilet. Then I pushed back a panel in the ceiling. The phone went up first and then the envelope. But the envelope had passed through too many greasy hands and the adhesive that had kept it closed was no longer quite sticky enough to do the job and, as I raised it to the ceiling, the money began to slide out of the envelope, slowly at first but then a sudden torrent, all those grubby previously owned twenties sliding past me and drifting down, coming in to land across the floor of the restroom. I was down on my knees, gathering them up when I saw Mary standing there.

She took it all in. The open ceiling panel, still pushed back and gaping black inside, and the twenties scattered across the floor and clutched in my fists, and the look of total panic on my face.

'I can explain,' I said.

She raised her hand for silence.

'I don't want to know,' she said, turning away.

It was time to choose our man. Mary and I scrolled through the faces of the men, looking for the male Angel Eyes for next month. We had always had a good laugh doing the choosing, Mary and I, but my old friend was a long way from me now.

'Not him,' I said. 'And not him ... not him ... how about him?'

He was a brooding male-model type with a beard so meticulously trimmed that the hair seemed almost pubic.

He looked like nothing but trouble and in the past Mary would have told me exactly what was wrong with him, and we would have had a good laugh about that pubic beard, but not today. Now her hand moved lethargically on the Magic Mouse, the long sleeve of her NASA T-shirt slipping up her arm, and that was when I saw the bruises.

I took her wrist and she pulled away, surprisingly strong, but I held her with both my hands and I would not let go and finally she relaxed, and let me roll up the sleeves of her T-shirt. And there they were – brown, yellow and black bruises, round like coins, the bruises that are left by fingertips, running all the way up her right arm where the men had pulled her and held her down and tried to do whatever they were planning to do.

I felt it all rise up inside me – disbelief, and hurt, and anger, and the feeling of stupidity – the bitter cocktail of the betrayed.

'I don't believe it,' I said. '*You're* the Accidental Dater?'

Mary did not speak, she just kept staring at the handsome male model grinning inanely on the screen from behind his pubic beard.

'I wonder if he really looks like that,' Mary said eventually. 'And I wonder if that is even his photograph, and I wonder if he has a wife and children at home, and I wonder what he and his friends would do to you if they got you behind locked doors and halfway to drunk or with a roofie dropped in your Sauvignon Blanc, and I wonder what kind of sick porn gets him hard.'

I shook my head, the words not coming, and I breathed long and hard.

'This is our *business*, Mary.'

I was still holding her and finally she yanked her bruised arms away from me and rolled down her sleeves.

'Are you fucking insane?' I said. 'Angel Eyes is our livelihood and you're trashing it! What's wrong with you?'

She looked at me, her eyes burning with resentment. '*It was my idea*, Tara,' she said. 'When we were a couple of young freelancers doing odd jobs on women's magazines even as they were all folding, you knocking out your crappy little pieces on commitment while I showed the old people how to plug in their computer, back when we were wondering what we were going to do for the next fifty years ... a dating app was *my* idea, Tara!'

I flashed back to those days and it was true that Mary – shy, homely Mary, the IT genius of the women's glossy magazine market, my colleague-slash-friend Mary, my office buddy Mary, who was prone to comfort eating but who could code like some teenage tech bro from Silicon Valley – had initially suggested the idea of a dating app to me.

As I recall, we were standing in line at the Pret a Manger used by the painted worker bees of Vogue House, counting out the meagre coins for our lunch, when Mary came out with the immortal words, 'We should do an app, Tara!'

'But *everyone* was talking about doing an app in those days,' I reminded her.

'Yes, but *we* did it! And you loved the idea of having your own business – remember? Because of your dad, because you thought you had all this go-getting entrepreneurial DNA in your Anglo-Irish blood – *but it would never have happened without me*. A dating app, Tara – it will always be a bit of a joke to a woman like you, let's face it.'

'It's not a joke to me! How I support my family is no joke, believe me. I've worked as hard as you for all this – and you're wrecking it!'

She smiled slyly. 'You don't *need* a dating app because the men will always come and find you. But I *believed* in Angel Eyes and I made it work. All that stuff about starting the company so you could find someone for your friend, Ginger – it's a great story, and maybe it even crossed your mind once that you could find Ginger someone, but none of this would have happened without *me*. I even went on dates! All those dates! That's how much of a true believer I was! Did you ever need a dating app, Tara? Ever upload a Tinder profile in your pampered life? Didn't think so. But we're selling a lie here, Tara. There's no romance out there, there's no love to be found in the faces of strangers.' She began absent-mindedly scrolling through the men on screen. 'Not him ... not him ... not him ...'

Then she abruptly quit and turned to me. 'I just can't care any more,' she said.

'Because you can afford not to care,' I said angrily. 'But I have a family to support.'

She shook her head.

'I didn't want to hurt us,' she said. 'That was never the plan. All I wanted was to meet someone *nice* – that's all. Someone like Christian. A guy like that. A good man.' Her face frowned at the mention of his name. 'But someone like Christian doesn't want someone like *me*, Tara. They want someone like *you*. Even that photographer – he didn't want me in the picture, did he? On that day. He wanted *you*.'

It took me a moment to realise that she was talking about the photo shoot in our early days, when that magazine was doing a piece on dating apps, and I ended up on the cover because the photographer and his assistant thought a solo shot of me was a better look.

'You think I cared about being on their stupid cover?' I said. 'That stuff is all totally meaningless!'

'Yes, it's so meaningless that you had the cover framed and stuck on your wall in your home, Tara.'

She stood up and I realised with a stab of panic that she was leaving me, and leaving the company, and I knew that I would struggle to run Angel Eyes without her.

'Mary,' I said. 'I'm sorry if you've felt undervalued and unappreciated. By me, and by these creeps you've been dating and writing about, and by that fucking photographer all those years ago.' I could not believe we were talking about a dumb photo shoot from the distant past but I saw that was where it began, the hurt she had been cultivating for all these years. 'I wish I had walked out of that shoot if he didn't want the pair of us on the cover.'

'Then why *didn't* you, Tara? Come on – you *agreed* with him – it was a better cover with fat old Mary kept out of the picture.'

'Mary – please don't go. This place revolves around you.'

'Thank you for saying that but it's too late.' She touched me lightly on the shoulder. 'You're spoilt, Tara. You've been loved from the start by so many people. You've always got whatever you wanted. You were the little girl with a horsey in her back garden. You were so loved by your parents—'

'Have you met my mother?'

'Your dad, then, although I am sure your mum loves you in her own way. Everyone loves you! Christian, certainly, my God, and every boy and man you ever met since you were about fourteen, and me and everybody at Angel Eyes. Skyla, Michael. When we met – when we first got chatting at that magazine – I was so *proud* to be your friend, Tara! It was like having the sun coming out when you were around. What's it like to be that loved, Tara? To be so indulged, to be so valued? You've had *so much*. Don't you see? But you took it all for granted, you were careless with it, you got a bit bored. All of it. And I think that when someone is loved as much as you are, they start thinking that being loved is the natural order of things. And believe me – it's not, Tara. You're not a bad person, Tara, I know that. But you're spoilt rotten and, in the end, you've let everyone down. Those men – I should not have had to suffer all those humiliations, not if you were really my friend. If you were there for me. But you take the love that is given to you and you spit it back in our faces.'

'That's not true.'

'Come on, Tara – isn't that exactly what you did to Christian?'

She stared around her, as if wondering what she should take – the mouse mat with an image of her cat, her chipped NASA coffee cup, a framed photograph of the pair of us laughing taken at that magazine shoot – and with a small sigh she turned away, as if resigned to leaving it all behind. Then at the last moment she hesitated and picked up the mouse mat with the picture of her cat.

And that's when I knew she was really going.

'I *need* you, Mary!' I told her.

It was my one last desperate shot at getting her to stay. And it was also true.

'But Tara lives her life like Tara doesn't really need anyone,' Mary said. 'And now Tara's going to get what she deserves.'

30

TARA

When Mary was gone I sat in stunned silence until Skyla appeared in the doorway.

'You need to turn on the TV,' she said.

'Not now,' I said.

'You really need to see this, Tara,' she said.

The British soldier, Alfred Oakley, had been released from police custody, and now he stood behind his lawyer, as if at attention, a proud man. *Breaking news,* it said on the bottom of the screen. *Iraq veteran homeless hero on bail charged only with theft – not murder.*

His lawyer was speaking, and he told the story of a disabled war hero, suffering from wounds that would last a lifetime, physical and mental, and the press – that pack of blood-sucking hyenas – listened in respectful, almost sentimental silence as the lawyer told how Alfred Oakley, MC, had been cruelly treated by a callous world and persecuted by a stupid, vindictive police force anxious for an arrest for murder, even if it was the wrong man, when all this disabled war hero had ever done wrong was pocket a watch he found lying on a room service trolley while attempting to feed himself with half-eaten scraps that were going to be thrown away.

Then suddenly there was DCI Stoner filling the screen, the press nowhere near as respectful now, shouting their rude, unruly questions at him and shoving their cameras and phones almost under his broken nose, as DCI Stoner tried and stuttered and failed to read from a prepared statement, his tough old face flushed scarlet with humiliation, and the spring sunshine, and what might have been rage.

The police came after lunch. A small convoy drove slowly into the mews, an unmarked BMW with DCI Stoner in the front passenger seat and then a police car with its blue lights pulsing, and a large white van bringing up the rear. But no sirens, and no drama, and it wasn't like the movies, there was just the sense that they were – finally – going to get it right this time.

The blue lights revolved in the late afternoon shadows of the mews as we stood inside the door, Skyla, Michael and I, my sense of dread rising. And I could not believe that Mary would have called them, even anonymously, to tell about the money and the second phone in the ceiling, I could not believe it even though there was no other explanation. But such is the nature of betrayal, I was learning, here was the mean heart of treachery. You can't believe it, it dumbfounds, it flabbergasts, even when it is happening to you. You never see it coming when they stab you in the back, do you?

DCI Stoner got out of his unmarked car and DI Ure got out of the back seat. Uniformed officers began emerging from the white van, opening kitbags that contained white suits and blue boots and gloves. They did not seem to be in any kind of hurry.

DCI Stoner and DI Ure walked down to the office. 'Is there anything you want to tell me?' he said.

I looked at the officers getting into their white suits. 'I didn't do anything,' I said.

He exchanged a look with DI Ure. He had recovered from the public humiliation of the morning but there was weariness about him now, as if he was sick of lies, and wanted this thing over and done.

'Mrs Carver,' he said. 'Don't look at my officers – *look at me*. Is there anything at all you would like to discuss with me? Is there anything I need to know before we begin?'

Before we begin?

'No,' I said.

He nodded to DI Ure, who went to the door and lifted her head to the officers waiting at the start of the mews. The search team came inside and now they moved with a degree of urgency as they unplugged computers, emptied filing cabinets and piled the bulkier items into black rubbish bags and the smaller stuff into transparent evidence bags that were sealed and signed and carried away. They picked the place clean.

A couple of them must have gone straight to the staff toilet because one of them came back with the second phone already sealed inside a signed evidence bag and the other had left the brown envelope unsealed inside its own plastic evidence bag so that you could see the thick wad of notes poking out.

DCI Stoner held out his hands. He was wearing a pair of blue latex gloves now. He looked carefully from the evidence bags to me and back again at the money and the phone.

DI Ure was smiling at me. Skyla and Michael were watching wide-eyed as our world was taken away. DCI Stoner looked – more than anything – disappointed in me. So here was yet another person I had let down. I don't know why they always seemed so surprised.

'You're going to need that lawyer now, Mrs Carver,' DCI Stoner said.

31

TARA

The affectionate twinkle in DCI Stoner's eye had been replaced by a cold dead light and, as he sat across from me in the sick yellow light of the interview room, he was never more like the bully who pretends to be your friend right up to the moment he has you pinned down in some isolated part of the playground.

'Do you remember when I came to your home, Mrs Carver?'

He waited as I stared at him across the worn Formica table and then finally nodded.

'*For the tape*,' DI Ure snapped, bored beyond belief, leaning back in her chair, as if these proceedings did not concern her. 'You can't just nod or shake your head. How many more times? We need to hear you *for the tape*.'

I looked at her, at the red hair, her black-rimmed glasses, the thin razor-cut of her mouth and my face flushed at the open contempt she displayed for me now that her worst, meanest thoughts had all been confirmed.

'Yes,' I said.

'I asked you if James Caine ever gave you a phone,' DCI Stoner said. 'And do you remember what you told me?'

I nodded.

'Yes,' I said quickly, for the tape.

'And now we find a second phone,' he said, taking a breath, as if he had grown weary of my lies. 'When you had denied having a second phone. When I had *specifically* asked you if James Caine gave you a second phone as he did to all his women.'

All his women.

I said nothing. My lawyer, family stalwart Kevin Steel sitting silent by my side, had coached me well. I knew what was at stake here, I knew exactly what DCI Stoner had planned for me.

Life imprisonment for conspiracy to murder.

Life imprisonment for perverting the course of justice.

It turns out – who knew? – that you do not even have to kill someone to get put away for so many years that your small child would become an adult and a stranger to you. You only have to think about it.

And they knew – the police *knew* – that I had thought about it.

'If I ask you what you were planning to do with £10,000 in cash stashed in the ceiling with this second phone, are you going to lie to me yet again, Mrs Carver?'

And this was what I feared now. Not DCI Stoner. Not his snide, speccy sidekick. Not the law. Not jail. These were all concepts my mind could not quite grasp. *But losing Marlon.*

I could understand losing Marlon.

That seemed real. It even seemed likely.

'Did you talk about killing James Caine with your husband?' DCI Stoner said, and I hated him now, I hated him with that timid vehemence you feel for the thug who once pretended to be your friend, and then turns on you without warning. I saw that DCI Stoner wanted both of us, even if it was nothing like real justice, even if Christian had always been one step behind what everyone else knew, even if it was all untrue. Even if – and this was what made my nails dig into the palms of my hand until I saw the red ridges of blood rising up beneath the skin – it meant my son losing both his parents.

DCI Stoner did not give a damn about Marlon and the justice system did not care about our son.

And I wondered – where's the justice in that?

'You see it all the time in cases like this,' DI Ure said, and I hated her too. *Cases like this*. 'The woman turns against her lover. She then asks her partner for protection, revenge and restoration of her honour. It's how couples often resolve their issues in cases like this – the woman plays the victim and the third party gets hurt.'

'My husband knew nothing about any of it,' I said.

'So what was the ten grand in cash for, Mrs Carver?' DCI Stoner said, going through the gears now. 'What service was that going to buy you?'

I felt the panic surge.

'Was that a figure suggested by your husband?' DI Ure said. 'Ten grand? Did Mr Carver think that would get the job done?'

'This is what I think happened,' Stoner said. 'You wanted James Caine dead – or warned off – or punished – or any combination of the above. And you were prepared to pay someone to do it. Is that about right?'

'James Caine was threatening to take everything away from me,' I said, and I felt Kevin's sharp intake of breath beside me.

Shut up. Shut up. Shut up.

But I didn't shut up because they poke you, they probe you, they goad you, and then you find that you are talking and you can't stop because it's *your* side of the story and you want it known.

You want the bloody tape to hear.

'My family. My sanity. My self-respect. My happiness.' I felt the words wedge somewhere halfway down my throat like a chunk of broken glass. I was not going to cry in front of them. 'My health,' I said.

'Caine was a deeply unpleasant man,' DCI Stoner said, suddenly all sympathy. 'He was doing to you what he had done to all those other women.'

'Yes.'

I hated my voice. The self-pity in it, the weakness, the fucking pain. I felt my lawyer exhale. It was not quite a sigh. Poor Kevin! It was more like someone had kicked him in the stomach.

'Controlling you,' DCI Stoner said, as if we were friends again. 'Manipulating you. Torturing you.'

I stared at my clenched fists on the table. My knuckles were white. I was aware of the pain in the palms of my hands where the nails dug in deep. I wanted the release of confession, I craved it, I ached for it.

'You wanted someone to kill this bastard,' DCI Stoner said, not a question now.

'He deserved to die,' DI Ure said, urging me on, unconvincingly acting as if she was on my side at last. 'For what he had done to other women. And for what he was doing to you. And to your family.'

'So how did you contact the hitman?' DCI Stoner said, almost conversational.

'And we'll take a break there,' said Kevin, smooth as a game show host.

Detectives Stoner and Ure leaned back, exchanging a look, pleased with a good shift.

The room Kevin and I went into was identical to the one we had just left.

My lawyer paced the tiny space. 'You need to stop talking,' he said. '*Please*. You're holding their coats while they build a case for conspiracy to murder. That's a life sentence, Tara, and even if you don't serve a full term your son will be grown-up by the time you get out.'

My eyes stung.

'I want to tell them the truth.'

'The truth is the last thing you need,' Kevin said. 'Conspiracy to murder is when a person – or more than one person, such as you and Christian – decide to carry out a course of action that will result in the unlawful killing of another person.'

I felt like I wanted to tear the skin from my face. 'But James Caine was driving me crazy. I was desperate. People say it all the time, don't they? *I will kill you.* It was an emotional response, a natural human reaction, not conspiracy to murder!'

'Look – it's conspiracy to murder if you hire a hitman and he never comes anywhere near to doing it, OK? Try to understand that, Tara. Or if you pay him the money and the hitman decides not carry out the killing. It's *still* conspiracy to murder. If they can make that stick – it's not good. Do you understand?'

'He's not a hitman,' I said. 'He's—'

Kevin raised a hand for silence.

'Please, stop talking,' he said. 'And you're right – people say it all the time. *I'll kill you.* But here's the difference between most people and you – because most people don't have ten grand and a second phone in the ceiling and an ex-lover with his skull smashed in, OK? And all this stuff about James Caine being a monster – *it just doesn't work for you.*'

I was stunned.

'It doesn't work for me? Why the hell not?'

'Because it gives you more of a motive to kill him,' Kevin said simply. 'Or to get someone to do it for you.'

'We've got your accomplice,' DCI Stoner said when we went back to the interview room, starting to enjoy himself, it seemed. He glanced at DI Ure. 'How many CCTV cameras in this country, Gillian?'

'Oh, lots,' DI Ure said. 'Too many, really. Sometimes you have to wade through two hundred hours of CCTV for the ten seconds you're looking for.'

'And how many CCTV cameras are there around the Langham Hotel?'

'Let's see – there are cameras outside the main entrance, outside the side entrance to the bar, around the back at the service entrance, at the entrance to the spa – and that's without neighbouring CCTV outside the BBC and the various restaurants, offices and embassies that are in Portland Place.'

'We've already got you and your friend Mrs Sallis – Ginger – entering the bar's side entrance of the hotel on CCTV,' DCI said. 'And earlier in the day there are CCTV images of your husband outside the hotel, although there is no evidence of him entering – *yet*.'

He let the word hang between us, trying to frighten me, but I thought that perhaps he was not quite as confident as he seemed, just like every other bully who ever lived.

'As you can imagine, Mrs Carver, our people are currently wading through a few hundred hours of CCTV images.' He paused. 'But the thing about CCTV is that it is endlessly fallible. What can go wrong with CCTV, Gillian?'

'Blurred images,' DI Ure said, stifling a yawn. 'Black screens. Horizontal lines. Faulty cables. Erratic infrared sensors playing havoc at night. Tapes getting wiped because of storage problems. Sometimes they forget to turn it on. And sometimes bad people have the wit to change clothes and cover their face.'

'So you see, Mrs Carver – CCTV is not the eye of God. CCTV rarely works quite as flawlessly as it does in the movies. But that said, with all those cameras surrounding that world-class hotel, we are cautiously confident that if you entered that hotel earlier than your visit in the evening with your friend Mrs Sallis, then sooner or later we will find CCTV footage of you doing so.'

He grinned at me.

'Fingers crossed, eh?' he said. 'And so I must ask you to think very carefully before you reply – when we have finally looked at all the CCTV, am I going to see you going into that hotel either alone, or with your husband, or with some third party?'

'No,' I said without hesitation, holding the big detective's mocking gaze, suddenly getting that old familiar feeling.

I seemed to feel it all the time these days.

I wanted to kill the bastard.

32

CHRISTIAN

Late in the evening, Tara's parents came to the house.

We stared at each other on the doorstep, struck dumb by the turn our lives had taken. This fit old man with a kitbag thrown over his shoulder and his wife, the Debbie Harry of the Home Counties. Leo and Jen. I didn't know what to say to them.

'She didn't do it,' I said. 'It's not her fault.'

Tara's mother snorted with derision.

'It's *never* Tara's fault,' Jen said. 'I've been hearing the same thing long before you arrived on the scene, young man. I have been hearing it for *thirty years* about innocent little butter-wouldn't-melt Tara!' She shot a ferocious look at her husband. 'And I'm sick of it.'

Then Marlon was there with his new book, Buddy padding behind him, and Jen was expressing wonder and delight, her loving hands in her grandson's golden mop. She took his hand and they went off to the living room, but Leo lingered on the doorstep.

'Marlon all right?'

I glanced back into the house.

'He's five years old, Leo. He doesn't understand any of it. He will be all right until his mum doesn't come home. And then he's not going to be all right.'

'How about you?' A beat. 'Any luck?'

'What?'

'Any luck with finding a job?'

I saw that the old man was in a state of shock. He was on autopilot now.

'Leo, I was a music journalist. It's like being a milkman. That job doesn't really exist any more.'

'Oh, yeah, right.'

And I suddenly realised that Leo was not coming inside.

'I'm going to the police station,' he said, and I almost told him that it was pointless, and a waste of time, and he was just banging his bald head against a brick wall. But I didn't say any of it because I knew that nothing would stop Leo from going to the police station.

Because that was where they were holding his girl.

TARA

It was Big Dave who had driven me to the estate the day after my dad's sixtieth birthday party.

'Do you want me to come in with you?' he said.

'Wait for me,' I said.

Less than one hour from our home in Camden Town there was an estate – four blocks of low-rise flats that had been scheduled for demolition almost from the moment they were built half a century ago, four blocks of miserable grey concrete facing a wasteland where someone had set an ancient computer on fire. In one corner of the wasteland, a gang of children on bikes watched me get out of Big Dave's car. Under their hoodies, the colour of their skin was varied as an old Benetton billboard. They looked past me at Big Dave.

Big Dave was standing outside his car, exuding a quiet menace, and watching. He nodded at them, and there was respect and warning in the gesture, and the kids hiding their faces on their bicycles did not approach me. Nobody approached me.

Once you got into the flats, what you noticed was the wind and the music. There was no apparent reason for the wind, you could not work out where it was coming from, and yet it whistled down the concrete corridors, as if the estate had its own mad weather system. There was music that echoed from somewhere above me, always the same song, which was no song at all, more like the sound of a nail being pounded into something that had died a long time ago.

I found the flat number. Among all the boarded-up homes and drug start-ups and crack dens and tiny pensioners who had somehow missed the final evacuation to the suburbs, there was an actual number. I stopped in front of a door with a cage in front of it. I pounded on it until the music stopped inside and Mad Dave came to the door.

Mad Dave. Poor Mad Dave. He looked so ill it broke my heart. The drugs had taken everything from him apart from his old-world courtesy and his shy decency.

He invited me inside his home and made me a cup of tea, all apologies that it was only 'normal' tea, although I have never been an alternative tea girl in my life. Oh, Mad Dave! I never wanted their fair-trade herbal teas! They can keep their chamomile, Mad Dave. And God knows I never wanted to drag him into this. But, it has to be said, as he fussed with milk and sugar, Mad Dave looked like a suitable candidate. If you were going to pay someone £10,000 to kill someone, Mad Dave might be your first choice, or perhaps your last. Because he looked like a man with absolutely nothing to lose.

And Big Dave had confided that it would not be the first time that someone had asked Mad Dave the same favour that I was about to ask him. Big Dave did not go into details – the less known the better – but there had been a dealer around Chalk Farm who had been particularly violent to a young woman that Mad Dave was soft on. Apparently, it had not ended well for the dealer. So it salved my conscience now that I would not be asking Mad Dave to do something that he had never done before.

'There's a man,' I said, as we settled to our tea. 'And he's killing me, Dave. This man. I feel like he's killing me.'

Mad Dave listened to my tale of woe. His face – even now, even after all this time – blushing a pale red, more of a rose, when I briefly told him about what had happened on that night in Tokyo.

'Does your dad know about this, Tara?'

'My *dad?* What do you think?'

'I think – move on. I think – forget it. Ignore all this and hope he goes away. But – not this, Tara. What are you suggesting exactly?'

'But I've got *this*,' I said, showing him the envelope, tearing it open and pulling out a fat fistful of twenties. All those faces of the Queen looking young and smiley and gorgeous. 'It's ten thousand pounds.'

He looked at the envelope.

And shook his head. But then he took a breath.

And then Mad Dave took the money.

Later, after they picked him up, Mad Dave told the police that he took the money because I had wandered into a place where they would kill me for fun, or for ten quid, let alone ten grand. So Mad Dave was doing me a favour taking my money.

He may even have been saving my life.

Mad Dave told the police that he was a registered heroin addict, not a hitman, and he had the NHS methadone prescription to prove it.

He also told them that he had known me since we were both teenagers and that he believed that, in my heart, I did not really want anyone killed. He said he hoped that if he took the money then this wicked man who was tormenting me would eventually leave me alone and find some fresh victim.

It might even have all been true. I like to think that it was.

Mad Dave certainly refunded the money in full rather than spending it on drugs, which must have taken a superhuman effort on his part, and that moves me more than words can say, because I am not sure that Mad Dave would have done that for anyone else in the world.

CHRISTIAN

There was an overweight sergeant on the front desk who cut me off as soon as he understood that my wife was in custody and that I wanted to see her.

'Does she need an appropriate adult?'

'What?'

'Is she under eighteen or a vulnerable adult and therefore in need of an appropriate adult to be present during her questioning?'

I stared at him.

'Hello?' he said. 'Hello? Is she under eighteen or a vulnerable adult?'

'No,' I said.

'Then you're not seeing her,' he said. 'Look – *sir* – I don't doubt your missus is innocent. Everyone who we bring in here is always totally innocent. But we have the right to hold her without charge for twenty-four hours. If she is not under eighteen or a vulnerable adult, you can talk to her on the phone as long as she does not choose to talk to someone else. She gets one call. Good day.'

'Fat man?' Leo said.

The desk sergeant stared at him with disbelief.

'You're not listening to my son-in-law, fat man. And I think you're being very rude.'

Leo was taking something out of his kitbag.

A claw hammer.

No, it was a nailing hammer, the hammer for banging nails through the horse's feet so that the horseshoes stay on, and with claws for breaking off the excess nail.

It was small and vicious looking, like a miniature pickaxe.

'Are you listening now to us, fat man?'

The desk sergeant was listening now.

'My daughter didn't kill anyone,' Leo said. 'Because I did.'

'Drop the weapon!'

The sergeant had a Taser in his hands, aiming it at Leo's chest.

He reached under the desk and hit a button that let off an alarm and then there were other officers, and there were handguns pointed at us.

'Drop the weapon! Drop the weapon! Drop the weapon!'

And they were screaming and we were getting down on our knees but Leo would not let go of the nailing hammer and he was talking but nobody was listening to him.

'On your face! On your face! On your face!'

And then we were on our bellies and I felt a boot smash down into the back of my neck, and my face was twisted sideways, and I caught one last glance of the nailing hammer before another boot stamped down hard on Leo's hand and he cried out with pain and then the nailing hammer was kicked away.

And as my arms were pulled halfway up my spine and the handcuffs snapped on, I knew that on the end of that horseshoe nailing hammer there would be tiny traces of hair and blood and bone and brains, all the forensic remains of James Caine's ruined skull.

LOSING

1 Month Later

33

TARA

'How do you plead?' the court usher asked my father, and in the front row of the public gallery in Court Two of the Central Criminal Court, my mother screamed.

It was a cry of rage more than grief, and the sound was shattering in that intimidating place of black robes and horsehair wigs and hushed, oak-panelled formalities. Then a female security guard was edging down the aisle towards us, and escorting my mother from the public gallery as if she was the victim of a sudden catastrophic accident. My mother was done up to the nines in her favourite sky-blue Chanel suit, her hair blonder than it had been for years, the glamour of her appearance in stark contrast to her hunched, stumbling gait as the security guard led her away with a tenderness that made tears spring to my eyes.

My head told me to go with her, and so did my husband's eyes, to run to her side and comfort her in the weirdly busy corridors of the Old Bailey where witnesses and police and barristers mingled as if it was always rush hour in the criminal justice system. But I made no move to go to my mother.

Holding Christian's hand too tightly, I turned back to look at my father standing in the dock as his gaze drifted from the usher who had asked the question to the judge, who was peering at him over the top of her reading glasses.

She was a small, beaky, bird-like old woman – although of course godlike in the theatre of the court, wearing the robes of a superhero and perched, it seemed to me, so much higher than anyone else in that terrible place of Regina v Doherty.

My father drew a breath as he looked up at the public gallery.

The seat that my mother had relinquished had already been taken by a serious young woman scribbling notes. A law student? There were all types in the house today.

At the other end of the front row, Sandy Caine and her lanky, frown-faced daughter sat with their eyes boring into my dad. The two Daves were together immediately behind Christian and me. A few rows behind them, beyond the faces of strangers who I had never seen in my life – the law students, the curious, the ghouls, the great gawping unwashed who had queued early for a seat to the show – Ginger and Spike were huddled together. The tears were streaming down Ginger's face, her eyes swollen with misery.

Ginger was crying far too much for the father of a friend, you couldn't help noticing. She caught my eye and quickly looked away, back at my dad.

Down in the well of the court, Detectives Stoner and Ure were on one side with the prosecution team while Kevin Steel, our lovely Geordie solicitor, sat behind our barrister, who I had not seen in his full horsehair and black-robed kit until now.

There had been a time when I thought our barrister would save us, a time I had felt something resembling hope, when there had been some discussion about my father pleading manslaughter on the grounds of diminished responsibility. Both the barrister and Kevin had seemed keen.

'We'll have a con about dim rep,' Kevin had said, in that cool, arcane language that makes no sense to civilians who feel their lives are being shredded.

In criminal law, Kevin explained, diminished responsibility is a potential defence when a defendant argues that, although they broke the law, their mental functions were diminished or impaired at the time, and because of their unbalanced mental state when the crime was committed, they should not suffer the full weight of the law. Dim rep, Kevin called it, all dreamy as if it was a beach he remembered from a blissful holiday island in Thailand.

Dim rep would have been nice. Especially when bolted on to factors reflecting personal mitigation – such as my father's age, his previous good character, his lack of a history of violence or prior convictions.

But pleading dim rep depended on a qualifying trigger, Kevin said. Something to light the touch paper, as it were, and when a father was confronting a man who was abusing his daughter, it was not difficult to imagine how a qualifying trigger could come up. Dim rep would have been so lovely! Dim rep would have meant a few years inside instead of what was left of a lifetime. Dim rep would have meant my father being released before Marlon started big school.

But Maple's nailing hammer put paid to all that.

If we went for dim rep then the prosecution would maintain that the nailing hammer had been taken to the hotel with the intent to kill. Kevin said that the nailing hammer meant that diminished responsibility was never going to fly. Because the nailing hammer screamed – premeditation.

So it was murder. And despite the optimism that ebbed and flowed, the hope that rose and fell in my family's conversations with Kevin and the barrister, the charge could only ever be murder.

My father smiled up at only me, although all eyes were on him.

What did they see?

A working-class man, the dark suit he was wearing usually only brought out of the wardrobe for weddings, funerals and landmark birthdays, a man who seemed fascinated by these proceedings, as if they were not about him and the rest of his life. An intelligent man who had never received much of a formal education, a man who was still powerful as a bull at sixty, a man who – I knew in my soul – would never need a horse nailing hammer or indeed any weapon to overpower someone like James Caine who had been made soft from a lifetime of desks and screens and profitably shuffling numbers around.

I saw all of this and I saw something else.

As we sat and waited for Leo to answer the usher's question, I saw my father more clearly. I saw him, in truth, for the first time. I saw his love for me, in all its purity and strength and madness.

My father was undiminished in this courtroom. He was unafraid as he stood up straight in the dock, a proud man, with the kind of pride that can slide into vanity.

I did this for my family.

I did this for my daughter.

I had never loved him more.

And at the same time I understood why my mother's love for him had faded, why it had turned into something else, something sour, degraded, degenerated, turned bitter and old. I understood the arguments between my parents that I had grown up hearing, and much later, the ferocity of my mother's late-night denunciations of my father when I was coming home after being out all night, nothing on my self-obsessed mind apart from what was in the fridge and then sixteen hours kip.

There were many fine things about my father but he lacked the self-awareness to see what my mother saw, the thing about him that drove my mother nuts, the thing that had been wearing away at our family for years. My father was one of those family men who – ironically enough – rarely stay at home with their family. The dedicated breadwinner who didn't see his child before bedtime. Possibly some of the time my father was busy because he loved us so much, and because he was providing for us, but then there were other times when he probably just wanted to escape us – my mother's mood swings, my wildness, and all those times when I bought the ticket. Who wouldn't want to escape us?

Because work life is always so much easier than home life. Work is easier to be good at, I know; work is easier to get right. The mistakes you make at work do not echo through a lifetime, the mistakes in the professional world do not inflict deep wounds that must be carried to the grave. Even when work is tearing you apart, it is still the car crash you can walk away from.

Sometimes my father had needed a break from all that he loved and here was another reason why my mother's love had been worn away. There had always been women, I saw now. My father had always had his women. And I suddenly knew who had told my father that James Caine was tormenting me, and I suddenly knew who the older married man was when Ginger had an affair in the difficult early years of her marriage. Her only lie to me had been – *you don't know him.*

The women. My father's women. Far too many, and far too close to home.

Two rows behind me, Ginger wept, and I wondered how long their affair had lasted for. Long enough for tears, long enough to put her off being unfaithful forever, long enough for Ginger to view infidelity as the place where marriages go to die. I understood now the curious intimacy between them, the way Ginger rushed to my father's side at parties, and the glint in my dad's eye – I had put it down to paternal affection! – when he looked at her. And there must have been other women. Plenty of them. And I wondered – of course I did – if my mother was sour because my father had strayed or if my father had strayed because my mother was sour.

The two Daves had been afraid that I would think they told my father about James Caine, but I knew those kind-hearted, overgrown boys would never have been able to find the words to reveal the brutal truth.

It was Ginger. She had told him. She had told my father about James Caine. She had told my dad that this business class bully was tormenting his daughter.

Ginger wept and I wished I could hold her in my arms and wipe away her tears. Did she think I was going to hate her? There are some people who are so deep inside your life that all you can ever do is love them.

I turned back to the court. Our barrister had drawn himself up straight, waiting for the hammer to fall.

The women, I thought, all those women. But in the end, there was really only one woman who owned my father's heart.

And it wasn't my mother. It wasn't Ginger.

It was me. My father loved me best, and that is why he stood in that courtroom, his bald head gleaming, that is why he had done this thing.

He spoke in a strong, clear voice.

No fear, no regret and no sound in the courtroom apart from the soft broken sobbing of Ginger.

'Guilty,' my father said.

34

CHRISTIAN

There are children at the prison.

This is the first thing I notice.

All the children are penned into the waiting room and bound for what they call the visits room, children of every age from tiny babies, sleeping or squawking in the arms of young mums and youthful grandmothers, to teenagers hunched miserably on the edge of adulthood.

There are children everywhere.

They make a lot of noise when you are trying to remember the rules.

Because there are so many things that you cannot take into the prison. No phones, no keys, no credit cards, no cash, although you can take £20 in coins – per table, *not* per visitor – to be spent in the visits room's vending machine. And it is not called the visiting room – it is the *visits* room.

There is suddenly so much to learn, so much to remember, so many things to get right. No gang colours, football shirts or ripped jeans are allowed. No short skirts or see-through blouses. You cannot wear metal hair clips, pins or badges. You cannot bring your own food and drink. You are not allowed sunglasses, hats or scarves, apart from those worn for religious reasons. And – my all-time favourite – you are not allowed to wear more than one pair of trousers.

And you cannot bring gifts.

But you can bring a child to prison.

You can bring all these children.

I watch Tara store her personal belongings in a scarred metal locker while a German Shepherd moves among us, its nose sniffing for drugs, and I know that she is thinking exactly the same thing as me.

Will we ever bring Marlon to this place? Our sweet, gentle boy?

It did not even cross our minds to bring Marlon today. Marlon has stayed at home with his grandmother, and his dog, and his beloved books. But if Marlon is ever going to see his grandfather again in the coming years, then he is going to have to see him here.

It creeps up on you slowly, so slowly.

The brute fact of prison.

You see the high walls and the barbed wire, and you look at all these children in the waiting area, and it is like a growing pressure on your heart, slowly increasing as you pass through the numbing bureaucracy of visiting someone inside.

This is what life will be like now.

For Leo, and for all of us who love him.

Your passport is scrutinised. Your name is checked against the list of visitors. Your belongings are locked away. Then there is all the waiting around – so much waiting around – and then come the steel doors, all those steel doors, and you pass through one and hear it loudly slam shut and lock behind you, as if you too have time to serve.

Tara and I pause before a metal detector.

'Shoes off?' Tara politely asks a female prison guard.

The guard grunts a bored affirmative.

Tara passes through the detector and it begins to beep.

She holds up her arms while the guard searches her and turns back to look at me, trying to smile, and that attempt at a smile – she doesn't quite manage it – makes my throat close up.

Tara's skin, I see, is flawless. All the things she has been through have not left a mark on her face. Why have I never noticed that before? I should have noticed her perfect skin before now, I think. I should have loved it.

Before our perfect world started falling apart.

*

It had been two weeks since Leo had been given a life sentence for the murder of James Caine, and he was ready to talk about the practicalities of his new life.

'There are two one-hour visits every four weeks,' he said at our table in the visits room. 'You can send as many letters as you like but they're read by the staff. There's some email scheme coming in, apparently, but it's not live yet. They can't open letters from your solicitor. You can't call the prisoner. We have to call you.'

But despite his chatter, some light had gone out in him, I thought.

He looked from Tara to me and back again.

'What does Kevin say?'

This was what concerned him most of all. Leo was worried about DCI Stoner. He was frightened that the authorities had not quite finished with our family.

Leo wanted to know that Tara was not going to be prosecuted, that Stoner was content with the conviction for murder, and that Tara was in the clear, no matter what reckless conversations she may have had with the two Daves.

'No more charges,' I said, meaning no obstruction of justice, no fleeing a crime scene, no conspiracy to murder. Tara was clear of all that. 'Kevin said the police and CPS wanted what he called a realistic prospect of conviction,' I said. 'And that wasn't Tara.' I hesitated for a beat. 'That was you.'

Leo nodded, sat back, satisfied. He was thinner than I remembered. Always lean and hard, his face had taken on a hollow-cheeked gauntness. The skin seemed stretched tauter across that bald head. He stared off at the children's play area, lost in his thoughts.

'Dad?' Tara said, trying to bring him back with her own list of practicalities. 'Big Dave is keeping an eye on the business until you decide what to do. And Mum says she's all right for money.'

'My boys have got enough work until the summer,' Leo said, distracted. 'After that ...'

It was hard to talk in there. The proximity to all those other people, some of them in tears, some of them raising their voices in anger and frustration, the mask-faced scrutiny of the guards. The noise of the children in the play area.

'I love you, Dad!' Tara said, too loud, too breezy.

He smiled at her. 'I know, angel face.'

'And, Dad – please, Dad – are you all right?'

I saw all the roles that Leo had been removed from. The roles he had removed himself from. Breadwinner, builder, businessman. That had all been stripped from him. Husband, father, grandfather. But his daughter still looked at him as if he was the king of the world.

Leo glanced across at the play area again.

'We can't move from the table,' he said. 'The inmates, I mean. So the children – the little ones – don't understand why their daddy doesn't want to play with them.

It's confusing for them! It's upsetting! Of course it is. So you can never bring Marlon here. Never. You know that, right?'

And at last, when he spoke of Marlon, Tara unravelled.

Leo took her hands. A guard looked, then looked away. Because holding hands was the only physical contact that was permitted during the visit, although hands must be visible at all times. Leo and Tara kept their hands on the plastic tabletop. So that was allowed. Their visible hands.

'I wanted you to watch Marlon growing up,' she sobbed. 'I wanted you to be there for him. The way you were for me. The way you were always there for me. Even if you were busy – even if you were not around – I knew that you were still there for me.'

Leo smiled sadly. 'I was never going to watch Marlon grow up, angel face,' he said.

She did not understand.

And neither did I.

'There's not enough time,' he said. 'You have your time and then your time is done.' He shrugged. 'We ran out of time – that's all.'

And that's when I started to understand what he was trying to tell us.

Leo was dying.

*

'He was always so proud of his yearly medical,' Jen told us back at home, snorting with a kind of derisive affection, a gesture learned during many years of married life. 'His blood tests! His cholesterol! His bloody biochemical tests of his liver, kidneys, calcium and all the rest of it. He waved his results around like they were an Academy Award.'

'Flying colours,' Tara said proudly. 'Always the flying colours. The doctor always said he was healthier than men half his age.'

Jen exhaled. 'But nine months ago he had his annual medical and his PSA score was off the scale,' she said.

Tara and I looked at each other. *Nine months ago?*

'Do you know what PSA is?' Jen said.

It rang some dark, distant bell. But Tara and I were still too young to be experts on all the things that can kill you. That stuff – the language of mortality – takes years to creep up on you.

'PSA is the protein produced in the prostate gland,' Jen said. 'Prostate-Specific Antigen. The PSA is the blood test for prostate cancer.'

Tara stared at her mother. *Cancer? What the hell are you talking about?*

'So when the PSA score shot up they give Leo an MRI scan and a biopsy,' Jen said. 'And it wasn't good.'

And so the totally unimaginable suddenly becomes a cruel fact of life.

'And then they tried to recruit Leo to the booming prostate cancer industry,' Jen continued. 'Remove or irradiate. Chop it out or burn it out. But your father learned that both surgery and radiation result in side effects that he found unacceptable. Impotence, incontinence. He googled it. And personally I can't think of anything your father would be less likely to sign up for.'

'It's better than being dead, isn't it?' Tara said furiously. 'It's better than *cancer.*'

Jen shook her head. 'Not to a man like your father.'

Marlon and Buddy burst into the room.

'We're hungry,' Marlon said.

Her eyes bright with tears, Tara inserted her finger in our boy's dimple as she scooped him up.

'I'm going to kiss you *right there*.'

When Tara and Marlon had gone to look in the fridge, Jen and I looked at each other.

'So Leo knew he was dying when he killed James Caine?' I said.

Jen nodded. 'Yes.' She touched her too golden hair, and I saw a flicker of pride in her pale blue eyes. 'But – knowing my husband – Leo would have done him anyway.'

I watched Tara move through the evening – ordering a takeaway, getting Marlon ready for bed, checking in with Skyla at the office – numb with the knowledge that her father was dying.

When Marlon was fed, read and tucked up in bed, she went online. Exactly what her father would have done. A practical response to what life had thrown at her. Educating herself about this latest kick in the head. Weighing up the options.

But there was one thing no search engine could find her.

'Why didn't he tell us he's sick?' she said.

'Maybe he couldn't find the words. Or maybe he thought it made him look ...' I hesitated to use the word *weak* about Leo. 'Less strong,' I settled for. 'Less strong than he wanted to be for you and your mother and Marlon. And maybe he thought it was nothing to do with us. Maybe he just wanted to deal with it himself. Make his own choices.'

'But how can you keep *cancer* a secret from your family?'

'He was trying to protect you. To put himself between his family and the world.'

Like he did with James Caine, I thought. *Just like he did with that bastard.*

I took Tara in my arms, and kissed her on her cheek, and caught my breath to feel my lips on her perfect skin.

'I never told him before today,' she said, burying herself in my arms, both of us loving that old familiar feeling. 'That I love him, I mean. Just the one time. That's not much, is it?'

'With a man like your dad, once is plenty.'

As tired as she was, as upset as she was, Tara had the old light in her eyes, the light that had made me fall in love with her.

'Guess what?' she said. 'We finally ran out of Prosecco. Can you believe it? But there's a bottle of Pinot Noir that's come all the way from New Zealand.'

'I don't care what we drink,' I said.

So we shared the bottle of Pinot Noir together, and we came together, and we slept together as we had on so many other nights, and when the shallow sleep of dreams that I would never remember jolted me awake, the room was still dark, and the night still here and I found that Tara and I were holding hands. It always felt like a miracle to wake when she was still sleeping and discover that we were holding hands.

For I knew that you can love a lot of people in your time. But there's only ever one person who will hold your hand when you are sleeping.

35

TARA

'You told my father,' I said. 'You told my dad about James Caine.'

Ginger picked up one of the bottles of Australian Shiraz that she and Spike had brought round and examined the label. She unscrewed the top and poured herself a large glass. I watched her drain it.

'Sorry about that. Obviously, I never dreamed—'

'You told him,' I said. 'And now – all this.'

'I told your father what you were going through because I was trying to help, Tara. And I told him because I knew he would want to know. And I told him because you were killing yourself and I didn't know what else to do.'

We turned our heads to the living room, as the laughter of Christian and Spike drifted to the kitchen. I felt a flash of irritation with the pair of them. What was so funny?

I took the bottle from Ginger and poured myself a glass.

'And what did you *think* would happen?' I said. 'After you told my father that some man was making my life a misery? What did you *think* he would do?'

'I don't know!' she said. 'I thought maybe go to see Caine with those scary guys who used to work for him – the two Daves. One look at them would have been enough to get him running back to Brighton.'

I shook my head. 'My father doesn't need the Daves to back him up. Not with James Caine or anyone else.'

I was aware of the insane pride in my voice.

'I just hoped Leo would do something to make it all stop,' Ginger said. 'I didn't think he would use a bloody pickaxe to do it.'

'Nailing hammer.'

'Nailing hammer. I called him as soon as it began, as soon as I knew, after you showed me the photographs of you sleeping, remember? After we were in the cafe. I didn't get a chance to talk to him at his birthday party because of all those people – and then you flaking out – but I phoned him again right before you and I went to the hotel together. And Leo told me – he *swore* to me – that he hadn't been up there because he knew it would get out of hand, and he said that there were other ways to get Caine to back off.' She held my gaze. 'Leo told me he hadn't been to the hotel, Tara,' she said.

'And you believed him?'

'Leo never lied to me.'

'Oh, I forgot – the special relationship between you and my father.'

She said nothing.

'Wow, Ginger! All that stuff you told me about infidelity! All your hard-earned wisdom about the high price of fucking around! And I never realised where you got it all from, not until I saw you sitting in the public gallery when my dad was standing in the dock. Then I knew everything.'

She stared at her hands, her wedding ring glinting, and then looked at me with eyes hooded with embarrassment.

'Neither of us wanted it to happen.'

'Oh, that's all right then.'

'It was over in the course of a summer.'

'A summer fling.'

'Something like that. Spike and I were having our problems – and so were your dad and mum.' She reached for the bottle of Shiraz. 'It's all years ago now.'

'But it always makes me wonder, Ginger. Is my mum toxic because of my father's women? Or did my father run to those women – like you – because my mum's toxic?'

'Jen's not toxic. It's just *hard*. All of it. Finding someone. Staying together. Keeping the passion. Staying faithful. *Wanting something that you already have*. Come on – you should understand that, Tara.'

And I did.

'But you should have seen him in that prison, Ginger. I never saw anywhere like that place. It's like there's no air in there, you can't breathe inside all those walls and locked doors. I hate to see my dad in that place, Ginger, I hate it so much. It feels like lives have stopped in there. He doesn't deserve it, he's a good man, a kind man, and I know he doesn't deserve to be punished like that.'

'Sorry,' Ginger said, her voice cracking. 'Sorry that I told him about you and Caine. Sorry me and Leo had ... our thing. Sorry about all of it.'

I poured the remains of the bottle into my glass as a gale of dumb laughter came from the living room.

'I'm proud of him, Ginger. Proud of what he did for me. Proud of what he's doing for me.'

She lightly touched my arm and I grabbed her hand and pressed it against my cheek. She came to my arms and we embraced. We were both crying now.

'I told him because he loves you, Tara, and I told him because I love you, too.'

I nodded, unable to speak. And then yet again, we heard the laughter of the men in the living room. Our heads turned towards the sound and, in that moment, they felt like total strangers. Our husbands.

CHRISTIAN

Spike sprawled on the floor with a glass of red wine in one hand and an original vinyl copy of my *Highway to Hell* LP in the other.

Marlon and Buddy sat either side, staring up at him with naked adoration.

'Now this record,' Spike told them. 'This record is stone-cold musical genius.'

He examined the LP's cover, one of those Seventies group-picture photo shoots that looked as though it had taken all of five minutes. The band hadn't even bothered to put Angus Young in the schoolboy uniform he wore on stage, although Angus was the only one who had made a modest effort, wearing a pair of plastic devil horns, the kind you might see worn on a hen night in Blackpool. Only Bon Scott, the singer, had a grin on his face. Bon Scott, who would be dead within the year. The rest of the band stared sullenly out from under their mousey mullets. I felt a surge of love for AC/DC, and for Spike.

'Best Australian band ever,' I said. 'And that's their best record, released in 1979. Their breakout LP. But *genius* might be very slightly overstating it.'

'Are they Australian?' Spike said, examining the record. 'I never knew. But it's genius, as I say.'

I had missed him.

And I had missed all of this – a drink with friends, talking about music – even if my friend was talking rubbish about music. He began singing – or rather, he began impersonating the opening riff to the title track.

'DER! DER! DER!'

It was more than a joy to see him. It was a relief. From the moment Tara came home from Tokyo, there had been so many tears. Seeing my friend slightly drunk while he talked about AC/DC made me smile again.

'It's really good,' I said. 'It's great, even. I love AC/DC too. But *genius*? It's all pretty simple. That opening riff?'

'Great riff! *DER! DER! DER!*'

'Spike, I could teach you to play that guitar riff in half an hour. It's just three open chords.'

'Yeah, and when we've done that you can show me how to run like Usain Bolt or paint like Picasso.'

'No, it's simple! Let me show you.'

I fetched my old Fender Telecaster and a little 15-watt practice amp. I strapped it on Spike and showed him how to arrange three fingers into an open A major. I gave him a light pick.

He shrugged his shoulders, surprised at the weight of the Fender.

'You hit that A chord three times, very fast, and then – very quickly – you mute the strings by placing your palm on them. Press down the meat of your hand. That stops the chord ringing out and you get that great dynamic crunching sound. *DER DER DER* – mute – then silence.'

He hit the strings too hard, including the thick E string, which he was meant to miss, and the little practice amp howled discordant metal feedback.

We fell about laughing, Buddy barking, tail wagging like windscreen washers, Marlon covered his ears, laughing wildly, overexcited and up way past his bedtime.

Then we saw Tara and Ginger standing in the doorway, staring at us without expression, and our laughter immediately faded.

'It's your turn tonight, Spike,' Tara said.

Spike chose Argentinian.

Groans.

Spike was the only red-meat eater among us so the rest of us had to search through the Malvinas Hermanos menu for chicken, fish and vegetarian alternatives. When we had phoned it in, Spike wanted to continue his guitar lesson.

Tara shot me a warning look.

'A bit late, mate,' I said. 'Some other time.'

Spike looked at Tara and then back at me.

'Show me then,' he urged. 'You do it.'

I put on the Fender, turned down the volume on the practice amp to one and hit the A chord three times. It sounded like the opening riff to 'Highway to Hell' played in a library.

Tara lifted her chin. 'A bit late, darling,' she said sweetly.

In the secret language of our marriage, Tara only called me darling when she was right on the edge of being really angry with me. I reluctantly slipped *Highway to Hell* back into its place on the shelf with all the As. I would have liked to have put it on really loud. I hadn't heard that record for years.

A red-wine stupor settled on us as we waited for our dinner.

The album that Ginger had put on – *Blue* by Joni Mitchell – had stopped some time ago. Marlon was finally in bed. Buddy sighed in his sleep. It did not seem appropriate to put anything else on. Because Tara was talking, dry-eyed, about her father. Not about prison. Not about his crime. She spoke of Leo's illness and about the choice he had made to let the cancer take its course.

'Whatever they do – surgery, radiation – there are risks of side effects. The kind of side effects that my dad will not contemplate. And so he does nothing, and that comes with a risk too – the risk of dying.'

'I'd do the same,' Spike said, full of red-wine bravado. 'Incontinence? Impotence? Sod that lot for a game of soldiers!'

Tara was unimpressed. 'It's really easy to *say*, Spike. Hard to do. Talk is cheap. To *know* there are things you could do, and then choose to take your chances with the cancer.'

Ginger abruptly stood up, and fled the room in tears.

'What's she upset about?' Spike said, his face darkening, and I saw that he knew that his wife had been with Leo. Somewhere somehow – and probably not very long ago – Ginger had told him about her affair. Or he had guessed. Or he had pushed her into a confession after all those bitter tears at the trial.

'Shouldn't that food be here by now?' I said, changing the subject. 'It's been over an hour.'

Spike looked at his phone, suddenly furious. I don't know how much of his anger was about his delayed steak and how much was about his wife going to bed with the father of her best friend. But as Spike got on the phone to the delivery service, there were the sudden lights and the insect buzz of a scooter on the street.

As I was collecting the order, Spike pushed past me.

'Where you from, mate?'

'Kabul, sir.'

'Come via Kabul tonight, did you?'

'Excuse me, sir?'

'You speak English, mate?'

'Leave him, Spike,' I said. 'Let's just eat.'

Tara and Ginger were laying the table when we went back inside. Ginger red-eyed, Tara rubbing her back.

We began unpacking our Malvinas Hermanos dinner and Spike exploded.

'They forgot my empanadas! You can't have an Argie without empanadas!'

Tara laughed. 'God, Spike, you were still putting tomato ketchup on your pasta when we first met you! And now you're having a nervous breakdown about your missing empanadas!'

The air seemed to go out of him.

'I know I'm a peasant, Tara. You don't have to remind me.'

'Oh, come on! You're not a peasant. It's just – God, give them a call and tell them there's something missing from the order!'

'That doesn't work! That never works! Because it takes another hour to get here again!' He shook his head, ripping open the Malvinas Hermanos containers. 'I know you've had a hard time with your dad and all, but I'm entitled to complain when Osama bin Laden makes me wait all night for my dinner.'

'Park the casual racism, Spike, I don't want it in my home,' Tara said. She began transferring the food to plates. 'But you're right, of course. What's happening to my dad is just like your missing empanadas. I feel your pain.'

His face clouded.

'Oh fuck off, Tara.'

I took a step towards him.

'Hey, Spike, not cool, mate.'

'Look, *mate*,' he said. 'Just because she walks all over you doesn't mean she can do the same to everyone else.'

And then he shoved me. Hard. In the chest. In my home. Pushing me back in my own house because my wife had insulted him, or he had insulted her, or because we had all drunk too much Shiraz. Or all of the above.

I grabbed him clumsily by the neck of his T-shirt and before I knew what was happening he had me in a headlock, staring at the ground, my glasses hanging onto my face by one ear.

The women were shouting.

Spike whispered in my ear as my glasses dropped to the floor.

'We both know I could have you on toast,' he said. 'Are you going to stop now?'

I grunted an assent and he let me go.

Then I threw a wild punch at his head.

He pulled away but my sloppy fist connected above his ear and sent a surge of pain down my arm.

And the evening went downhill from there.

TARA

'Forgive me,' Ginger said on our doorstep.

On the street Spike was standing by the back door of a black cab. Christian and Spike were embracing. They appeared to be drunkenly telling each other, 'I love you, mate,' over and over again.

The old shaven-headed taxi driver stared straight ahead, nodding along to a Mozart piano sonata on Classic FM, this not being the first time he had seen drunken men declare their undying love. Christian appeared to be in some pain with his right hand.

'What for?' I asked Ginger. It felt like there was so much to forgive. The affair with my dad. Telling him about James Caine. Our takeaway disaster tonight. The fight in our living room. 'I wouldn't know where to start.'

'All of it,' Ginger said. 'Forgive me for all of it.'

'There's nothing to forgive.'

It was true. As Ginger kissed me goodnight and hugged me hard, I understood why she had told my dad about James Caine, and I could even understand why she had an affair with him in the difficult early days of her marriage.

Women liked my father, you see – apart from my mother, of course. My dad liked them, too, and he craved a little sugar in his bowl, and he felt that he had earned it.

And I understood all of that, because I felt it too.

36

CHRISTIAN

Prisons don't have hospitals.

If an inmate needs serious treatment, such as surgery on the malignant tumour that is killing him, then he is moved to a regular hospital. But prisons do have in-patient beds like the one that Leo was sitting on now in his stripy M&S pyjamas, a tartan dressing gown tied modestly over the top, and a copy of *My Family and Other Animals* on his lap.

Marlon sat by his side.

The old man and the boy smiled at each other.

'Are you sitting comfortably?' Leo said.

'Very,' Marlon said.

'Then I'll begin.'

A few short weeks ago, Tara and I had been afraid that our son would be overwhelmed by today – by the forbidding Victorian hulk of the prison, by the tough kids running wild in the waiting area, bug-eyed with sugar and neglect, by the sight of his sick grandfather in his pyjamas, and by the sadness that settles on you in prison, there in every breath you take, the claustrophobic melancholy of life inside, that sense you never escape of human beings locked away from everything they ever loved.

But our boy was happy to see his granddad. It was as simple as that. And some special light inside Leo seemed to come on when he was around Marlon.

'What did you do to your hand?' Leo asked me.

I looked down at the bandage on my right hand where a couple of days ago I had clumsily hit Spike on his concrete-hard skull. I shook my head, finding that I didn't have the heart to discuss a badly sprained wrist with a man who had prostate cancer.

'He fell over,' Marlon said. 'Silly daddy.'

'Silly old daddy,' Leo happily agreed.

On the other side of the room, a young man was shivering and sweating in the small ward's only other bed. He could have been in the early stages of a fever or the late stages of withdrawal from heroin addiction. The prison visitor learns not to ask. When we had arrived, the young man had thoughtfully pulled the sheet up to his chin so that only his already skull-like face was showing. He had gaunt, sunken features, a face with a million miles on the clock, although he could not have been out of his twenties. He was thoughtfully making a real effort to stop his teeth chattering as Leo read to Marlon.

'Gradually the magic of the island settled over us as gently and clingingly as pollen,' Leo read. *'Each day had a tranquillity, a timelessness about it, so that you wished it would never end.'*

At the desk that passed for a nurse's station, Tara and Jen were in discussion with a young doctor.

The doctor looked exhausted. Jen was manically nodding, dabbing at her eyes with the tip of her little finger while Tara was white-faced and dry-eyed, only the tight set of her mouth revealing the effort she was making to hold it together.

And I never felt closer to her. It is not the years together that build a marriage, I saw now. It is these moments. All the big moments, like the first time I saw her face in the office of our old music paper, and the first time we went to bed, and the pregnancy and birth of our son. And then all the smaller moments that only seem huge later, like the time Tara got violently, projectile-vomit sick on vodka and I took care of her in a way that I later realised I could never have taken care of anyone else on the planet. They only come with time, all those moments. You can't find them in a bar or a club or on some business trip to the other side of the world. These moments were ours and these moments were mine. And here, in the conversation with that exhausted young prison doctor, here was another one of those moments that built a marriage. The moment when my wife was told that she would one day – possibly one day soon – be without her father.

'But then the dark skin of night would peel off and there would be a fresh day waiting for us,' Leo read, *'glossy and colourful as a child's transfer and with the same tinge of unreality.'*

Then Tara and Jen were walking towards us, their faces arranged to pretend that everything was unchanged and would stay that way forever.

'We could do with a real cup of tea,' Tara said, looking at me. 'Not that stuff from the vending machine. That would be really nice, Christian.'

Which was married talk for – *please leave us now.*

TARA

We watched them go.

And when my mother, my husband and my son had passed beyond the little desk that acted as a sort of pretend nurse's station, my father and I looked at each other. He indicated the copy of *My Family and Other Animals* that he still had in his hands.

'And we all thought he was only ever going to love one book. But now he loves lots of books. As long as they've got animals.'

'You stubborn old man,' I said.

He gently placed the book on the bed and I took his hands in mine.

'Dr Khan says that you shouldn't be in here talking about the results of tests,' I said. 'You should be in a proper hospital, and should be having *surgery*. Dr Khan says—'

He shrugged it off, all the sage advice of the medical profession.

'Dr Khan says that I should be on the chopping block. Dr Khan says that I should sign up for the booming prostate cancer industry. Dr Khan wants me to have surgery. Dr Khan wants to give me a cure that is worse than the disease. No thanks, Dr Khan. And I didn't want his tests in the first place.'

'But if you do nothing it could spread. And then it will be too late for surgery. It will be too late for everything.'

Leo shrugged. 'That's the problem with watchful waiting and active surveillance and all that. You run the risk that sooner or later the little bugger will get bigger.' All this without a trace of self-pity. 'But I'll take my chances.'

When I was a little girl, I could not imagine this world without my father in it and now it seemed so close that I could feel it breathing in my face.

'Are you in pain, Dad?'

'Only when I laugh.'

'Please *talk* to me! Don't joke, don't pretend it's nothing, don't just turn me away.'

'What do you want me to say? I'm not having surgery, Tara. It's not Dr Khan and the surgeon who have to live with the side effects.'

'The side effects? The side effect of surgery is that it will save your life!'

He snorted. 'What kind of life? A different life. A life that's not worth having.' He shook his head, and I knew he had spent hours thinking about this subject, lying awake in the middle of the night with my mother sleeping by his side in her hideous eternal-youth, skin-regime face mask. 'You've got to go sometime. All this clinging on to life however rotten it gets – it's just modern rubbish.'

He pretended to study *My Family and Other Animals*.

'Wanting to stay alive is modern rubbish, is it?' I said. 'A bit woke, is it, Dad? A bit enlightened? Is all this staying-alive stuff for the snowflakes, Dad?'

'Not accepting we all have our time is modern rubbish. Look – they're too quick to chop men up, Tara. The booming prostate cancer industry! Well, they're not recruiting me. Leo Doherty may have left school with nothing more than a certificate for swimming his width, but I know enough to keep off their butcher's block. There's no such thing as minor surgery. Only minor surgeons.'

'Dr Khan is trying to *help*.'

'If Dr Khan wants to help, then he should leave me alone and stop getting me to have all his tests and stop upsetting your mother and you.'

'What was it you always used to say? *I'm going to die a fit man*. Well, if you don't have surgery, you're not going to die a fit man, are you?'

'Well, at least I won't be a man in a nappy!'

The boy in the other bed – he looked like some kind of junkie – covered his head with his prison duvet. I realised that Leo and I were close to shouting at each other.

'Is that what really worries you, Dad? Incontinence? There's no shame in that if you're sick! You changed me when I was a baby, didn't you? Everybody was amazed. They all still talk about it. Leo changing nappies!'

He smiled at the memory, softening, and then his face clouded. 'It's a bit different though,' he said. 'Changing the nappy of a baby and changing the nappy of some old git who can't control himself.'

'You know what I think?'

'I think you're about to tell me, Tara.'

'I think it's the other side effect that really frightens you.'

He turned his head away, a cloud passing across his face. He didn't want to talk to me about sex.

'Those days are long gone,' he said.

'I just want you to live as long as possible.'

He grinned, cheering up. 'Me too!'

We were silent, finally agreeing on something. It was time to play my ace card.

'I've got some news.'

He brightened some more. 'Your business is picking up?'

'Not really. It's been better. But this is not about work. It's about me and Christian.' Dramatic pause. He was no longer pretending to read. 'We're trying for a baby, Dad.'

No reaction. I shook his hands, wanting him to see how great it was going to be, how much fun he would have over the next twenty years if he chose surgery, chose life.

He just stared at me blankly.

'A sister or brother for Marlon!' I said. 'Don't you want to watch them grow up? I know how much you love Marlon. And I know how much Marlon loves you.'

But my dad's face settled into the mildly disappointed folds that I remembered so well. It was the look he got on the many occasions when I rashly bought the wrong ticket. When I stayed out all night, when I got a crush on the wrong boy, when all the fun left me sick the next day, when I got engaged to the wrong man, when I didn't think about my business overheads. My father was about to give me the benefit of his hard-earned wisdom.

'Bad idea,' he said.

I was shocked. 'How can a beautiful baby ever be a bad idea?'

'Because a beautiful baby can't mend a marriage, Tara. Married couples who are having problems – they put too much weight on some poor unborn child. I'm sorry – I'm being honest now, Tara.'

'Oh, are we being honest now?'

'It's a bit late for anything else, don't you reckon?'

I looked back at the nurses' station. It was empty. The young junkie in the other bed had slipped into some chemically enhanced sleep. My father and I were alone at last.

'Then please be honest with me now – and tell me why are you doing this, Daddy?'

'Doing what?'

'What you've been doing since you turned up at the police station with that nailing hammer. What you did in court. What you're doing now. Taking the blame for someone else,' I said. '*Pretending.*'

Now my father glanced towards the nurses' station and then at the young man in the other bed and still he could not bring himself to tell me the truth.

'I don't know what you mean.'

'I think you do. Because we both know that you didn't kill James Caine. I bet you don't even know where that hotel is, do you? Where he died. Where he was killed. The Langham! I don't believe you went around there with Maple's nailing hammer. I don't think you've ever been there. Is that honest enough for you, Daddy?'

'It's in Portland Place,' he said without hesitation. 'About halfway between the Chinese Embassy and Oxford Circus. Right across the street from the BBC. I used to go there all the time, Tara. You can ask your friend. Ask Ginger.'

And I realised that the Langham was where my father must have taken his women. I abruptly let go of his hands.

He stared at them resting on the paperback as if he deserved nothing less. Then I could not stop myself. The grief rose up in me and choked my throat and filled my eyes.

'But I don't want you to die!' I said, and it was as stark and simple and heartbreaking as that, and I wept for him, and for myself, and for Marlon, and for the child who had not been born.

'Don't cry,' he said. 'You have your time and then your time is done. And that's true for all of us. You just don't realise it for the first, oh, sixty years or so.'

'But *not now!*' I said.

I could hear my teenage self, raging against all the injustice in the world. *It's not fair! I hate you!* Slamming out of the house in Bushey as I ran to whatever older boy was waiting for me on the pavement with his engine running. But there was nowhere to run to today.

'It's not your time yet, Dad,' I said. 'It's just *not*.'

'Don't be sad, angel face,' he said. 'You have to focus on what really matters.'

I wiped my nose with the back of my hand and I waited for him to tell me what really mattered and when he spoke, his voice was as soft as a prayer.

'You're safe,' my father said. 'Nobody can hurt you now.'

37

TARA

My business was struggling. Subscriptions were falling, advertising had fled, I had had to let Phil the driver go. He did not take it well. People always assumed that their job was going to last a lifetime, even though no job does. The younger you are, the better you understand that cruel fact of the working world. Michael had taken a 50 per cent pay cut while Skyla was thankfully still doing it for the experience. Christian and I had remortgaged the house and that was OK because we had been poor before, we had struggled before. But this time it was different. Things seemed to be coming to an end.

It was the candle shop that was dying today. Two women in their middle years who had moved into the mews six months ago with dreams of selling hand-crafted scented candles were now loading a Nissan Micra with boxes of unsold stock. One of them was in tears and the other looked stunned that their dream had died before the end of a six-month lease. Our little corner of the city was no longer a vibrant hub for quirky one-off shops and plucky start-ups. These days the mews was a small business graveyard. With the candle shop gone, only The Vinyl Countdown and Angel Eyes remained.

'The good news for you and me,' Wiggy from The Vinyl Countdown said, scratching thoughtfully under his Led Zeppelin US Tour 1975 T-shirt, 'is that people will always need love and music.'

If only, I thought.

'How's Christian getting on with *Weird Scenes Inside the Gold Mine*?' Wiggy asked.

'He wants to write something about it.'

Wiggy's eyes lit up. He had always been a fan of Christian's music journalism. 'Man, he *should*. What was it they said about The Doors? Three great musicians fronted by a genius.'

'But I don't know who would print it, Wiggy,' I said. 'That old world of the inky weekly music press doesn't exist any more.'

Wiggy and I hugged the candle ladies and then watched them drive away. As they left, a group of teen-agers drifted into the mews, the smell of their weed and resentment drifting down to us. This was something new, too, the mews as a place for bored youth to hang out.

'It's such a great album,' Wiggy muttered to himself, and went back inside his shop, humming 'When the Music's Over' to himself.

I sat at my desk, scrolling through the smiling, hopeful faces of the lonely as Skyla stood watching the kids at the end of the mews. There seemed to be more of them now.

'Did you see it?' Skyla said. 'Mary's latest Accidental Dater post?'

I shook my head. Preoccupied by thoughts of my father, I tended to avoid social media these days. Call it cowardice, call it a defence mechanism, but reading the snide and frequently obscene comments under our Angel Eyes Twitter and Instagram postings felt like inserting my head in someone else's sewer.

'You should read this one,' Skyla said. Then she hesitated. 'I'm worried about her, Tara. This one feels like it could be the last.'

So I sat in front of my screen, and I read about my old friend's latest adventure in the world of online dating.

Mr Fat Shaming met through Tinder.

I smiled to myself. Tinder! So Mary had finally given up on us.

Mr Fat Shaming was disappointed from the moment he saw me. His face fell. Then there was the flicker of anger. As if he had been cheated. As if I had been lying. As if he had been duped. But I just wanted to look nice in my profile picture. That's all. I didn't want to trick anyone, or mislead them, or lie. I just wanted to look nice, I wanted to look like someone who might be worth loving. Is that so much to ask? So now I sit in a hot bath in my crappy little flat, wondering if I would not be better off alone and if the world would be better off without me.

I should see her, I thought, suddenly, and I realised I was increasingly doubtful that people would always need love and music. I wasn't even sure exactly what I had been selling all these years. I had had a dream that romance would be only the start, and that Angel Eyes could eventually connect the world – not only potential lovers but employers and job seekers, house hunters and sellers, holiday homes and tourists, the lot. That was the dream I had – connecting the world. And the bitter truth was that I had not even been able to find my homely, kind-hearted friend one half-decent date.

'Tara?' Skyla said, and there was fear in her voice.

There were loud shouts outside, a growing frenzy, as if someone was working themselves up to violence. Night was falling and there were dark shadows on the mews, directly across from our office, their hoods pulled up, hiding their faces.

'Punish the guilty!' someone screamed.

So they were not just bored kids who had found an unoccupied corner of the city. They knew all about me.

'Michael, lock the front door and close the blinds.'

But Michael was slipping on his pre-faded denim jacket and clocking off forever.

'Sorry,' he said. 'Tara. It's been a blast. But this shit is not worth half-pay.'

And he ducked out the back door as Skyla and I stared at each other. Then a brick came through the big plate-glass window and we flinched under a spray of broken glass.

The brick skittered across the floor and landed at my feet and it wasn't a brick at all. It was a bottle and the bottle was full of colourless liquid that had a burning scrap of rag stuffed in the neck.

For a long moment it smouldered like a damp firework as the stink of petrol filled the room. Then the fire suddenly caught with a rush of air and spread across the floor like water.

Skyla was instantly on top of it with a fire extinguisher but then there was another one, smashing against my desk, and bursting into flames immediately, while on the screen, all those hopeful faces kept smiling as my business burned.

*

Later, much later, Wiggy covered his face in his hands and I held him as he cried his heart out. Apparently, all those thousands of LPs in The Vinyl Countdown had acted as an accelerant and made the fire burn fiercer and faster. Our end of the mews was quickly consumed by flames and was now a blackened husk, sodden and steaming. A lone fireman stepped through the gaping hole where the front door of Angel Eyes had been. The office was already unrecognisable, just a charred shell of what looked like a pathetically modest space, too tiny for all my big dreams of connecting the world, but beyond the shattered windows of The Vinyl Countdown you could still make out the bright primary colours of album covers that had been swallowed by the flames. We watched from the end of the mews until the roof collapsed, and then they ordered us further back.

'The police want to talk to you,' Skyla said. 'Both of you.'

I led Wiggy out of the mews, dazzled by the lights of the fire engines and police cars. Crowds of people were waiting beyond the emergency tape, their phones pointing at the smoking ruins.

DCI Stoner was on the street. He gestured at Wiggy.

'This the other owner? I need you both to come with me. We got the little bastards.'

He led us down an adjacent alley. Supervised by DI Ure and a few plain-clothes cops in trainers and jeans and T-shirts that showed off their body art, there were a line of youths on their knees, perhaps half the number of the mob who had been outside our office.

'There were more than this,' I said.

'This is what we've got,' DCI Stoner said. 'Can you ID any of them?'

'What have you done?' Wiggy screamed at them. 'What have you *done?* It's *madness!*'

'Do you know any of them, sir?' DI Ure said.

Wiggy held out his hands helplessly. 'They're just stupid kids.'

'Do you *know* them?' DCI Stoner looked at me.

But Wiggy was right. They were just stupid kids who did not realise how easy it is to shatter someone's life. Boys, all overgrown boys, on the spotty cusp of being beginner men. As racially mixed as you would expect in the heart of the city.

And then I saw her face. A long, gawky face that I remembered from my father's trial, staring at me from the other side of the public gallery, and earlier, trailing her mother, the professional widow, and looking at me with undiluted hatred. It turned out they were not all boys.

'The girl,' I said. 'Her.' Pointing my finger, seeing my hand shake with rage. 'I know this little bitch. That's his daughter.'

'James Caine's daughter?'

DCI Stoner stared at her. She bared her teeth. Stoner's heat-flushed features twisted into a grin.

'Don't buy it, do you, sweetheart?' he asked conversationally.

Amy Caine spat on the ground and glared at me with an undying loathing.

DCI Stoner turned to me.

'She doesn't buy it,' he said. 'This idea that the guilty have been punished. And neither do I, Mrs Carver.'

He nodded at DI Ure and she said, 'OK,' and the plain-clothes cops in their T-shirts and tattoos started lifting the stupid kids to their feet and dragging them away, their arms locked behind their backs.

DCI Stoner was staring at me, waiting for a response.

'I don't know what you're talking about,' I told him.

'I think you do. What kind of cancer does your father have?'

'The end-of-the-road kind.'

'That's what I thought. And the Caine family don't believe a word of it. It's too neat. Come on! The dying old man did it? That's very convenient for you and your husband, isn't it?'

I felt like clawing his face off.

'If you don't think my father would kill a man who wanted to hurt me, if you don't think that my dad could kill a man like that, then – believe me – you don't know my father.'

'I know it all worked out well for you and your husband.'

'My father is serving *a life sentence* – and it worked out well for me?'

'For you it did, and for your many admirers. And I would put any of them ahead of your dying dad. Like those men who worked for your father.'

He meant the two Daves.

'And that great big Aussie lump who is married to your pal, Ginger. That Spike guy. Did you know he nearly beat a man to death once? Ex-boyfriend of his wife, apparently, who wouldn't press charges.'

So it turned out that Spike had done far more to Omar than just have a quiet word.

'And then there's my favourite – your husband. All your admirers, Mrs Carver.'

'I don't have any admirers.'

'Oh, I think you do! A fine-looking woman like you? A lot of men want to get in your good books.' He came closer and for the first time I could smell the alcohol on him. 'And in your pants,' he said.

'You're drunk,' I said, taking a step back. 'And it's disgusting.'

'You know why I'm drunk, Mrs Carver? Because you get the call and you go. They don't ask you if you feel up to it tonight, or if you have had a couple of drinks, or if you feel like sorting out all the screwed-up filth that people do to each other. They tell you that a bunch of dumb teenagers are chucking petrol bombs through a few windows off Upper Street and you answer the call.' He wiped his face with the palm of his hand. 'You know how many crimes of passion I've seen? Plenty. Crimes of passion makes it sound more romantic than it really is. In real life, it's not romantic at all. All those angry men who found out their wives had been wrapping their legs around some other man. Most men – even the rational, quiet types who would not hurt a fly – it drives them *insane*. So the husband is always ahead of the father in the queue. Especially when dear old daddy is dying.'

I swung my fist at his face. The blow caught him high on the cheekbone and spun his head sideways.

He laughed at me.

And I could feel the panic gripping my heart and the heat of the fire still on my face and I could see the sneer on his mouth.

'It works for a lot of people if your old man takes the fall,' he said. 'And it works for you too.' He touched his face and looked at his fingers. No blood. 'But the truth will come out one day, Mrs Carver. And when it does – I'll be waiting for you. And your husband.'

38

CHRISTIAN

The car was back.

On what felt like the first real day of summer, my T-shirt stuck to my back with sweat as I watched the car from a corner of the window blinds. Camden Town seemed over-lit and airless, and the car baked in the heat on the far side of the street, directly opposite our house, making no attempt to hide. There was nobody in the passenger seat, which made it seem as though this was not an official visit. This was personal. And somehow, that was a lot worse.

Detective Chief Inspector Stoner, waiting for something. Waiting for some hidden truth to reveal itself. He was never going to let us go, I saw now. It should have ended with Leo going away, but it had not.

Every now and again, Stoner lifted a bottle to his mouth, his eyes drifting across to our house, his thoughts loud and clear.

Guilty.

Guilty.

Guilty.

'Sorry?'

The girl from Tara's office was suddenly standing beside me. Skyla. She was dressed in some sort of silky, floaty outfit, like a bridesmaid dress, and had a laptop tucked under her arm.

'The music?' she said.

Ah – the music. It was on loud – very loud. The Doors in their pomp. The volume I had grown accustomed to in the time that I had the free run of the house. Too loud.

She smiled apologetically. 'I was trying to make a few calls—'

'Sorry, I'm so thoughtless,' I said, and went to lift the arm from the record player and The Doors were suddenly silent.

We smiled at each other, both embarrassed. She had good teeth but one of the front ones was chipped, making her smile a little lopsided and gappy. I liked it.

'And are you OK?' I said.

She nodded towards the kitchen, where she was working now that their office was gone.

'Oh, I'm fine, all I need is a good Wi-Fi connection.'

'No, I meant – you know. After the fire. It must have been horrible.'

'We didn't have time to think about it. Tara and I. It's worse for our neighbour – for Wiggy. Angel Eyes can work anywhere, but Wiggy – he lost everything. Tara – your wife – has been … incredible.'

You too, I thought. Everybody loves my wife.

Skyla picked up the album I had been playing. Jim Morrison's face at its most thin and beautiful, his finely cut features swimming in an exploding galaxy of planets, or maybe it was just the dream inside your head.

'*Weird Scenes Inside the Gold Mine*,' she read, as if for the first time, as if it was a funny title for a record.

I nodded. 'The title is a line from one of their most famous songs, "The End". They used it in *Apocalypse Now*. This is an important record because it was the first compilation they released after Jim Morrison died in a bathtub in Paris.'

I felt my face growing red as I realised that this young woman in a pink bridesmaid dress had never heard of Jim Morrison. I ploughed on. 'So it's a celebration of genius, conceived in grief.'

Once upon a time, this pretentious bollocks would have gone down quite well with the girls. Oh, where had those glory days gone? Skyla smiled politely.

'The Doors, yes,' as if, now she came to think of it, they did ring a distant bell somewhere. 'I think my dad liked them. Or maybe my granddad? They did "LA Woman", right? The Billy Idol song?'

'Yeah. Well.' I was trying hard not to be too pedantic. It was hard. 'The Doors did it before Billy Idol. It's a Doors song. Not – you know – a Billy Idol song.'

And I realised that for some unknown reason it was important for me to make this young woman see that I was not just a stay-at-home dad listening to old rock music way too loud.

'I'm writing something about *Weird Scenes Inside the Goldmine*,' I said, trying to sound casual. 'I'm getting back into my journalism. If I can. If anyone will have me.'

'But it's so great what you've been doing with your son – with Marlon! Taking care of him while Tara builds up the business! Not many men could do it. The guys I know – well, they're overgrown children, really. They can't take care of themselves, let alone a child.'

Who were these men – these overgrown boys? Where did she meet them? What were their unsuccessful chat-up lines? I was ridiculously proud that they could not do what I had done with my son.

'To see a man as the primary carer for a child,' she said. 'It's special.'

A primary carer. Is that what I was?

'It was kind of imposed upon me,' I said. 'Upon us. After we lost our jobs on the music paper.' I still shuddered at the memory of the print plunge, and waking up in the middle of the night wondering how we were going to support ourselves for the next half a century. 'Our industry – print journalism – didn't exist any more. Not in the same way. We were like those starving Red Indians – Native Americans, I mean – driven from our happy hunting grounds at the end of *Dances with Wolves*.'

'I've seen that one,' she said, as if *Dances with Wolves* was from the silent era.

'But Marlon's great,' I said. 'Our boy's not a difficult kid. I always love hanging out with him.' I shrugged, smiled. 'It was just the way things worked out.' I hesitated, then reached for the profound cliché. 'Life is what happens when you're busy making other plans.'

Her brown eyes were wide. 'Wow. *That's so true*. Life *is* what happens when you're busy making other plans!'

'That's a John Lennon quote,' I said quickly. 'I didn't make it up.'

She looked a bit disappointed. 'The Beatle that got shot,' she said.

'That's the one.'

Then we both stared thoughtfully at the cover of *Weird Scenes Inside the Goldmine*.

'Tara and I are just different,' I said.

She's driven. I'm parked.

'I could never do what she did – start a business,' I went on. 'Have that idea, that vision, and build it up from scratch. You watch – a fire is not going to stop her.'

'No,' Skyla smiled.

'The truth is, I was happy to give up work, especially towards the end when I was on a national newspaper. All those people doing work they hate so they can buy stuff they don't need, the years slipping away. I was happy to bail out and look after our son.'

'But now you're ready to get back into it!' she said brightly, as if it was that easy, as if life were a series of choices taking us ever closer to total fulfilment.

And we could use the money, I thought.

But it seemed wrong to mention the need to earn a living. It seemed vulgar to mention the longing for legal tender to this young woman.

I gently replaced the needle on the final track of disc two, turning the volume way down to a respectable level. We listened to 'When the Music's Over' for a while.

'He sounds like Frank Sinatra,' Skyla said.

'Who does?'

'Jim! I can imagine him singing "That's Life".'

I laughed. It was an astute thing to say. The world thought of Jim Morrison as a blues-based, crawling-king-snake rock god but it's true there was always something of the Las Vegas crooner about that baritone.

'So what are you writing?' she said. She didn't seem in a rush to get back to work.

'A think piece, we used to call it. Back in the days when we used to think.'

'For your old music paper?'

'That ship has sailed. It was free, and then it went online, and then it died. There's no more music press. I don't know where this piece would go. I thought about trying to get it in my old national newspaper, but I know they've had a lot of budget cuts up there after losing so much of their advertising revenue.'

Skyla pulled a face. 'Do a podcast,' she said, and she made it sound like the most natural and easy thing in the world.

There were maybe ten years between us but she made me feel like a High Court judge peering over my reading spectacles.

'And what is a podcast?'

'M'Lud, a podcast is a series of digital audio episodes on the wireless ...'

'I wouldn't know where to start,' I said.

'But you've made a start already!' she said. 'Because you have *something to say* about *something you care about.* That's the hard work done right there! The rest is just managing the tech, and that's the easy bit. Maybe get a better microphone, download some free software and spend a weekend learning how to use it. Save your MP3 files. Edit.' She nodded at the vinyl spinning on the record player. 'Add the music. Find an online platform who will distribute it to streaming services like Spotify and iTunes.'

I felt like I should be writing this stuff down.

Skyla's fingers were flying across her laptop, keen to show me something that explained how easy and perfect it was all going to be.

'Ten million people listen to podcasts every week. There is a big growth in – you know – *older* listeners. My dad listens to podcasts and he's like, *fifty* or something. No offence.'

I had to smile. 'None taken.'

'A classic rock music podcast is *perfect*,' she said, with the kind of unequivocal enthusiasm that I guessed she brought to every working day, and I could understand why she was Tara's last remaining employee. 'I bet a lot of people would love to hear you talk about *Weird Scenes Inside the Goldmine* and The Doors and Jim Morrison and play the music and share your passion with the world.'

I watched her on her laptop. She seemed so young and fresh and untouched. She was a smart, beautiful young woman in a weird pink bridesmaid dress and nothing bad had ever happened to her.

I watched her face as she called up some of her favourite podcasts.

This could work, I thought. This could actually work.

This was my way out.

This shining, hopeful, gap-toothed new day.

But when Skyla had gone back to the kitchen to carry on with her work and I had gone back to mine, I went to the window and the car was still there, and DCI Stoner was still taking a hit from the bottle on his lap, and he was still staring at our home as if he knew one thing with total certainty.

Guilty.

Guilty.

Guilty.

Then I was heading to the door with Skyla's voice calling to me from the kitchen, the first time I had ever heard her say my name, and my blood was up because the detective in the car wanted to take away my future.

I was ready to rip his throat out. And I felt that way right up to the moment he got out of his car and stood there, waiting for me, his big hands hanging loose by his side and the vodka on his breath. I was not going to rip this man's throat out. Not today.

'You haven't been totally honest with your wife, have you?' he said. 'Get in the car, Christian. I want to show you something.'

I looked at the familiar roads flashing by. Stoner was driving too fast. He was not wearing a seat belt. The smell of vodka filled the car.

'What kind of cancer does your father-in-law have again?' Stoner said.

'I have to pick up my son soon,' I said.

'This is not going to take long.' He grinned. 'It's not going to stop you doing your house-husband chores, OK? You know the park? That's where we're going. So he's refusing treatment, is he?'

I didn't have time for this.

It would be Marlon's going-home time soon.

Stoner drove faster.

'He's refusing surgery,' I said.

'Staring down cancer.' He shook his head in admiration. 'He's a brave old man, your father-in-law. I don't think he took a nailing hammer to James Caine's skull. But then that only makes him even braver, wouldn't you say?'

We had reached the park. Stoner pulled up across the street from the playground. It was that mid-afternoon period when the swings and slides and roundabouts were still annexed by the youngest, pre-school children.

'You see that couple with the two little girls?'

A tall, athletic-looking black man and a small, neat redhead were gently turning two small kids on the roundabout. Two girls, a toddler in the early staggering stages of walking and the older one about four.

'You know who that is?' Stoner said. 'Of course you don't know. How could you possibly know? But have a guess. Go on.'

I stared at the drunken cop's face and for the first time I wondered if he was insane.

'Listen, I'm going to go now,' I said, 'I have to pick up my son. I can walk home from here.'

Stoner pressed a button and the central locking clicked shut.

'That woman is *my wife*,' DCI Stoner said. He stared thoughtfully at the family in the park. 'He's a big guy, isn't he? Fit. Works out. Free weights, all of that. Naturally strong. *But I took him*.' DCI Stoner stared at me. 'I went to his place of work and I gave him a good hiding because of what he was doing with my wife behind my back. He dropped the charges but the bitch still had a restraining order put on me. Did you know they could do that? They can get a restraining order put on you *even if you're not convicted of anything.* Where's the justice in that? Just for sending a few hundred text messages! And you know why I beat him?'

'Because you can do what you like,' I said wearily. 'Because you're a cop.'

DCI Stoner shook his head. 'That's the irony, Christian! I'm a cop – *but so is he!* That's the funny thing! That's how my wife knew him. We all worked at the same station. I was a detective, he was a uniform, and she was on the clerical staff. No, the reason I beat him even though he is twice my size is because it *mattered* far more to me than it did to him. To him, she was just some bored married woman he was knocking off.'

'Their relationship looks like far more than that.'

His face clouded with annoyance.

'Whatever it became *later*, once she got her claws into him, at the start my wife was just a bit on the side. Believe me. And to me – well, my wife was my sun and my moon and my stars. And that bastard took it all away.'

I looked at the two mixed-race little girls on the roundabout.

'She doesn't look like your wife,' I said quietly. 'She looks like his wife.'

DCI Stoner's mouth tightened. 'Are you trying to provoke me? My *ex*-wife.'

'Ah.'

'Because I want to show you – *I understand*. I understand the way that James Caine made you feel. I felt the same way. If you didn't want to kill him, you would be different from every other man on the planet. You wouldn't be human. That guy and your wife – the mother of your child – they did what they did while you were putting your little boy to bed. Then he came to your home. Then you confronted him in the street. And then, when it was all too much to take, you went to his hotel to sort him out. That's true, isn't it?'

'I have to pick up my son.'

The children would soon be coming out of school. I imagined Marlon's face scanning the grown-up faces at the gates, and failing to see me, and his smile fading to concern.

I tried the car door. Still shut.

I reached for the central locking button but Stoner seized my wrists.

'My son,' I said. 'I need to pick up my boy, he will be waiting for me, he will be scared.'

'Until that poor bastard of a soldier showed up,' DCI Stoner said, 'it was all on you.'

We were being watched by the family in the playground now. DCI Stoner's ex-wife was staring at him, a look of pure terror on her face. Her phone was in her hand as her husband herded their two small daughters away from the roundabout.

'I have to pick up my son,' I said, shoving my fists against his chest, banging them against him until he released his grip. 'I mean it. Let me out of this car or …'

'Or what, little man? What are you going to do to me?'

'If my son is upset because I'm not there, then I swear to God …'

'Go on, go on, you can do it!'

'You're a dead man!'

'That's my boy,' Stoner chuckled. 'That's all I wanted to hear. That's all I needed to know. Good for you, little man. We're done now.'

His phone was on the dashboard.

He picked it up, stared at Voice Memos for a moment and then pressed the red button to turn off the recording.

We both looked up at the sound of the sirens.

And then the police were there.

But this time they had not come for me.

The family watched from the playground as Stoner was taken away. I felt like I should apologise to them but there was no time. I ran all the way to the school. In the end, it was not too bad. I was not late. The going-home bell had just stopped ringing.

And as I walked home holding hands with Marlon, my boy chatting about the story I would read him at bedtime, I dropped DCI Stoner's phone down a drain.

39

TARA

'I've got you,' Uncle Jack said, hoisting Marlon onto Maple's back.

Everything was too big. The horse, the saddle, the long drop to the dirt of the round riding pen, and Maple's mouth, that great gaping endlessly moving hole with teeth the size of Stonehenge.

Marlon looked petrified. But one of Uncle Jack's hands hovered behind Marlon's back and the other soothed Maple's muzzle.

'I've got you, I've got you, I've got you,' Jack chanted, and Maple stared thoughtfully at me – *Wasn't that you on my back once upon a time?* – as the look of frozen terror on Marlon's face dissolved into an expression of disbelief and finally settled into something akin to wonder.

Uncle Jack glanced over to where my mother and I were leaning against the wooden railings of the riding pen.

'Boy's got a good seat,' Uncle Jack said, and my mother and I quietly applauded. Maple slightly lifted her head and Marlon beamed, his face ecstatic under my old pink riding helmet.

'With the reins,' Uncle Jack told him, 'you pretend you're holding an ice cream cone in your hands and you don't want to tip your ice cream over, do you?'

I smiled. 'Still using the old ice cream tip, Jack?'

'It's still good advice, young lady.' He nodded at Marlon. 'OK, now horses move away from pressure so when you want old Maple to start walking, you just give her a gentle little nudge with your heels. She'll feel that and she'll know it's time to go. No need to do it very hard. No need to hurt her. Gently, gently. Can you do that, son?'

Jack began leading Maple around the pen.

'Don't lean forward,' Uncle Jack said, and my smile grew bigger because all this was exactly the advice he had given to me more than twenty years ago. 'Don't slouch. Sit tall and relaxed.' Uncle Jack glanced down at the stirrups and made a slight adjustment. 'You don't have to stuff your feet all the way in. And when you want to stop ...'

Tighten your tummy muscles, I thought. *And rock back.*

'Tighten your tummy muscles,' Uncle Jack told Marlon. 'And rock back. Try it.'

Maple came to a gentle halt. Marlon was wide-eyed. 'I'm doing it!'

'Time to go home soon,' I said. 'Your dad will be waiting for us.'

'Just a bit more, Mama,' Marlon said.

Marlon had always been wary of Maple, which I saw now was my father's fault for always being far too desperate for Marlon to share our family's love of horses. With the best intentions in the world, my dad had forced Maple on Marlon right back from when he was a toddler, trying to get him to feed the horse carrots and chunks of bread and lumps of sugar before he could even feed himself. But it was different now that my father was away – and that is what we all said, that my dad was 'away', as if he was on a journey with no known return ticket in sight – and Marlon being more relaxed around Maple was only the start of it. Some ancient barrier between my mother and I seemed to be coming down at last. I looked at my mother's fabulous face. Her hair was still blonde, with a little help once a month, the teeth in that striking face were still dazzling white as she grinned at her grandson, and the neat figure was still trim enough to turn heads when she walked into a room.

'Mum?'

'What?'

'Why did you stay with Dad?' I asked.

She turned to look at me, her smile fading.

'Why did you stay with him when you knew he was unfaithful?'

She turned away, and I could feel the barrier coming back up.

'Why does Christian stay with you?' she said in that old tone of voice, the irritated, disappointed, don't-push-me-too-far voice that I had grown up hearing. But I had thought about her question a lot.

'Because he knows I made a mistake,' I said. 'And because he knows I love him.'

'Ah, love! That explains everything.'

'And because he knows I regret it.'

She turned to size me up, unsmiling now.

'Do you? Do you really, Tara? Or do you regret getting caught?'

'I regret all of it. I will be sorry about it for the rest of my life. But it was different with Dad. All those women over all those years. It wasn't just a one-off mistake, was it? It was a way of life.'

'Not for years now.'

'Because he got sick.'

'No, before all of that. Because he got older and wiser and got it out of his system. And he saw what we had – in the end.'

I laughed with disbelief.

'In the end!'

My mother did not reply immediately. She waved and smiled encouragement to her grandson, progressing at a stately pace on the far side of the riding pen, before looking at me, surprisingly calm, not remotely irritated by her mouthy daughter now, as if she had known some hard truths for half a lifetime that I still had to learn.

'Yes, Tara – *in the end*. You want to know – why did I stay? I stayed because it was my home. It wasn't just about me and my hurt feelings, was it? It wasn't just about me and my broken heart. It was about having a daughter who would be changed forever if I kicked him out or if I walked away. You would be a different person if you hadn't grown up on – I don't know what to call it – that rock, that foundation of family. And he always came home. And he never fell in love. Not with any of them. It could have been a lot worse. Your father could have been like other men, trading in his family every few years for a new one. Starting a new franchise of younger wife that doesn't look so different from the last one and having more kids. But he always came home to us. To you and me, Tara. There may have been lots of other women but he only had one home. And it's hard, isn't it? It's hard for everyone.'

'What's hard?'

'Marriage. You and Christian must be going through the same thing or you wouldn't have – what would you call it? Strayed.'

'I still love my husband.' I felt my face flushing. 'In every way.'

'Of course you do, dear,' she said, the old impatient tone creeping back into her voice.

'I don't want to argue,' I said, almost desperate. 'I just want to understand.'

We watched Marlon's slow procession around the riding pen and I thought how much my father would have loved to see his beloved grandson riding Maple and my vision blurred with tears.

'I miss him,' I said. 'I miss Dad.'

'Me, too,' my mother said briskly. 'He's a good man. He's a good man who has done some bad things and he has tried to make up for them.'

'He shouldn't be in that terrible place.'

We watched Marlon and Maple gently padding back towards us, Uncle Jack murmuring his words of encouragement and advice.

'Your father was trying to protect you.'

'I know.'

'That's why he went to that hotel. That's why he had to have it out with that bloody awful man.'

I hesitated. 'But Dad didn't kill him, Mum.'

She stared at me with disbelief. 'Then who did?'

Marlon laughed, a wild joy in his laughter, and we looked up to see the old man and the boy and the horse.

'I've got you,' said Uncle Jack, his face close to Maple's, and it felt like they were words that had been there all my life, soothing me, assuring me that I was not going to fall, that I was not alone, that everything was going to be all right in the end.

'I've got you,' Uncle Jack said. 'I've got you, I've got you, I've got you.'

I stood at the big French windows and stared out over the empty field. In the far distance, Uncle Jack was leading Maple into her stable. My mother was putting on one of her records. Dolly Parton began pleading with Jolene not to take her man.

My mother loved country and western music, all of it, from Patsy Kline and Dolly Parton all the way through to Emmylou Harris and even early Taylor Swift. All that big blonde hair and steel guitars, motel rooms and smoky bars, wronged women and wayward men – *Story of her life*, I could not stop myself thinking – but it was only now, with my father away, that my mother felt free to play her music.

'Are *you* all right, Mum?' I said, and she looked at me as if it was the last question she was expecting.

'The thing about this illness business is that you are not ready for the sadness,' my mother said. 'You know that illness is going to be full of pain and anxiety and distress. But the sadness of it all, that's what catches you off guard. I think about everything your dad's going to miss. He wanted to watch Marlon grow up. He wanted to see you settled.'

I rubbed her arm and I could not remember the last time I had touched her and I thought – *am I still not settled?*

'Mama?'

Marlon was in the doorway in his pyjamas. There was a line on his forehead from his pink riding hat. He held out his arms.

'Basically I'm not tired.'

'Basically you *are* tired,' I said, going to him, scooping him up in my arms. 'But you're also excited after doing all that great riding. Your head's a washing machine with all those thoughts going around and round.'

'Want Grandma to put you to bed?' my mum said.

'Both of you,' he ordered.

My mother led us upstairs to the master bedroom. It still seemed strange, entering this Chanel-scented inner sanctum. My parents' bedroom had seemed like some secret palace when I was a child. It still did, I realised. My mum's bottles of scents and creams and lotions and potions on the dresser, the colour and season coordinated walk-in wardrobe, that smell of a sophisticated pampered wife, mother and woman. There was little trace of my father in here.

'Make spoons,' she instructed.

The three of us curled up on top of the bed. My mum on her side, Marlon in the middle and me where my father should have been. They were both exhausted and I listened to the sound of their breathing as they slipped easily into sleep, and I must have dozed off too because somewhere between sleeping and waking I sat up realising that there was someone at the front door. The bell was ringing, a chiming melodic run that was as twee as a 'welcome' mat, old-fashioned and strange as it echoed in the big house, like a call to church on Sunday morning or a dream of childhood.

Christian was on our doorstep.

'I'm so sorry, Tara,' he said.

And I fell into his arms and let him hold me as if he would never let me go because I knew from the moment I looked at his face that death had come to our door.

40

CHRISTIAN

DCI Stoner was right.

I had not been completely honest with my wife.

And I felt bad about that. No, lights years beyond bad.

I was deeply ashamed of the secrets I had kept from Tara.

I was ashamed that I had somehow become something less than the man I wanted to be.

But there were lies that I had told, and there were rooms that I had been in that Tara did not know about.

Yet as I stood at the ground-floor window of our house, watching the empty street, wearing the black tie of mourning that I had not worn since my mother's funeral, I felt the first faint spark of hope.

For the first time in a long time, it felt like Tara and I were going to be all right. And maybe that's the way it works – if you love someone, if you really love them – then you can get through anything.

What gave me hope was that DCI Stoner's car was gone from our road.

According to what I had read online, it had not been the first time that he had watched his ex-wife and her family in the park.

Some reports suggested that it wasn't even the first time that week.

And then there was his bombardment of text messages, his aggressively familiar comments left on social media, his drunken phone calls in the middle of the night – the great sour avalanche of disappointed love.

All in direct violation of the restraining order against DCI Stoner having contact with his ex-wife.

She told one newspaper that, in the face of his never-ending harassment, only her two small daughters had stopped her from contemplating suicide.

Our old lawyer, Kevin Steel, had called to say that if DCI Stoner was convicted of breaking his restraining order, then he faced a maximum penalty of six months' imprisonment if he was tried in the Magistrate's Court, and five years if he was tried before a jury in a Crown Court.

So whatever happened, DCI Stoner was unlikely to be taking up a resident's parking bay in our street any time soon.

And for the first time in a long time, I felt free. Perhaps Tara and I could make it through all of this, I thought.

Fat Phil's car pulled up. A one-off job. He got out, hiked his trousers up over that belly like a prize marrow and frowned at our house. He saw me at the window and raised a hand in salute. He wasn't laughing at me now.

I went to find Tara.

She was sitting on our bed with Marlon on her lap, and my heart ached to see the pair of them in the bleak uniforms of mourning.

Tara's black dress.

Marlon's white shirt and clip-on black tie.

They were both too young for those clothes.

I got down on my knees in front of them. They held each other so tightly, and so still, that they seemed like one person.

I placed my hands on their hands.

'Everything's going to be all right,' I promised.

Tara nodded. She did not seem convinced.

And then we went to the funeral.

TARA

We came down the aisle of the church and it was like leafing through one of those old-fashioned photo albums where suddenly you are being stared at by faces from your past, all those people that drift in and out of your life. But the faces were all older now, sometimes shockingly so; all those women who had worked with Mary and I around ten years ago when there were still jobs for us at the glossy magazines – editors, photographers, journalists, stylists – all those smart, single city girls who assumed they had a job for life.

As I was handed an order of service, some of their heads turned to register my presence in the church, a few whispers passing through them, and the eyes that I caught had a cold hard light. I had made no space for these people in my new world. Not as friends, not as colleagues, not as even the vaguest of acquaintance. It was true. I had not made any attempt to stay in contact with any of them. I had not returned their messages or emails asking for a drink, or a job, or a kind word. Too busy, too selfish, too Tara.

Christian scooped up Marlon, our boy suddenly wide-eyed and awed at the strange theatre of the church, and all these solemn adults, and the palpable sense of sadness. Mary's parents were in the front row – her fierce heavyset mother and her thin, diffident balding dad, like a married couple in one of those old seaside postcards, I always thought – their faces etched with the unbearably raw grief of parents who have to bury their child. We took our place in a pew towards the front of the church and I swallowed the cruel finality of the day.

Mary was gone.

Christian put Marlon on his lap and held him, gently turning his face from the coffin that waited by the altar, as I looked at the order of service. Mary's face was grinning at me from the cover and I remembered exactly when that fleeting happy moment was captured and I knew she had never looked lovelier. It was the day we went to the photo shoot for the magazine cover and we had both tried to look our very best. Mary had been cutting down on the carbs for a couple of weeks, she had had her hair cut and her teeth whitened. We had gone for a facial together and I recalled the pair of us rolling down Oxford Street with our newly exfoliated faces, howling with excitement. The photo was taken when they were still setting up for the shoot and I was in that picture too, although of course I had been cropped out for the order of service. But I knew I was there at the moment the photo was taken, and I could still see one hand lightly resting on Mary's shoulder. Then five minutes later the photographer's assistant broke the news that they were only going to be using me for the shoot. And, looking back, I don't think I saw my old friend ever smile quite like that again.

I looked around the church. It was a full house today, because Mary was loved and she deserved to be loved – smart, kind, funny Mary – and I remembered the real laugh Mary and I had every month looking at the faces of the men, all those vain smiling men, and we sometimes laughed until we wept. There were a lot of people in the church who had worked with her. Nobody who ever worked with her ever disliked her. I could see Michael and his boyfriend on the far side, sitting with Skyla, who was already in tears, and there were people who had worked with Mary all the way back to her first job on some long-gone women's magazine, and then towards the back were Ginger and Spike, who had met Mary when we were setting up the business, and who knew that she was the rock I built everything on. All come to say goodbye, Mary, goodbye.

Mary had dropped in front of a train on the Underground. A tragic accident, we were told, one of those random assaults of bad luck that can rip apart any life at any moment. Not suicide, that was the line, definitely not suicide, because there were no notes, no bitter recriminations, no acknowledgement that the last blog from the Accidental Dater read like a suicide note. 'Excuse me,' two witnesses had heard Mary say, the inquest was told, 'Excuse me,' and then she was falling, falling, falling as the train was coming into the station. But it was an accident, that was the verdict, and that's what we said, and that's what we would say for the rest of our own lives, and do our best to believe it because anything else was too horrible to contemplate. But I contemplated it anyway, and I knew I would contemplate it forever, and I would always feel that I could have said something or done something so that it did not have to end this way. Because I knew what had happened, or I thought I knew, and I tried hard to push that knowledge aside, and I wanted to be wrong. But this I knew to be true – I should have loved you more, Mary.

I should have walked out of that photo shoot when they only wanted me in my little black dress and the smile that I have been perfecting since I was fifteen years old. I should have told them to stick their magazine cover, and I should have chosen you, and chosen friendship and – even if it was beyond my power to find you a man like Christian, who was always your idea of the perfect man – then I should have told you once in a while that I could not have done any of it without you. I should have been kinder.

'All these people,' someone murmured respectfully in the row ahead of us, and I recognised her as a photographer who ten years back had been the Ecstasy-chugging, Kate Moss-skinny, platinum-haired toast of Soho, and was now a middle-aged frump with some old dad by her side. 'It's exactly what Mary would have wanted.'

Exactly wrong, lady! The irony of this packed church was that Mary would have wanted none of this major drama. Too much of a fuss, right, Mary? When David Bowie died, Mary was very impressed by how little fuss there was – a direct cremation, they called it. No flowers, no service, no big send-off, nothing like this, Mary. Bowie's body went straight from the hospital to the crematorium in a cheap coffin and then the ashes were returned to his next of kin. Mary thought that was the way to check out. 'When I go, I'm going like Bowie,' she told me, and I had worked up the nerve to mention it to Mary's mother in our short, frosty phone call when she asked me to say something at the funeral. At first Mary's mum did not understand what I was talking about.

'A direct cremation is what David Bowie had,' I said. 'It's what they do with the homeless. And it's what Mary wanted.'

'The homeless and David Bowie?' snorted Mary's mum, and I could imagine the henpecked dad in the background, ready with a docile 'Yes, dear,' to whatever his wife decided. 'Mary was neither homeless nor David Bowie.'

It was stupid of me to even suggest a direct cremation. Mary's mother was a conventional soul who was always a little sniffy about the digital dating business her daughter and I had founded together. But to tell you the truth, when Mary's mother and I had that conversation, I was aware of how much easier it would be for me to be spared the ordeal of a big funeral, and all those disapproving faces, and all the terrible weight of guilt and grief I felt for my dead friend. Good old Tara, eh Mary? Always thinking of herself! Even now! So here is your big day in church, Mary, and I am sorry it is not a white wedding with a guy who looks, thinks and loves like Christian, and I am sorry you did not get another fifty years, and I am so sorry it ended the way it did between us, and I am sorry because I know in the end anyone gets sickened by all those useless apologies that can't erase the past. Sorry is just kindness that arrives too late.

And so it was a big service. The church. All these people. The little booklet. Entry music. Welcome and Introduction. Hymn, Eulogy, Reflection, Prayers, Poem. As Marlon sucked his thumb and rested his sleepy head against Christian's chest, I flicked through the eight-page order of service because I was the Poem.

The vicar welcomed us, and we followed his lead as we sang, we prayed and we reflected. Please stand. Please sit. *Sun and moon, bow down before him. Give us this day our daily bread and forgive us our trespasses. I was a stranger, and you took me in. Amen.* But the hymns and the prayers and the readings washed over me. It was only when we listened to Mary's favourite song – 'Wild is the Wind' by David Bowie – that I felt her watching.

And then I was on.

Christian squeezed my hand in encouragement. Marlon stared at me wide-eyed with wonder. I licked my lips and went up to read. I looked out at them, all those faces from a lifetime, and the simple fact that they had all come here today for Mary meant more than anything that could be said, sung or prayed. It meant more than the flowers. I wanted to tell them all of that but there were no words to say it. I looked at Mary's parents in the front row, both of them watching me. They were numb but not undone. Not here, not today. That was not their family way, they would do their mourning behind closed doors, and it felt like the worst thing in the world to be burying your child. I looked at my

Marlon, my son, my beautiful boy and I knew how life would end for me if I had to do what Mary's parents were doing today.

And then I read.

'Death is nothing at all.
It does not count.
I have only slipped away into the next room.
Nothing has happened.'

Someone was crying too loudly towards the back of the church.

'Everything remains exactly as it was.
I am I, and you are you.
And the old life that we lived so fondly together is untouched, unchanged.
Whatever we were to each other – that we are still.'

And I didn't believe it, I didn't believe a single word of what I was saying, because to me it felt like the changes never stopped coming, it felt like life never gave you a chance to catch your breath. I felt like I knew all of these faces in front of me today but they were all changed, every one of them, all older, more beaten down, disappointed with the way things had worked out, faces that told you that time was running on and running out, the old certainties always sliding away. Ginger watched me and some kind light in her eye gave me encouragement to go on and get it done so that we could all go home. Kindness is so underrated, Mary, I see that now. But although they sat together today, I knew that Spike had moved out, and their marriage was coming apart under the impossible weight of historic betrayals, and it was another reason to feel that Henry Scott-Holland's death poem was a pack of sugar-coated lies.

'All is well,' I said.

> 'Nothing is hurt – nothing is lost.
> One brief moment and all will be as it was before.
> How we shall laugh at the trouble of parting when we meet again!'

The sobbing from the back was growing louder. Heads were turning to see who was crying. It was all wrong, this hysterical, broken-hearted wailing coming from the back. It was the ultimate funeral faux-pas – for the outsider to show more emotion than the family. It was Skyla who was in tears. I almost smiled. Skyla was so young, so untouched, she probably still had healthy grandparents. Skyla's first hamster was probably still in robust health.

Then it was over.

I was exhausted by it all, I could not face the thought of watching Mary's coffin being lowered into the ground. I just wanted to go home. I wanted to take off these miserable black clothes and order a takeaway and huddle in our nest. I wanted wine, I wanted life, I wanted to be with my boys.

But Skyla was coming down the aisle, going against the tide of people leaving the church, still sobbing uncontrollably as if Mary had been her next of kin.

Too bloody much, quite frankly, I can clearly remember thinking as Skyla went to Christian and he took her in his arms and she stayed there.

And the moment seemed to freeze.

As if she was his, and he was hers, as if she wanted to stay in his arms forever.

I felt Marlon take my hand as I stared at them and they broke away from each other, too quickly, not meeting my eye. But I knew everything and I did not have to look at his phone, I did not have to trawl through the deleted messages and his call history and the reckless texts, all those sweet Wi-Fi nothings that are so hopelessly, endlessly romantic to the sender and the recipient, and so pitilessly, murderously cruel to the one who suddenly learns that she is living in a shattered home. There was no need for any forensic examination of my husband's iPhone. I did not have to go shopping for pain because it was delivered to my door.

The pain came and found me.

41

TARA

My mother gently tapped on Maple's hind hoof with the nailing hammer, as delicate as a dental hygienist cleaning under a particularly tricky bridge. Her shiny crimson nails glinted in the fading sunlight of the stable, expertly closing the gap that had worked loose between shoe and foot.

'In the cold weather,' Uncle Jack said, 'me hands seize up a bit.'

'It's not a problem,' my mother said.

'It's the arthritis,' Jack continued. 'All right in summer, they are.'

'Jack. Stop. I'm happy to do it.'

My mother was a horsewoman too.

This fact was often forgotten in our family. My mum had been a pony club regular before she had started school, but her history of riding and showing had been overshadowed by my father's romantic nostalgia for rosy-cheeked stable lads riding an Irish draught mare bareback as they went off to court the beauty at the next village. But although my mother's love of horses grew in a very English middle-class suburbia, rather than mucking out in Irish racing stables, it was no less real. I watched her run the palm of her hand over Maple's hoof. The shoe now looked like an extension of Maple's foot.

'Look at how concave her foot is,' she said. 'Lovely.'

'Good feet, old Maple,' Jack agreed. 'Horses can have flat feet like people. And the flatter they are, the more problems. Look at all the weight she has to carry.'

My mother straightened up. 'Leo used to say – no feet, no horse.'

Dressed in skin-tight Sweaty Betty leggings and top, my mother looked particularly gorgeous today. Hair and make-up were always a major operation for my mother, but you could tell when she had made a special effort.

Her face lit up as a car pulled up in front of the house.

Spike.

My mother's one-to-one yoga class with Spike. She touched her hair, examined her face in the hand mirror.

'The highlight of my day,' she said, and there was a time in my life when I would have cringed inside to hear my mother say that ninety minutes on a yoga mat with a man half her age was the highlight of her day.

But now I found it brought tears to my eyes.

She handed Uncle Jack the nailing hammer.

'Careful with that,' my mother said. 'It's bloody sharp.'

After I had cleaned Maple's tack I walked down to the house, my clothes damp from the warm water I had used to clean bridle, bit and saddle. The smell of saddle soap and leather conditioner on my hands was like a memory of childhood.

I could see my mother and Spike through the window.

He was stretching her out at the end of their session, his large body bent over her neat little prone form, and he grinned with great amusement at me through the glass, as if I was interrupting something.

And as if he could have my mother if he wanted her.

I kicked off my riding boots at the door and went to the kitchen to drink tea and stay out of their way. When I came back, my mum was giving Spike an Air Mail envelope – such was her delicacy giving money to the help – and they were scheduling their next session.

Then she had to run to pick up Marlon from school and bring him back for tea.

I walked her to the door as we discussed Marlon's stuffed itinerary of playdates, pick-up times and parties, swimming class, violin lesson and drama club. Bringing up a six-year-old was like being the PA of some multinational CEO.

But Marlon was our great project. He was what we talked about. After a lifetime of antagonism, child care had brought us together and as I waved off Jen, I knew that she was a single parent's greatest ally – the doting grandmother. And I would always be grateful to her.

Spike was rifling through the fridge in my parents' large open-plan kitchen like an overfamiliar lodger.

In the distance, Uncle Jack was stabling Maple.

Spike turned to me, a can of Sapporo in his hand. 'You don't mind?'

It was a big can of beer. How long exactly was he planning to stay?

'Thirsty work, stretching out your lovely mum.'

It felt like he should be gone by now.

But he flopped his large body on the sofa, legs spread wide, can in hand.

'Alone at last,' Spike said.

'There's always Uncle Jack,' I said, trying to pretend this wasn't awkward. 'And Maple.'

'You know what I mean,' Spike said, unsmiling. 'Long time no see, Tara.'

That was true. When you lose your partner, you lose a network of shared friendships. All those double-dating nights, Christian and me, Spike and Ginger, – in restaurants before Marlon was born, from Deliveroo after he was born – were gone forever.

'You look good, Tara.'

'Spike?'

He waited.

'Don't flirt with me, OK? I'm not my mum. I don't need you to compliment my Downward Facing Dog.'

He stroked his stubbled chin.

'Me and your mother – now there's a thought. Can't be easy, having your husband inside for life. Got to be lonely. And of course it would even up the score with Ginger and your dear old dad.'

There was a nastiness to it that I felt I had never seen from him before. But that wasn't quite true because then I remembered the night when Ginger had asked him to go to the hotel, to do to James Caine whatever he had done to her ex, Omar, yet another man who would not take no for an answer, and I recalled how Spike had looked at me that night. As if he could see right through me, as if he was seeing me for the first time – what an easy slut I really was and always had been.

The silence grew.

I glanced out of the big windows at the back of the house towards the empty field. Uncle Jack and Maple must be back at the stable. Spike was right then. We were alone now.

He sipped his beer, taking his time.

'I'm not having sex with you, Spike,' I said, smiling, to show him how absurd it was to even dream it.

He grinned.

'Christian still with his child bride?'

'That was a one-off, I think,' I said, far more lightly than I felt, because it still hurt, and it was going to hurt for many years yet. Although the flirting between Christian and Skyla may have started under our roof, and maybe even the early kissing, the final betrayal was consummated at her little room in her shared flat and not in our home. That was Christian's story, and I believed him. It had come out during one of the endless talks we had when at last I knew – those tear-sodden, heart-ravaged talks that lasted for hours, that last all night, those talks that make you feel as though you are being flayed alive.

Christian and Skyla didn't do it in our home. They didn't do it in our bed. They didn't do it in the house where Marlon slept and played and grew. And all at once that was very important and didn't matter a damn. It was important because knowing that they had been together in our home would have been a monumental act of disrespect and at the same time it didn't matter a damn because all his promises to me were still broken.

I remembered the ride home from the funeral. Christian speechless, staring at my legs in the black tights, as if he missed me already, as if he knew what he had lost. Or maybe he had been staring at nothing, maybe he had been thinking nothing except this:

She knows.

My wife knows.

But it was a new world already in that car, with Fat Phil checking me in the rear-view mirror and me trying very hard not to cry, and Mary gone, and our business with her, and now Christian, the love of my life, revealed to be not much more than just another guy, mounting the first young woman who looked at him wide-eyed and promised to restore his battered self-esteem in her shared flat, or maybe he just wanted a little sugar in his bowl, or maybe he wanted to even the score between us, or maybe it was a bit of all of the above, and it was all so sad that I could not speak, there were no words, because apart from everything else, I knew I had lost my best friend in this new world.

How much we throw away, I thought. How much we waste. And I wept when we were home and our front door closed behind us and Marlon scooted off to his room, desperate to get out of his funeral kit, I wept because I knew that Christian and I were doing something to our son that would change him forever. Marlon had always been a happy, easy kid, a bit quiet, unsuited to the rough-and-tumble of even the softest play areas – he had a particular terror of bouncy castles. Every film upset him – *Happy Feet* was a horror story to Marlon, because a small penguin gets bullied by bigger birds. He was a gentle soul. And I did not want him to change. And I knew he would. Infidelity – what we had done to each other – was nothing compared to what we were going to do to our son.

I watched the field. I found I liked watching the field more and more. The field never changed. Not like everything else. The field looked exactly like that when I was growing up. And I remembered – after I knew what he had done, and after we realised that we were falling apart and nothing would ever put us back together again – Christian and I crying in perfect harmony.

'I'm sorry!'

'Me too!'

And then we would cry some more because, in the end, we could never be quite sorry enough, we would never be so sorry that everything was as it was before. There are lines that we cross, I saw now, lines that mean you can never find your way home again. We had crossed those lines, my husband and I, and we wept for our home, for our boy, for each other, for ourselves, and for all we would never have again. You can talk about it for the rest of the night or the rest of your life. But once you cross the line, there's no way home.

'You once said – most relationships don't end too soon,' Spike was saying, bringing me back. 'Most relationships go on for too long.'

'I don't remember saying that to you.'

'You said it to Christian. When he was moving out. He told me one night. In his cups.'

Now I remembered. I was trying to hurt Christian. I wanted to hurt him. I wanted to break his heart because he had broken mine. You will say anything when you want to hurt someone bad enough.

'I didn't think you two would ever split up.'

He handed me the can of Japanese beer. I took a sip and passed it back.

'Me neither. But as soon as there's a third person in a marriage, it starts to come apart. Even if they're only there for one night. Even if they are a mistake. You break the spell. That's what happens when you let the third person in. And once you break the spell, anything is possible.'

'Yes, but it's like that old saying – why would you go out for a cheeseburger when you've got steak at home? And the answer is – because nobody wants to eat steak all the time, right?'

'No, that's not it. We don't do it because we want a change of diet.'

'Then why?'

'Opportunity,' I said. 'We do it because we can.'

And then we live to regret it, I thought, and then we live to ask ourselves – was it worth it for a few hours of something masquerading as fun and a lifetime of lies? And you know the answer better than you have ever known anything.

'Opportunity,' Spike said, as if that was his cue.

He slowly got to his feet and came towards me, putting down his beer, his smile spreading across his face.

'Opportunity,' he said. 'I like it.'

But I was so done with all of that. I was trying to focus on the things that mattered now. How was I going to raise my son? How was I going to make a living now that my business had collapsed? What would happen to my dad? What was I going to do with my life for the next fifty years now that I had lost Christian? Who would love me now?

Spike stood in front of me. He licked his lips.

'Spike? Enough. I've got stuff to do.'

He looked offended.

'But I was there for you, wasn't I?'

'You and Ginger were always there for me.'

He gathered his thoughts. You could watch them gathering on his stubbled, beach bum face.

'You must have heard the rumours, Tara. During the investigation, I mean.'

I remembered Ginger's panicked face.

Keep them right away from Spike.

Don't mention Spike to the law.

'There were rumours about a lot of people,' I said. 'The Daves. Christian. But there's only one man they put away.'

His face winced with what looked like a flash of jealousy.

'Do you really think your daddy did it?'

'My father would die for me.'

'Ah, but would he *kill* for you, Tara? You think Leo went to that hotel and topped James Caine?'

'My father pleaded guilty.'

I bought the ticket, Daddy.

But you paid the bill.

'Because he loves his little girl,' Spike said. 'And because he was afraid her happy home was going to fall apart if her husband got collared.'

He slipped his hands around my waist.

I tried to pull away, but he wouldn't let me.

He was far stronger than me. And what scared me was that Spike looked like a man who believed he was collecting a debt.

'Ginger's my friend,' I said.

'That didn't stop her with your dad.'

The field behind the house was empty. I listened for a car on the drive. But there was no car on the drive. Nobody was coming.

'Your father's not a killer, Tara, and neither is Christian – whatever that old copper may think. They put him away, didn't they? How long did he get?'

'Five years.'

Five years for DCI Stoner, which meant he would be out in less than three. Would a few years be enough to stop him torturing a woman he didn't know how to let go of? In my experience, that kind of man never leaves you alone. They think they own you. Maybe they would have to lock him up again. Maybe somebody would have to teach him a lesson he would never forget.

'Look – your dad's a good guy, Tara. And Christian is a sensitive bloke. He's my friend. But I'm not like them.'

'You're not good or sensitive?'

'That's right, Tara. I am neither good nor sensitive. I'm a rough boy. I put ketchup on my pasta. Remember?'

He pulled me closer and I felt him harden against me. His mouth was against my neck, nuzzling me as if he had waited years for this moment. His hands were in my jeans, inside my pants, on my buttocks, squeezing too hard, digging in his fingernails, his arms locked around me.

'Get the fuck off me, Spike!'

'Ah, you could make a dead man come, Tara.'

And I felt a wave of pure panic. Would he rape me? Would he really do that to me?

'I'm not going to force myself on you,' he said. 'What kind of man do you think I am? But I want you to want me. And don't you want to thank me, Tara?'

'What – *stop!* – what should I be thanking you for?'

'What do you think?'

Then he was pushing up my top with one hand, batting off my hands with the other, much too strong for me, and he pulled up my bra, releasing my breasts, and he was bending over, his mouth was on them as he began yanking at my trousers, struggling with the brass button on my jeans, wrenching at it with all his strength until the brass button of my Wranglers went across the room like a spent bullet. Then he had the zip of my trousers open, and he was pulling them down, over my thighs, murmuring with pleasure against my ear when he caught a glimpse of my pants.

'Spike – *stop!*'

'I am not going to make you do anything you don't want to do,' he said, working at my top again and, surprisingly deftly, he unhooked my bra at the back and my breasts were suddenly free and his mouth was on my mouth, his tongue forcing its way in. I twisted my head away and screamed at him.

'Look,' he said. 'We both know you owe me, don't we?'

'No,' I said. 'No, it's not true.'

'Tara?' he said, breathing. 'You wanted Caine killed and you are glad the bastard is dead. And you are happy that somebody had the guts to cave in his rotten head. *Aren't you?*'

My voice sounded pathetically small.

'Yes.'

'So who do you think really went to that hotel room?' he said. 'Who do you think ended that man because he wouldn't leave you alone? Somebody did it, Tara! And it wasn't your father and it wasn't your husband. You know Ginger was terrified the law were going to come for me. You've heard the rumour, I know you have.'

Then I got my knee between his legs and brought it up as hard as I could. Not a perfect shot, too much impact was wasted on the top of his thigh, and he was still holding me very close, but it must have caught him on one side of his scrotum because the wind went out of him with a rush and he doubled up, moaning with pain.

I moved away from him, breathing hard.

I pushed my hair from my face, seeing the fight go out of him as he sucked up the pain. I did up my bra, pulled up my jeans and pulled down my top, all the while watching him try to ride out the pain. And then I laughed at him.

'Oh, Spike!'

He looked up at me and in a flash I saw in his eyes that he suddenly wanted to be out of here, that he wanted to be somewhere else, and to never see me again in his life.

'Come on,' I said. 'Talk to me about that night, Spike. Tell me all about it.'

'No,' he said, still hunched over with the pain, pulling up his tracksuit bottoms, his rough face flushed with shame and fear. 'I don't want to talk about it.'

He was rolling up his yoga mat, snatching up his phone, desperate to be out of this house, to never speak of this thing again but I followed him to the door as he fumbled with his car keys, all the swagger knocked out of him now.

'You didn't kill James Caine,' I said.

And I left the rest unspoken, and I would leave those words unspoken forever, and I would go to my grave without ever saying them.

But Spike knew. I could see it in his terrified eyes.

He did not kill James Caine.

Because I did.

42

TARA

'I just came from your home,' James Caine had said, and I saw how easy it was for him to take everything I loved away from me, and I knew that I would never be free, and I understood how much pain I was about to inflict on those who cared about me the most.

'I just came from your home,' he repeated. 'Are you even listening to me, Tara. *I have just come from your home*. I met your husband – Christian? And the dog. Christian gave me the grand tour.' He chuckled knowingly. 'I saw the bed, Tara. Your marital bed.'

And at first I had believed that it was a lie, one more in James Caine's litany of poisonous lies, all those lies that he used to torment me. But for once Caine was telling the truth. I walked in a dream through the cool shadows of the stable. Uncle Jack came forward to take charge of Maple and Marlon skipped after them.

I retreated into a dark corner as James Caine kept talking.

'There's a framed magazine cover of you in the hallway,' he said, proving he was telling the terrible truth. 'I like you in that little black dress. Have you still got it? I would like to have you in a room for a couple of hours wearing that dress.'

My heart had clenched like a fist.

'It's not true,' I said, my knuckles white as I gripped my phone, knowing it was true.

'Yes,' he said. 'We – my family – are looking at properties in your area. I might make your husband an offer.' A short laugh. 'For the house, I mean!'

And I was struck dumb because he had all the power and I was nothing now.

'We need to talk to your husband,' James Caine said, always keen to kick me hardest when I was down. 'Christian. We need to talk to Christian together.' The familiarity turned my stomach. 'It's not fair for Christian to not be aware of what's going on. And frankly, Tara, I need to know where I stand.'

He was all business and common sense and I felt like I was losing my mind.

His voice was full of what sounded like real hurt. It was as if we were entering a difficult period of our relationship, as if we had truly been together, as if he mattered, as if he could take the place of Christian.

My head reeled. How had this happened?

'I don't want to have to tell him alone,' Caine said, and then the little lash of the whip to keep me pliant. 'But if you push me – I will.'

I could imagine him on the doorstep of my home. I could see him totally clearly, I could see him standing there and ringing the bell and Christian opening the door and the two men looking at each other before James Caine spoke, shoving our dirty secret into the light.

He would be doing to me what Ginger had originally wanted us to do to him. But we were never going to do it, I knew, we were never going to turn up on his doorstep in Brighton to terrify him into leaving me alone. I was not that brave, and I had too much to lose. But he could do it, I saw now, and I knew that the one with less fear is the one with all the power.

'Hello?' he said. 'Hello? Hello? Talk to me, Tara.' And then the flash of temper.

'If you don't cooperate, I'll tell your husband and he will throw you into the street like the whore we both know you are.'

'Please don't,' I said. 'Please, James.'

He laughed, as if I had got down on my knees and begged.

'Come to the hotel. I want you to spend the night. Just like Tokyo.'

I did not recognise my voice. 'All right.'

'Dress for dinner, OK?'

I was flooded with terror. What if someone recognised me?

'Are we going out?' I said.

'We're eating in my room.' A pause. 'Sorry I lost my rag for a second there,' he said, suddenly oozing regret. The abuser who finally gets his way is always all apologies, I understood now. 'I care about you, Tara. That's all.'

I watched Uncle Jack and Marlon laughing as Maple snorted, tossed her head and leaned forward in the hope of a treat.

'When should I come to the hotel?' I asked.

'You'll come when I tell you,' he said.

I felt empty, and defeated, and sorry, so sorry, as I watched Marlon with Uncle Jack at the far end of the stable. The old man was fishing in the multiple pockets of his threadbare jacket, producing bits of carrot and apple and lumps of sugar like a magician, pulling them out and then handing them to Marlon, who was shyly offering them to Maple, back in her stall now but with the door still open.

My father had just tried to give Marlon his first riding lesson and it had all ended in tears and failure and Marlon's naked terror of Maple. But already, under Jack's wise and gentle guidance, Marlon was drying his eyes and smiling as Maple snuffled up the treats he offered in the palm of his hand. Uncle Jack glanced back at me as I called my best friend, not knowing what else to do.

'James Caine came to my home,' I told Ginger. 'While I was up at my parents' place with Marlon. Told Christian some bullshit story about wanting to make an offer on the house. Christian must have let him in, showed him around.'

'Does Christian suspect anything?'

'I don't know what Christian thinks, Ginger. I'll find out when I get home. Caine told me to come to his hotel.'

'If you go to his hotel, then I'm coming with you,' she said. 'You have to make him leave you alone. You have to take control. You have to look him in the eye and tell him to back off. Meet me outside my flat tonight. Late. After dinner.'

'I think he wants me there before then.'

'Well, fuck what he wants, Tara. Come tonight. Park outside the flat. You don't have to come in. I want to keep Spike out of it. I'll tell him – I don't know – we're going for a late drink. Spike believes whatever I tell him. Then we'll go to the hotel together.'

She rang off.

Marlon was laughing now and my heart ached because I remembered that feeling when Maple realised that it was sugar in the palm of your hand, how eagerly she hoovered it up, and how much her tongue, lips and breath tickled. I stared at the scene at the end of the stable. Uncle Jack placed Maple's favourite blue blanket on her back and showed Marlon how to close her gate. Then Uncle Jack took Marlon's hand and led him out the far end of the stable where there was an incinerator bin smoking in the spring sunshine. Uncle Jack supervised Marlon as he dropped dead branches into the bin and then the pair of them stood back, watching the dead branches begin to burn.

I slowly walked down to Maple, standing in her stall.

She lifted her lovely head with a soft snort, always happy to see me. *It's you again.* Uncle Jack stored a box of treats opposite Maple's stall and I found a wad of bread and slipped it into her mouth, feeling the saliva slick against my hand as she took it. I pressed my hands against the long sweep of her beautiful face and those bottomless black eyes blinked at me once.

'What am I going to do, girl?' I said.

I stood there in the half-light of the stable, comforted by the old familiar smells of leather and hay and soapy water and horse and the wood burning in the incinerator bin. The smell of horse above all. I could hear the voices of Uncle Jack and Marlon as they stoked the fire, my son chuckling, happy again. My old saddle was on a stand, the worn leather gleaming with glycerine saddle soap. I walked slowly along the shelves that my dad had put up years ago, full of well-ordered boxes of bridles, bits, shoes, sponges, blankets and brushes.

I found the toolbox.

I picked up a nailing hammer.

There were a few in there, and I chose the oldest-looking one with a square nose on its steel head, and sharp jaws for pulling out nails and a worn wooden shaft.

I stood there with the hammer in my hand and then I saw Uncle Jack staring at me in the stable's doorway. Beyond him, Marlon had his back to us as he lobbed a dead branch into the incinerator bin. For a long moment, Uncle Jack and I looked at each other and then he came closer and watched me as I slipped the old nailing hammer into my bag.

'Want me to call your dad?' he said.

I shook my head. 'No thanks, Uncle Jack.'

My father could not help me today.

I drove Marlon home and found Christian in a funny mood, distant and distracted and rather cold, although perhaps anyone would be like that after living with me for enough years. He seemed to have no real suspicion about the true identity of the man who had come to look at our home that day. Or at least he gave no sign when I fobbed him off with a story about some random social media stalker who had been trailing me around online. Perhaps it is easy to believe what we are desperate to hear.

I told him I needed to go out later – the burglar alarm kept going off at the office and I was going to have to go down there and investigate. Christian merely shrugged at my carefully prepared lie.

When Christian and Marlon took Buddy for his late afternoon walk, I had a shower, trying to wash off the long day – the time spent driving fast and worried sick on the motorway between Bushey and town, and all the rest of it – my doctor's appointment in Harley Street, Marlon's disastrous riding lesson, James Caine's verbal punishment and the fear Uncle Jack saw in my eyes when he offered to get my dad to help me. But somehow the day's dirt seemed to stick to my skin no matter how hot the water, and no matter how hard I scrubbed. I dressed in a default little black dress with my favourite tailored jacket from Stella McCartney thrown over the top.

I looked in the mirror and I saw it wasn't enough. I was consumed by the sudden urge to hide my body, to hide my face, to hide myself. Everyone would be looking at me and no one must see.

So I dug out a long green Prada raincoat from my youth. I put it on and found a Tokyo Giants baseball cap that I had brought back as a souvenir from Japan for Christian and he had never worn. I tucked my hair up inside, pulled it on low over my eyes, gave myself one last look. I resembled a boy in an Eighties synthesiser band – Pet Shop Tara – and then I quickly left the house, my hair still damp, before my family got back from walking the dog. Leaving was easier if I did not have to look at their faces, if I did not have to lie to them any more. I was sick of all my lies.

It was early evening when I arrived at the hotel. James Caine opened the door in his bathrobe. He smirked as he stood aside to let me enter. I didn't want to hurt him. I just wanted him to leave me alone. I wanted him to stop torturing me. I wanted him to understand why this could not go on. Most of all, more than anything in the world, I wanted him to stop threatening to turn up on my doorstep and say things to Christian that would make my husband look at me in a different way for the rest of our lives. But I knew that James Caine saw exactly what Uncle Jack had seen when he looked at me in the stable.

Fear.

Because everything frightened me now. I was scared that Christian was going to know the truth about me and what I had done, I was scared of coming to this hotel room when I should have been preparing for an early dinner with my family, I was afraid of James Caine's physical strength, and his cruelty, and I was afraid that I was too weak to stop him doing whatever he wanted to do to me.

I had told myself – and I would have told Uncle Jack if he had asked me – that what I carried in my bag was purely for personal protection, an insurance policy against rape, murder and being tossed naked into the street. Because I knew he would want to touch me. But I had made up my mind. I had to make him understand that I had a life and there was no space in it for him or anyone else. He turned as I entered the room, his bathrobe flapping open, one hand on himself and the other pressing a button by the door.

The red *Do Not Disturb* light came on.

I shook my head. 'No.'

And he laughed in my face because he had heard it all before from lots of other women in many rooms just like this one. 'No? You're telling me no now?'

'You have to leave me alone,' I said. 'I want my life back.'

But he was in total control.

'You want your life back? Ah. You want your life back. But your life is mine now, Tara. You don't have any other life.' He reached out and squeezed a nipple, hard enough to make me cry out in pain. 'And it's not over until I say it's over.'

I was still gasping with pain as he turned away.

'Now I'm going to take a shower and when I come back I want to find you out of those stupid clothes and down on your knees—'

And then the nailing hammer was out of my bag and it was in my right hand as I struck James Caine in the back of the head. My aim was wild and he was walking away from me but the head of the nailing hammer still cleaved through the back of his skull with surprising ease and he stumbled forward, blocking his fall with the coffee table. A complimentary fruit bowl went flying. He stared up at me with disbelief, his hand touching the back of his head and coming away covered in blood.

'Whore,' he said, slowly rising to his feet.

And so I hit him again.

I flew home. Not to my home in Camden Town where Christian and Marlon were waiting for me but to my first home, the home where I had been a child, the forever home where I had grown up. From the cars on the drive I could tell that my parents were home but it was a big house where a family could easily avoid each other and I went out to Half Acre Field without having to see them, to talk to them, to lie to them. There was no sign of Uncle Jack up at the stable. But the incinerator bin was still burning. I took off my long green Prada raincoat and threw it into the bin. Then I threw in the Tokyo Giants baseball cap. I felt a sudden blast of hot breath by my side and gasped with fear.

Then Maple was licking my neck, nuzzling my face and I could have wept with love for her. My old Prada raincoat was burning nicely as my father walked out of the big glass doors at the back of the house and slowly crossed the field.

He nodded at the incinerator bin.

'Having a bit of a clear-out?'

I said nothing. We both watched my raincoat burning in the incinerator bin. The baseball cap was slower to catch fire, but then I saw the golden letters of the Tokyo Giants curl, and blacken, and then they were lost in the flames.

'Jack's down at the house,' he said. 'We were just having a chat about you.'

'Why?'

'He said that you're scared.'

'Not any more, Dad.'

'You sure?'

'Yes.'

My father slipped an arm around Maple's neck and kissed her forehead.

'Maybe you should be,' he said.

The nailing hammer was at my feet. My father watched me pick it up and go to drop it in the incinerator bin.

'No,' he said, taking the hammer away from my hand.

'Dad—'

'That shaft is made of hickory but the head is high carbon, heat-treated steel. Do you understand what that means, Tara? It means it is never going to burn, OK? It's going to sit in the bottom of that bin until someone finds it or until you fish it out of the ashes and drop it down a drain or in a skip. Which they will also find if they look hard enough. You could burn it for a hundred years and not destroy high carbon, heat-treated steel.'

He nodded, ending the debate. 'Leave it with me, angel face. I've got it. You going home now?'

'I'm meeting Ginger at her place,' I said. 'She's really worried about me.'

He smiled, the smile that said I didn't have to worry about anything hurting me while he was in the world, and I watched my father walk into the stable with the nailing hammer in his hand.

And then I drove to see Ginger.

43

CHRISTIAN

Last night I dreamed that I lay in the darkness of our old house in Camden Town, waiting for my wife.

Marlon slept peacefully by my side, Buddy snored at the foot of the bed, and as I waited for Tara to come to me, to return to our home, to sleep by my side again as she did on more than three thousand nights, I listened to the weather – the sky full of thunder, the seasons turning, a storm preparing to break – and I took the measure of my life.

And found it wanting.

As a younger man I had thought that the world would have more use for me, would be more impressed by me, would be eager to raise me up and enrich me but none of those things had happened and as the years flew by with increasing speed, I knew as I lay there in the darkness that they never would.

But then Tara was in the doorway of our bedroom, a slim silhouette in the light that seeped in from the street, and I felt the old feeling that I always got when I was around Tara, it surged up in me, and filled my heart.

I felt like the luckiest man in the world.

She slipped into bed, our son between us, and I did not need to count my blessings because they were both in my arms.

When we were in bed on such a night, when Marlon was still so small, our family felt like one body tangled up under the duvet. We were a jumble of warm limbs and breath and love. Nothing ever felt more right.

They were the measure of my life, Tara and Marlon, in my dreams and all my days, together and apart, forever and ever.

Then Tara spoke softly in the darkness.

'I don't think I can sleep tonight,' she said.

'Then just rest your eyes,' I said.

I reached across Marlon to take Tara's hand, and I smiled to myself as I felt her fidget but then settle, relax and finally slide into sleep, and I knew that even if she should turn her back on me in our deepest rest, or if I should move away from her in the dead of the night, then we would somehow always know to reach out, and we would always find each other again, and I would still be holding my wife's hand when morning came.

10 Years On

THE ONE BAR, TOKYO

TARA

He is simply Marlo now, not Marlon any more, almost sixteen years old, taller than me for two summers, and I watch him standing outside Shibuya station, frowning at his *Rough Guide to Tokyo* as the crowds go about the business of the night and the rain comes down in sheets, drum beating on all those convenience store umbrellas, transparent as cellophane.

'Can you find it?' I ask, and Marlo sighs with that special kind of exasperation that is unique to a teenage boy addressing their slow-witted parent. I lightly punch his arm. 'Be kind,' I tell him, and he smiles that slow, shy Marlo smile that always makes me forgive him.

The name we gave him at birth was packed away somewhere between the end of Lego and start of troubled skin. His choice, of course. And *Marlon*, we saw immediately, my ex-husband Christian and I, was never really him. That was just our idea of who he might grow up to be, our juvenile Brando fantasy for our baby boy. *What are you rebelling against? What you got?*

No, a young Brando was not him, not this gentle soul frowning at his guidebook, squinting behind his glasses, although it might have been me once, long ago, coming home from some club as my father was setting off to work in his van with the two Daves. There was a time when I was up for rebelling against anything they had. But my son is a far sweeter teenager than I was, and I am proud of the man he is going to be, the man that I am raising. He *will* be kind.

'It's somewhere over there,' I say vaguely, pointing beyond the great neon-lit mountain range of department stores, restaurants, cafes, noodle joints, love hotels and all the epic activity of central Tokyo.

Marlo rolls his myopic eyes, bleary with jet lag behind his specs, and although he doesn't actually tut, he comes quite close.

'Somewhere over there, *right*, Mum,' he says, unimpressed, and now he has his phone in one hand, his thumb tapping a frantic blur, his guidebook in the other, and a see-through umbrella balanced on one bony shoulder.

I leave him alone to concentrate and look at the city I have not seen for ten years. The lights of TV screens ten storeys high flare and blur and melt in the driving rain as we stand at the crossroads of the world, my beautiful boy and I, trying to find a bar, one bar, a special bar, out of all the thousands of bars in Tokyo.

Then suddenly there is the unmistakable tremor of an earthquake.

I feel it rattle through me – that old, almost-forgotten feeling of a train passing right in front of your face – and then after a few long seconds it has passed.

Marlo looks up at me with concern.

'Just an earthquake,' I said. 'Happens all the time. It's nothing. It's not the big one.'

The earthquake is already over and the crowds at the Shibuya crossroads have not even paused. The great tectonic plates deep below the earth have shuddered but are now still.

Marlo closes his book, puts away his phone and adjusts his see-through umbrella. His first earthquake has shaken him and for a moment I recognise the look on his face. It was the look he used to get entering a soft play area when there were bigger boys casually bouncing up and down.

He pushes his glasses up the bridge of his nose and gets a grip.

'Dad's waiting,' he tells me.

My father did his time but he did not die in prison.

The cancer inside him, the tiny part of his body that was betraying him, could not kill him. The policy of watchful waiting had worked out well. But Dr Khan, who had urged my father to go for surgery, was not so fortunate and died from a stroke at just forty-nine.

'Bloody tragic,' my father said.

He had been a model prisoner. Always good with his hands, the prison workshop was his natural habitat, and younger men who had no clue what to do with their hands apart from take another selfie flocked to him to learn about metal work, and dovetail joints, and taking apart the engine of a car and putting it back together. After a few years, he was encouraged to take a Certificate in Counselling and Mentoring (duration 200 hours, Level 4 Prisoner's Education Trust). My dad liked to boast that it was the first qualification he had earned since the certificate for swimming his width at school more than fifty years ago. I imagined him helping lost young men to find themselves, but he said it wasn't really like that. Mostly, he taught them to read and write. But that was no small thing, my dad said.

The years passed and he missed his home, he missed his work, he missed watching his grandson grow up. But most of all, he missed my mother. Prison, my father said, was not really about being locked up – it was about being locked *away* – locked away from everything you loved. That was your punishment.

And my mother blossomed without him. Always a beauty, she somehow applied an emergency brake on the ageing process as she entered her sixties.

There were men in her life. I suspected the use of a dating app, but she laughingly denied it. She said she met them at her gym. 'Or just – you know – in *the world*, Tara. The old-fashioned way of meeting people, darling!'

It may even have been true. Most of them were silver foxes with a few bob in the bank and not too much extra flesh on their old bones, although some of them were ten, fifteen years younger. I watched with admiration as her hair got blonder and her teeth got whiter and her body got firmer. But my mum kept all of her suitors at arm's length, and she never missed a visiting day with my dad.

His minimum term of ten years was fast approaching. After that, he could apply for parole and release on licence. And after ten years, my mum was still waiting for him to come home. They had chosen each other, long ago, for better or worse, home and away, all of that.

And so he did his time for the thing he claimed that he had done. It all helped – the workshop, the mentoring course, the young men who looked at him as the two Daves had once looked at him. But most of all, it was my mum who got my father through his time, knowing that she was waiting for him. And, in my experience, you can get through anything if you know that someone is waiting for you.

Christian sits by himself in The One Bar.

His weekly podcast – Way Back Wednesday, a loving and surprisingly successful curation of traditional late-twentieth-century rock music, that beloved and dying art form – has brought him out east for the first time.

A band – one of those bands that he was young with half a lifetime ago, some of those boys he was wild with

– have had an unexpected hit single on the back of a remix of one of their old tunes by an excruciatingly trendy Grime artist. Their new record company has sprung for Christian's flight and accommodation and in return he is doing a Way Back Wednesday special on them. It is a happy coincidence that his trip more or less coincided with Marlo's sixteenth-birthday present from his besotted grandmother.

Christian had floated the idea that Marlo might come to a gig with him, but this wasn't going to happen. Christian had hoped Marlo would share his love of music, just as I had thought that he would eventually fall in love with horses, but Marlo was one of these children born in the twenty-first century who grew up totally smitten with anime, manga, Studio Ghibli, J-pop, all of the soft power of Japan. He had always wanted to see the country that filled his dreams.

And his father has always wanted to see this bar, this strange bar where they only play one band (Led Zeppelin), and only serve one kind of wine (Australian Shiraz), and only have one thing to eat on the menu (truffle pasta).

For a moment Christian doesn't see us standing in the pink glow of The One Bar's doorway and I watch him, lost in the music. The song playing is the other side of Led Zeppelin, that reflective, folky side that was always so important to the band, Jimmy Page sounding as wistfully tender as Joni Mitchell on *Blue*. I can't quite place the track. Something from *Houses of the Holy*? I used to *know* this stuff, I think, as I watch the sleek, well dressed young couples sipping their red wine and eating their truffle pasta.

Christian is the oldest person in the bar, and the scruffiest, and the only person who sits alone. He wears the leather jacket and jeans that he always wears these days.

And then he sees us, and his face lights up.

And he smiles, and we moved towards him, all of us smiling, and I feel happy and sad all at once because for those few moments as we cross the bar to Christian, it really feels like we are a family again.

'We got lost!' I say.

Marlo gazes around the bar, grasps the concept and, despite his worship of all things Japanese, finds it baffling.

'Having a good time, kiddo?' Christian asks him.

Marlo grunts an affirmative, not convinced by the bar's central thesis.

'But why would you want *just one thing?*' he says, dipping his head to his phone as his father stares at him, his smile fading. I know what Christian is thinking, *Why don't you turn off the bloody phone for five minutes?*

But he doesn't say it. Christian is making an effort. When he sees Marlo these days – and it is much more sporadic than when Marlo was little, and we arranged his social life for him – Christian is constantly *making an effort*. Their relationship is more combative, more prickly than I would like, and it may get worse before it gets better. Despite the ten years since we parted, Christian has never considered himself an absent father, he was never going to embrace the cliché of the absent parent who overdoes the kindness. If anything, he is a far sterner father than when Marlo was little and they were spending their days together while I was out working.

And then Marlo's face breaks into a smile. 'This is Shibuya, right? We're really close to Mandarake.'

Christian and I look blank, glance at each other for help.

'It's quite famous,' Marlo says with infinite teenage patience. 'Mandarake is the best place in the world to buy manga.'

'Comics,' Christian says.

'No, Dad. Not comics. *Manga*.'

This is what Marlo lives for, this is where he looks for all the things that feed his soul. I remembered how we looked to America for our music, our films, our heroes – well, Marlo's head is pointing in the opposite direction. Marlo looks East. It's why my mum – 'Why *shouldn't* I spoil him?' she asked me – shelled out for two tickets east for his sixteenth birthday.

'Is it all right if I go?' he asks me.

Not his father – me. I am the parent with the power of veto. Like Russia at the United Nations Security Council.

'But you only just got here!' Christian protests, trying hard to keep the shrill note of parental outrage out of his voice and not succeeding at all.

'Are you all right getting back to the hotel by yourself?' I ask.

My boy doesn't quite roll his eyes. Instead he smiles, as if we both know the answer to that one. We watch him go. We watch him until he is out of sight. Then it is just the two of us. Not what we planned or expected.

'I thought we were all having dinner,' Christian complains, more hurt than I want him to be. 'It's the only chance on the trip. For the three of us to be together.'

We stare at each other, lost for words. When Marlo was younger – when he was still Marlon – there would be handovers. But that's all done now. There were *my nights* and *your nights* for Christian and me but now they are all *his nights* – Marlo's nights. He travels the city alone, he makes his own way in the world and there is no reason for Christian and me to ever see each other any more. It's only because we are all in Tokyo at the same time that we are having this failed attempt at a family reunion.

Christian sighs. 'How's he doing?' he asks me. 'I worry about him.'

'He's self-conscious about his skin. He doesn't know what to say to girls. He doesn't like wearing glasses.'

Christian self-consciously adjusts his glasses.

'But he's doing good,' I say. 'His skin will clear, although he doesn't believe it. And he will learn what to say to girls and girls will love him, because he's lovely. He's fine, Christian. Don't worry about Marlo.'

He is kind, I want to say. *He will be a good man. Like his father.*

But I don't say any of it. I cling to the small talk. Much safer.

'How's the band?'

'They're having an early night. They were talking about going down to Roppongi, but we're off to Osaka tomorrow.'

'Big in Japan, are they?' I say, smiling.

'Small to medium in Japan.'

The waitress brings a round of Shiraz. We order truffle pasta. And Christian takes a breath and starts talking. He has been sitting in this bar waiting for his ex-wife and his growing son and unlike me, he is skipping the small talk.

'One of the guys in the band I'm out here with wrote a book. It did quite well. Among – my kind. In this book the guitarist – who was also the band's only songwriter – told the story of how they broke up. And it was so familiar – so much like the way a million bands have broken up – that it felt like a fairy tale, Tara. When they started, when they were young, when they thought they were going to be as big as Blur and Oasis, the guitarist-stroke-songwriter was taking pills while the rest of the band were out drinking. So he was staying up all night writing songs while they were caning it, then sleeping it off the next day. And there was jealousy, anger and resentment. And it all fell apart very quickly and they didn't get together again until they played at the singer's funeral last year. Fifteen years later. And the thing is, when they played together at the singer's funeral – *they couldn't remember why they had broken up*. Coming apart just seemed like a form of madness.' He sips his Shiraz. 'And it reminded me of us.'

I laugh. 'You think we're like some old Brit Pop band?'

'I can't remember why we came apart.'

I remember. I remember it all. But I am too old to care about being cool. I am too close to the end – or at least the middle – to play games. Christian is right. There is no time left for small talk.

I miss us. I miss our home. I miss our life. I miss all that we lost and even though I know it is never coming back, the irrecoverable past, and I know that I will miss it forever. I compare every man to the one I lost. I compare every place I live to the home we had in Camden Town. And every new place, every new man, they are always wanting.

I look around The One Bar. I had loved this bar at first sight. One band, one wine, one pasta. And I knew that the reason I had gone looking for it all those years ago, and the reason that I had loved it, was because it felt like a bar that had been invented with Christian in mind.

'Bloody good bar,' he murmurs, sipping his Shiraz, nodding along to 'Whole Lotta Love' as the waitress places two plates of steaming truffle pasta before us.

What I had missed over the last ten years, most of all, was the sense of being exactly where I was meant to be. But for a while now I have had the feeling that the best is over, I have been nagged by the sense that life is winding down. It is only when I look at Christian's face – Clark Kent pushing forty – that I believe that there is hope. But of course I am not allowed to say any of that.

I know that, biologically, life is finished with us. But I can't help feeling that we, this good man and I, are not quite finished with life.

'We should have come here ten years ago,' I say. 'I mean it, Christian – we should have come here years ago!'

'There's a saying,' he replies, then pauses for a bit as he finishes a mouthful of truffle pasta. '*The best time to plant a tree is fifty years ago – and the second-best time is now.*'

'One of John Lennon's?'

'Could be,' he says. 'Somebody wise.'

We sit there in silence, eating our pasta, drinking our wine, listening to the music and thinking about the best time to plant a tree.

'Listen,' we say, both at once, then laugh with mutual embarrassment.

'You,' he says. 'Go on.'

'No,' I say. 'You.'

'When we've finished our dinner, do you want to go and get a drink?'

And now I am Tara, the old Tokyo hand.

And now I take control.

'You're spoilt for choice,' I say, and I tell him about the block of tiny bars called Golden Gai in Shinjuku, where there are only two or four seats in every bar, and all of those micro-bars have a theme, reflecting the owner's lifetime obsession, and we might even be able to find that magical little block if we look hard enough and if we don't mind too much about getting lost.

And so we step into the Tokyo night, the pair of us looking at the rain under my see-through convenience store umbrella, and although we are not young any more, and although we are not even together any more, I can't deny the feeling of belonging that I know I will never find anywhere else, or with anyone else, and for one sweet moment anything seems possible in a city where the past and the future seem equally alive, and as Christian slips his arm in mine I know that anything could happen by the end of the night, even a shared bottle of Prosecco.